Greatest
Of All
Time

Also by Alex Allison

The Art of the Body

Alex Allison

Greatest Of All Time

dialogue
books

DIALOGUE BOOKS

First published in Great Britain in 2025 by Dialogue Books

1 3 5 7 9 10 8 6 4 2

A CIP catalogue record for this book
is available from the British Library.

Hardback ISBN 978-0-349-70454-8

Typeset in Berling by M Rules
Printed and bound in Great Britain by
Clays Ltd, Elcograf S.p.A

Papers used by Dialogue Books are from well-managed forests
and other responsible sources.

FSC
MIX
Paper | Supporting
responsible forestry
www.fsc.org   FSC® C104740

Dialogue Books
An imprint of
Dialogue
Carmelite House
50 Victoria Embankment
London EC4Y 0DZ

The authorised representative
in the EEA is
Hachette Ireland
8 Castlecourt Centre
Dublin 15, D15 XTP3, Ireland
(email: info@hbgi.ie)

www.dialoguebooks.co.uk

Dialogue, part of Little, Brown Book Group Limited,
an Hachette UK company.

WARM UP

1

Before he was everyone's, he was mine.

2

During his years in Milan, the media nicknamed the manager *L'oracolo*. He was a footballing savant – it was said he could visualise a full ninety minutes entirely in his mind, each moving cog in the beautiful machine.

There were two weeks remaining before our pre-season tour and I had been summoned to the manager's office for a favour. With a reserved smile, *L'oracolo* gestured for me to take a seat, indicating that he would need a moment before we could begin.

The manager's hair was notably thinning and he had begun to round at the middle, his ageing body flattered by fine Italian tailoring. This was a man who exuded authority, justly earned through decades at the highest level of the game. Above his bookshelves, a newly framed print: the final day of our previous season; fans swarming the pitch as we confirmed our survival. While I absent-mindedly inspected his photos and the spines of his books, the manager typed dramatically at his keyboard, before turning the laptop to me, showing a serious, but handsome teenage face.

'This boy from Monaco, he is the one for us,' *L'oracolo* said, tapping the screen for emphasis. 'It is true what they say about him. The things he can do. What he is capable of.'

'What is it they say?' I asked, reading the boy's name and vital statistics from a profile below the photograph. We were the same age, the same height, within a few pounds of the same weight. *Samson Kabarebe*. 'I've never heard of him.'

'I promise that you will – whether he comes or whether he chooses not. The scouts – they say the boy has an arrogance. You have known the type, yes? You have seen it before, of course. All of the best, they believe in themselves. Like the best, he wants to play.'

The manager spoke English with zest, pausing for emphasis, weighing words in his mouth like treats.

'If he's so good, why's he barely playing for them?' I asked, pointing out the bold *six* in Samson's appearance stats.

'Come now,' the manager said incredulously, allowing himself a sly smile. 'We both know why! In this game, it is luxury to take the risk on such a young player! This manager at Monaco, you know him, yes? You know his, *how-you-say*, pedigree? He does not need this risk, you see? He likes his job very much and wishes to keep it. But for me, for this club: I am forced to take risks. This is our reality. If the owner says we cannot buy, we cannot buy. So, we beg for loans and we look to the academy for stars like you.'

I had been part of the club since I was nine years old, captaining our youth teams at every level. I grew up a ten-minute walk from the stadium, with our players postering my bedroom walls – players who had since actively distanced themselves from what the club had become. Amid an injury crisis last season, the manager had brought me into the first team, pushing and favouring me to the point that I had been accused by the squad of being a *teacher's pet*.

'So, I suppose I'm a big risk too?' I huffed, shifting back in my seat. 'Even if you trusted me with the ten shirt?'

'But of course! You are my favourite risk! My proudest risk! Last season, I trust you with this shirt because only you understand what it means. You know every legend who has worn this number. You have sung their names! And look at us now – another season in the greatest league! This is why it must be you to speak on our behalf.'

Pushing the laptop further towards me, the manager stood from his desk, buttoning his suit jacket.

'Speak with this boy, this Samson. You must say what it is like here. How it is different. How it is *better.* In Monaco, there are no real fans. Just the rich, you know? The wealthy and the impatient. They fight for nothing. You must tell Samson of our history. Sell the tradition of this place, this city! Tell of the way our players are worshipped.'

'Okay,' I said, hesitant. 'When do you want me to do this then?'

'I will call him now.'

'*Now?*'

'Yes, now,' the manager said, already unlocking his phone. 'Today, he expects this call. Is this a problem?'

'I mean, no, but . . . shouldn't we rehearse it or something?'

'It must be now. He is on his way to speak with others. His agent – if we wait, the agent will become – *how-you-say . . .* '

Leaning back on his heels, *L'oracolo* paused, rolling his finger like a reel, winding in the words.

'*Inside his head*, you know? You have your papa to agent for you, but you know how this is for the others. The influence of these agents. They will force what is best for their pockets.

There is a lot of money for this boy, you know? We must sell ourselves on the fight. We offer him our stage to perform, our voices to sing.'

The phone was already ringing as *L'oracolo* handed it to me. I angled myself away from his gaze, fixing my eyes on the laptop screen, upon Samson's photograph. When he answered, I introduced myself in a damp rush, launching into an elegy on the club, our past glories, our unrivalled resilience. Without pausing for breath, I enthusiastically listed off whichever positives came to my mind: our brilliant catering, our superb medical staff, the great dressing-room banter, our loyal fans. I emphasised that the Premier League was a war, all about power and endurance.

Before I left space for Samson to ask any questions, the phone was taken back out of my sweaty hand. The manager spoke briefly, even finding time to laugh, but the call seemed to end without a neat conclusion. I apologised, wiping my hand on my thigh, but *L'oracolo* assured me that I had done well. That it was exactly what he had envisioned.

3

There was a buzz among the squad. The latest *Football Manager* video game rated Samson at 184 out of a possible 200 on their *Potential* stat. I'd sought out videos of Samson on the internet, sharing them in the team chat. Collectively, we'd developed an impression of his skills.

On our third day in camp, Samson flew to Doha, chaperoned by his agent. Pausing from our drills, we watched on as he approached the training pitch, greeted by *L'oracolo*. The manager clasped Samson's hand in both his own, shaking gratefully.

'Where's this one from then?' asked our kit man, handing me a water bottle.

'Monaco,' I said, observing as Samson removed his sunglasses, hanging them from the collar of his sharp, white polo shirt. While his agent and the manager laughed and slapped each other affectionately on the back, Samson shifted his weight from foot to foot like an impatient child, glancing over to us, to the pitch.

'No, I mean, where's he properly from?'

'Oh, I think he's played for the French Under-19s, but the gaffer says his family's from Rwanda.'

'Where the fuck's Rew-ander?'

From what we'd gathered, the deal was confirmed, and Samson would be joining us on a season-long loan, playing in his natural position as a centre forward. The same position as me.

Bert, our newly appointed club captain, imposed himself beside me to grab the bottle from my hand and spray it over his head. The arid desert heat had already scalded him a tender, gammon pink.

'You ready to put this fooker in his place then?' Bert said, wiping off his face and grabbing my shoulder, squeezing firmly. 'He's here for your spot, you know?'

'Yeah, I know.'

'So what're you gonna do about it?'

'Whatever the gaffer asks me to do, I guess.'

'You guess? You guess, do ya?' Bert said, his grip tightening. 'You'll have to do a lot better than fookin' guess if your man's as canny as they reckon.'

'What am I supposed to do?' I asked, twisting free.

Bert leered in Samson's direction. 'You've got to show him who's boss, doncha? Put a hard one in on him early.'

'How's that going to help?'

'Here now,' Bert said, brandishing a finger in my face. 'Don't try getting smart with me, laddy. If I'm generous enough to offer advice, that'll be gospel to you.'

As the manager led Samson and his agent over, we hustled back to our drills. Quick-dash pass and plays, lay-offs and rondos. *L'oracolo*'s training routines were always varied – they anticipated our boredom, our dips in concentration, rotating through exercises at ten-minute intervals.

'Boys,' called the manager from the edge of the impossibly fresh grass, whistling us over like pack animals.

'This is Samson,' he said, ushering our new recruit in front of him as we gathered in a crescent, stepping forwards in turn to clap hands with him. Samson smiled warmly, seemingly relaxed.

'Welcome, big man,' Bert said, pulling him aggressively into a chest bump. 'How's your English?'

'About as good as his,' Samson smirked, glancing cheekily over his shoulder to the manager.

Our captain laughed and shoved him backwards. 'You'll do nicely. Ah like yas already.'

'You will remember this one, of course,' the manager said, as we touched for the first time.

'Ah,' Samson said, holding my eyes, '*L'ambassadeur – enchanté.*'

'Here, what did we just say about English?' Bert joked.

'Samson will join training from tomorrow,' the manager said. 'For now, you work another twenty minutes, then we finish.'

'*A demain,*' Samson waved, still eyeing the pitch as he walked away. His agent had paced ahead, walking briskly in the direction of the air-conditioned hotel, phone pressed to his ear.

'Before you go,' the manager said, casting himself in front of me as the rest of the team jogged back to our drills. 'There is something you must know. As part of our arrangement, we have given Samson the ten.'

'What are you talking about? What arrangement?'

'With Samson. This season, he will have the ten shirt.'

'Are you serious, gaffer?'

'It is given. His agent, they insist. You understand, of course?'

'No I don't fucking understand, boss. This is bullshit. He's fucking nobody – I earned that number. I've been with this club since I was nine, for fuck's sake.'

The manager puffed out his cheeks. 'You are upset, but it is already done. Samson will be the ten. That is my word.'

'I *earned* that fucking shirt. You even said so, remember?'

'My friend, you have earned nothing yet in this club. Understand? Maybe in time, but for now? For now, you have earned nothing. What I said to you was true – you understand why this number is important, so you must also understand why we give the shirt to Samson.'

'Well,' I said, stumbling for a rebuttal, 'we'll see what the lads have to say. The fans and all! The fans will be on my side.'

'Your teammates – they will think what I tell them to think. And the fans? What they desire most is hope. Samson is hope. You are known to them, and what they know is all mess. For years, all they know is ugliness.'

'So, I'm ugly too, yeah?' I barked.

'We speak later,' the manager said calmly, pulling up his waistband and walking off the pitch. 'Thank you for this understanding.'

'This is *bullshit*,' I shouted after him, hearing the squall of petulance in my own voice.

4

Through my childhood, we couldn't afford to attend many games, so any visit to the stadium was a major treat, an occasion to be savoured. We would arrive two hours before kick-off, carried through the wait by the club's emotionally charged and bass-heavy pre-match playlist. By my side, my father clapped along, tapping out an anxious, discordant rhythm with his work boots.

I loved being there, singing our club songs, the din growing as the ground filled, anticipation rising, our voices swelling in one familiar tongue, roaring the names of our heroes in that hallowed temple, embracing an identity larger than our differences. I keenly felt the responsibility of being a good fan, the pressure to play my part, to influence from a distance, to fill the space between us and them.

Dad preferred to sit in the North Stand, where we could watch the players emerge from the tunnel, their faces intimately familiar even from sixty metres. No matter how badly we were getting beaten, Dad never left a game before the full-time whistle. We paid good money for those tickets, and we'd get our full value. All he demanded in return for his devotion was effort – for the players to apply themselves. To play for the badge.

Once it became clear that I was a genuine prospect, Dad acted as both my biggest champion and fiercest critic. After one particularly comprehensive thrashing by the Liverpool Under-15 squad, on the drive home, I announced my decision to pack it in, telling him that I'd never be good enough, that I'd never be able to match their level. My father remained silent, refusing to deliver any platitudes or reassurances. He let me wallow in self-pity until dinner, then asked me what we were going to do to prepare for the next game.

For years, my best performances always came when Dad was in attendance. Those special occasions when he could skip work or slip away early from the construction yard. Under the scrutiny of my father, I kept my elbows in and my mouth shut. Scoring in front of Dad was all the sweeter, for he recounted my goals to the rest of the family with richly embellished detail, making ordinary strikes sound quite miraculous.

'You should have heard it, Lolly – his connection on that ball, so sweet it sung. Eighteen yards out, twisting and catching it on the volley. He couldn't have placed it better if he'd used his hands.'

That evening, I spoke with my father over the phone.

'He can't do this, Dad. You need to call and get on to him.'

'Sounds like it's too late though, son.'

'Bollocks, is it! You're my agent – you're supposed to have my back on this stuff.'

'I'm also a fan of the club, and I know that sometimes you've got to put the team first. Come on, lad. Don't go on being a petty shite about it. No one'll thank you for it. Put some faith in the gaffer. He's been around the block. He knows how to play these things a lot better than we do. You've fought for your place before, and you'll do it again.'

'It's not about my place though, it's about respect. He's mugging me off. It was my *fucking* number.'

'All right, son. How about this? We'll hold off until the game on Tuesday, then see how you feel. If you're still all fired up, I'll try to have a word.'

'But—'

'Just wait a few days, all right? That's all I'm asking.'

'Fine. Whatever,' I said, fighting the temptation to hang up dramatically. I took a long, deliberate breath – loud enough for Dad to take note. 'What's the news on my house?'

Purchased last season, shortly after *L'oracolo* brought me into the squad, I had agreed to a twenty-five-year mortgage on a property in the suburbs of our city – a commitment that could potentially outlast my playing career. The house was quaint – red brick and picketed, a garden large enough for goal posts. The interior was in the process of being renovated to my specifications. Or, more accurately, to my mother's specifications. I'd given her licence to live out her interior-design fantasies, albeit on a conservative budget.

'Your mam's been over there all day. She's getting herself in a state, faffing and fussing. The poor decorators. You know how she gets.'

'But will it be ready before the start of the season? The gaffer's always saying we need a stable environment to rest in.'

'It'll be ready when it's ready. Worst comes to worst, you have to live with your old mam and dad for a few weeks longer.'

'Great.'

'I know you like the idea of your freedom, son, but trust me, it's nothing but hassle.'

'All right. Thanks, Dad. Speak to you soon.'

'Love you, son. We're proud of you.'

5

For the duration of the Middle East tour, we were trusted with rooms to ourselves. During the season-proper, all but our most senior players would be forced to share rooms. Because of our club's location in the UK, the squad always travelled to away games the night before the match, staying in a moderately priced hotel. The owner justified his miserliness with the sentiment that sharing rooms held us accountable and out of harm's way.

Tommy, my roommate from the previous season, had recently been sold to West Ham for nine million quid. Tommy and I had developed a routine of playing *FIFA* from dinner until bedtime: a hundred pounds a game, with an extra five hundred if you lost by a margin of four goals or more. Tommy liked to play as Juventus, but I always picked our own club, putting myself at a significant disadvantage. But the novelty of seeing my digital avatar celebrate a goal never grew old. The game valued my digital self at thirteen million.

Following Tommy's departure, there were only two academy graduates remaining in the first team squad: me and Kyle, our reserve goalkeeper. It was Kyle who had taught me to kiss. He was two years older and therefore infinitely wiser. As we grew into our bodies, we'd spend stolen hours pressed against each other in toilet cubicles and laundry rooms, our voices changing, deepening with each whisper. Kyle kissed hungrily, eyes scrunched closed, counting my teeth with his tongue, batting away my hand each time I reached for more. Kyle cut things off abruptly, ending his experiment, graduating to kissing girls, seemingly having used me for all I was worth. Though it had been years since anything happened between us, there remained a complicit trust. A pact of mutual destruction.

We sat together for breakfast the following morning. I knew that Kyle would sympathise regarding the loss of my shirt.

'That shirt used to mean something,' Kyle said, chewing assertively on some toast. 'The other academy lads – they'd give their right foot to wear that shirt even once.'

'Not sure how useful they'd be without a right foot.'

'You know what I mean, dickhead.'

Across the room, uniformed servers stood with their backs to the wall, looking blankly into the middle distance like sentinels, springing to life the moment anyone approached their buffet, drawing their faces into affable, accommodating expressions.

I stirred my porridge.

'My old man reckons I need to just shut up and get on with it.'

'There are always other options.'

Kyle leaned conspiratorially across the table.

'Between you and me, I've started lessons with a Spanish

tutor. Twice a week. Supposed to make you more attractive to them lot in La Liga. *Mi nombre es Kyle. Juego al fútbol.*'

'This tutor – pretty little twenty-something bird, is she?'

'Yeah,' Kyle smirked. 'You know my type.'

Bert approached us from the buffet with a bowl of cereal and took the vacant seat beside me. I imagined Bert would be an aggressive kisser – inexact and boyish, partial to biting.

'Morning ladies,' he said, sitting and spreading his legs into my personal space. 'Hope yous are warming up your voices for this evening. Have ya picked out an initiation song for us yet?'

'I'm not singing again,' I told him.

'You'll sing when I tell you to.'

'Like fuck will I,' I said. 'No one wants to suffer through hearing me again anyway.'

'Yous don't know how good you've got it. It's just a little sing-song. Back in my day, ye'd have a broom handle shoved up ye jacksie and be made to dance.'

'Good thing you like that sort of thing anyway then, eh boss?'

'Watch it, ye,' Bert said, brandishing his spoon at me, flecks of milk spattering across the table.

'How do you reckon Samson will fit in?' Kyle asked.

'Always hard to say with the Africans,' Bert said. 'Some of 'em got a reet attitude at first, but we'll kick it out of him soon enough.'

I winced.

'I think he's French, actually.'

'*I think he's French actually,*' Bert repeated, mimicking my accent.

'Right,' I said, pushing away the porridge. 'I think I'm off then. No appetite. See you on the pitch.'

'*See you on the pitch,*' Bert said, continuing his impression, shoving me as I stood.

6

We were staying in a spa resort with two full-sized pitches, tucked away behind tennis courts and a polo field. The whole complex felt supremely clean and well maintained. Stepping out from the air conditioning alongside Kyle, we were besieged by a rush of baking, carrion dryness. Across an expansive plane, downtown Doha shimmered in the distance: glass monoliths looming like mirages, the horizon oozed like liquid metal.

Tuesday's game was an exhibition match against the reigning champions of the Qatari league. The fixture was to be played behind closed doors, with various emirs and sheikhs expected to attend.

When Kyle and I arrived at the training pitch, Samson was already there. He stood alone in the centre circle, dressed in our kit, doing keepie-uppies, alternating between feet, the ball tight to his boots.

'Fancies himself, doesn't he?' Kyle said. 'Bit keen – early to training on his first day.'

'Yeah,' I said, debating whether to confront Samson, measuring my fury.

'*All right, fella,*' Kyle yelled. 'You know we're not due to start till nine?'

'I know,' Samson called back, his focus unaffected, casually flicking the ball twenty feet in the air, then controlling with his left foot while shielding his eyes from the sun.

'Suit yourself,' Kyle said, jogging off towards the goal.

'They gave you my shirt number, you know,' I said, stalking forwards, trying to appear menacing.

'Yes,' Samson said, his eyes still fixed to the ball, now switching it from foot to foot, his lips pursed, a silver crucifix necklace bouncing off his chest with each kick.

'I thought you might apologise at least. Given that you stole it from me.'

'I am sorry,' Samson said candidly, bringing the ball down under his studs and extending his hand. 'Friends?'

I felt disarmed. I hadn't rehearsed for this. I had intended to hate him. We were meant to be rivals, not buddies. Seeing him stood there, with his hand out, I had no recourse. All my indignation had been muted.

'Sure,' I heard myself say. As I accepted his hand, Samson unexpectedly pulled me in for a hug. He smelled of lotion and coconut.

'The kit, she looks good on me, no?' Samson said, drawing back and smoothing out his shirt.

'Yeah,' I said, dazed by his warmth.

Samson nodded towards Kyle, who was stretching his hamstrings against the goalpost. 'Shall we shoot at him?'

'The rest of the guys will be here in a minute,' I said. 'We usually do a proper warm-up before we start shooting.'

'Nah, let's shoot at him,' Samson said, rolling his ball forward a few inches and taking aim.

'*EHH, KEEP-AIR!*' he called.

In one fluid movement, Samson arched his body back, swinging out his left arm while motoring his right foot under the ball, connecting with a thump that almost hissed with speed. The ball launched from the half-way line in an arc like a golfer's drive, fizzing through the air and finding the middle of the goal, past a scrambling Kyle, caught off guard by the audacity of the shot.

'Your turn,' Samson said, readjusting his crucifix and running off to retrieve another ball.

By the time the rest of the squad arrived, I'd witnessed Samson replicate the same technique a dozen times, his body snapping like elastic. By comparison, my own efforts whimpered meekly into Kyle's gloves.

Spotting us together, Jean-Claude, our first-team coach, paired me off with Samson to lead him through our standard stretching regimen: hips, calves and quads, then piriformis, groin and hamstring.

Jean-Claude had worked with *L'oracolo* for over a decade, leading his backroom staff at every one of the manager's clubs. He was privy to many secrets and trusted unreservedly.

As we stretched out our quads, Samson held my shoulder, purchasing for balance he seemed not to require, effortlessly limber, openly surveying his new teammates.

'*L'oracolo*, he is where?' Samson whispered, switching legs.

'I guess he's out with the club owner, doing meetings and stuff. Jean-Claude leads these sessions.'

'Never mind,' Samson said, running his free hand over his closely shaved head, 'I will make the fun today.'

We rushed through high knees, lunges, rotations and shuffles. Samson moved with a range of motion that seemed almost simulated – too measured and precise for an ordinary body. All eyes were on him, yet he seemed to derive pleasure from the attention. Throughout the warm-up, there was a smile on Samson's face.

'What's he so fucking happy about?' Bert asked me during a water break.

'Ask him yourself,' I said, spitting some water over my shoulder.

'You're supposed to be reet on him today, ain't you? Proper knacking him, like?'

'Nah, I'm over it.'

'Ahh, you've gone soft on us already!' Bert said, scratching at his groin.

'Competition's good,' I shrugged. 'No point being bitter, I reckon. Just more to prove.'

As we began our move-and-shoot exercises, Bert set the tone, targeting Samson – passing the ball aggressively, testing his control. Samson took everything in his stride, barely registering the collective scrutiny, dispatching goal after goal with alarming consistency.

Samson treated that three-hour training session as an exhibition of his art, a smile etched across his face. He nutmegged players during rondos, leapt over lunges, threw his body into every fifty-fifty. Jean-Claude loudly praised Samson's sprinting, his control, his balance.

'Tell you what, marra,' Bert said to me as we walked off the field, 'He's proper canny like, that one. Good lad too. Clearly loves his football.'

'Bit of a show-off though, right?' I said. 'Loves himself.'

'Aye. But with feet like that, you would, wouldn't you?'

7

Following a light lunch, I showered and changed into my swimming trunks, inspecting my tan lines in the bathroom mirror. Compared to Samson, I looked like a boy – lithe frame and narrow shoulders, a face that would struggle to purchase alcohol unchallenged. I could still get away with shaving once a week.

On my way to the pool, I knocked on Kyle's door.

'Who is it?'

'It's me, you mug. You coming down then? It's the best place to stay cool.'

'Nah,' Kyle shouted through the door. 'Head's pounding. Think I've got sunstroke.'

'I'm sure you're stroking something,' I said. 'If you change your mind, you know where you can find us.'

We had the pool mostly to ourselves. Just a few children in the shallow end, splashing and shrieking, occasionally chastised by a bored-looking woman in a one-piece.

Samson had claimed a sun lounger on the near side of the water. He was topless, lying on his back with his palms turned upwards, fingers softly curled, his head tilted to the side, the bud of a white AirPod just visible. His body glistened, a bottle

of sun cream tucked between the gap of his legs, almost inviting me to reach.

Registering my presence, he looked out from over his
sunglasses.

'Lie with me,' Samson said, pulling out one headphone
and reaching languidly to tap the vacant sun lounger
beside him.

'All right,' I said, my throat tightening.

'She's glorious, no? The sun?'

'Yeah,' I said, flattening out my towel and lying back. 'Hope
you're not expecting this in England.'

'I expect nothing. I come with no expectation.'

'Right.'

'Again, I am sorry about the ten. My agent, he says this is
good for the sponsors, you know?'

'It's fine,' I said, almost meaning it.

'This agent, he is gone now. He has other business. Now,
I am alone.'

'Well,' I said, a little flustered, 'Not alone. You've got me.
I hope we can do well together. I mean, as a team. It looked
like you were enjoying yourself out there today.'

'It is good. I like everyone. I hope they like me. You think
they like me?'

I paused – unsure of how to answer, struck by the vulner-
ability of the question.

'Yeah, of course. I think everyone's glad you chose us. We
need all the help we can get. It'll be a tough season.'

'Ah, but we like the tough, yes?'

'I guess so.'

In this position, facing that faultless desert sky, it felt easier to be near him. He was just a disembodied, beautiful, inquisitive voice.

'The goalkeeper, he is your friend, yes?'

'Kyle? Yeah, he's a good mate. We came through together. From the academy.'

'I hate goalkeepers,' Samson said flatly.

I laughed, reading the comment as jest, but Samson remained silent. I raised myself on one arm and peered over my sunglasses.

'You're serious?'

'Of course,' Samson said, unmoved. 'Goalkeepers, they are cowards. The keeper is afraid of real football.'

He batted his index finger through the air between us.

'We are the enemy of the goalkeeper. When I have a son or daughter, I would be ashamed if they hide in a goal.'

'That seems a bit harsh.'

'Do you have any kids?' Samson said, glancing over at the splashing children.

'What? No!' I said, a little too sharply, lying back down. 'No, I'm the same age as you.'

'Ah, but age does not stop a child, correct? A child, she happens so easily. I am sure many women, they love to have your child.'

'I don't know about that,' I said.

'Maybe you have different priorities, eh? Still plenty of time for children.'

'All I ever wanted was this,' I said. 'Football, I mean. My priority is playing for this club. To make my family proud, you know?'

'And you worry they are not proud?'

I spoke defensively, scratching my arm and mumbling something about my father and local tradition, then attempted to redirect the conversation.

'What's Monaco like?'

'My mama, she says Monaco is illusion,' Samson said confidently, fingering his crucifix. 'Monaco, it is as we say with the keeper – it is a place to hide – there is no substance to this city. The people, they worship themselves. They worship luxury. They have no purpose.'

'You Christian, then?' I asked, gesturing to his necklace.

'Catholic,' Samson said, 'But only when it matters.'

Only when it matters – easing back into a reclined position, I considered his words, the sun brushing over my skin. I lay there, warm and relaxed, bathing in the audacity of Samson's confidence, feeling emboldened by his mere proximity. Even God worked to his convenience.

Lost in thought, I fell asleep. When I woke, Samson was in the pool, his chest and shoulders above the water, hairless and gleaming, heading a ball back and forth with our Senegalese winger, Baba, who was counting their tally aloud in English.

'Forty-eight, forty-nine, fifty . . .'

I sat up and walked over, dangling my legs into the water, dragging my hand over the surface.

'Come to join us?' Samson asked, his eyes still tracking the ball.

'Fifty-six, fifty-seven, fifty-eight . . .'

'Maybe,' I said, twisting my body in a dramatic stretch. 'Just got to wake up a bit first.'

Baba stumbled backwards, losing his footing, allowing the ball to hit the water.

'It's his fault,' he said, pounding the water at me and kissing his teeth, 'He distracted me, eh?'

'I'm not taking any blame. And that looked boring anyway.'

'You are right,' Samson said. 'It was boring.'

'Fuck you both,' Baba said, wading slowly to the shallow end.

'They say I have to sing tonight,' Samson said, pulling himself out of the pool to sit beside me, his trunks slipping deliciously down his waist.

'Yeah,' I said, swallowing. 'Just a laugh. Everyone has to go through it.'

'What is it you sing?'

'Last season, after the manager brought me into the squad, I sang "Like a Virgin", by Madonna. I didn't pick it, they made me.'

'"Like a Virgin"? I don't know this song?' Samson said, kicking gently under the water.

'What? Come on, you must know it.'

'No – how does it go?'

I hummed the tune, then began to sing the hook of the chorus.

Touched for the very first time

Samson stuck out his tongue and burst into laughter, 'I'm joking, virgin boy. Winding you up, you know?'

'Oh fuck you,' I said, shoving him forwards, back into the pool, blushing fiercely.

After a short swim, we returned to our sun loungers and discussed music. Samson introduced me to some French rap, sharing his AirPods, sliding one into my ear and choosing the songs. My head was filled with a thick, foreign pulse, a rhythm within me that Samson controlled.

It felt intimate.

It felt good.

8

Upstairs in my room, I took my third shower of the day; my face lifted to the beat of the water, cleansing me of the chlorine and the thought of him, the sinews of his forearms, the sharp edge of his jaw, the soft warmth of his skin.

Stepping out from the steam, I examined my suitcase, agape on the hotel floor. I found myself inspecting my clothes, assessing for Samson's approval, imagining the fashions he would have been accustomed to in Monaco – a world of designer brands, ironed collars, subtlety and refinement.

Fashion was a freedom I had failed to fully embrace. In a world of strict schedules and even stricter diets, what footballers wear is one of the few ways we can exercise control and express our personalities.

I stood in front of the bathroom mirror and held up shirt after shirt, measuring the pastel blue and hot pink against my emerging tan. I felt unsure of what I was looking for – more feeling than thinking. More wanting and longing.

There was nothing special about my appearance except my height, and height alone is hardly worthy of compliments. I looked at my parted hair and willowy limbs and felt inadequate of reciprocated desire. In the end, I settled on a plain polo and smart jeans – sufficiently inconspicuous. Suitably adequate.

Downstairs, the hotel had decorated the dining room in our team's colours and arranged their furniture into two long banquet tables. There were four new players due to perform, one scheduled between each course of our dinner. As club captain, Bert acted as the evening's master of ceremonies. He'd scheduled Samson last, a sure sign that he'd be subjected to the harshest treatment.

'How you feeling?' I asked Kyle, taking a seat beside him.

'Better, thanks – head's still got a throb on. Probably just as well there's no booze.'

'If I were performing, I'd rather be pissed.'

'Well, being pissed couldn't have made you any worse.'

'Get to fuck,' I said, jabbing Kyle in the ribs and grabbing a bread roll.

As we ate, I chatted and scrolled absently through Twitter – a regular search of my own name: an endless parade of undulating opinion, veering from praise to dismissal and back again.

Passing behind me on his way to the toilet, Samson snatched the phone from my hand.

'Oi, what the fuck,' I said, my voice cracking.

'This is bad for you,' he said, examining the screen, tutting. 'These fans, they are idiots. They know nothing. Do not listen.'

'Give it here,' I said, attempting to hide my alarm.

'Be kind to yourself, eh?' Samson said, handing the phone back.

While dishes were cleared between each course, the evening's performers took their turn at the head of the tables, clutching water bottles as makeshift microphones and rushing a cappella through their allocated songs. Other members of the squad were elected to record or broadcast the proceedings on their phones, sharing the terrible singing and stilted dancing to their millions of followers.

As Mario, our new attacking midfielder, stepped up before dessert, ready to serenade us with his rendition of 'Uptown Girl', the mood in the room shifted. The club owner had arrived and was hovering in the doorway. He was accompanied by a man I recognised from pictures – it was the Oxford-educated son of the Emir. This was the sheikh who had championed football in his country. His well-groomed face was plastered everywhere in the hotel.

'Don't mind us,' our club owner announced. 'Just pretend like I'm not here.'

'That's what we always do!' shouted Bert, prompting the rest of us to fall about laughing, more riotous than the joke really merited.

'*Albert*,' the manager hissed, standing and hustling his way towards the door, approaching His Royal Highness and the owner in a deferential stance, attempting to shepherd them both away, into the corridor.

'I hope you have a pleasant stay,' the sheikh said warmly, stepping around the manager and raising his arm to the room with a smile. 'Good luck for next season.'

'Cheers, mate,' Bert replied on our collective behalf.

L'oracolo missed both Mario's song and the dessert course, but returned just in time to witness Samson being called for his turn. He swaggered up the table with his back straight, shoulders wide – a posture of pure chutzpah. Bert brought the room to an expectant hush.

'Well boys, we've reet been looking forward to this one, eh? Fancy feet here is going to be performing a proper banger. A real classic of the genre. For one night only, our very own Samson is joining the Pussycat Dolls, singing "Don't Cha".'

Hoots and cheers filled the room as Bert passed Samson a sheet of paper with the lyrics.

Samson examined the paper with a smile and brushed one hand over his head.

'Bof!' he said, removing a stone-coloured linen blazer and stepping up onto a chair. 'I will need the help. You make the beat, *oui?*'

'I think we can manage that, right lads?' Bert said, initiating a clap.

'Get on with it,' called Baba, his phone aloft.

Unfazed, Samson paused, closed his eyes, held the paper at arm's length, and started to sing. His voice was baritone, flat and toneless, but completely assured: each lyric sung with energy and purpose, each pause punctuated by a loose wiggle of his shoulders.

Between lines, Samson looked up from the paper and smiled down the table, blowing kisses and winking towards the coaching staff, dancing stiltedly on his chair, clearly enjoying himself, relishing his position as the evening's final course.

Beside me, Kyle whistled like a catcall, thumping the table and knocking over a glass.

Stepping down off the chair mid-verse, Samson strutted over to where the manager sat and forcibly pulled back his chair, raising one long leg onto the edge of his seat, hands on his hips, shimmying his upper body. The manager pulled a good-natured grimace and leaned away, continuing to clap, while the rest of us cheered and laughed. I mentally willed Samson to thrust – just once, for my sake alone.

'Here,' Kyle said, leaning over and cupping his hands to my ear in an attempt to drown out the whooping around us. 'Good job that sheikh's not seeing this, eh? They've got pretty strong ideas on how to handle any queer shit – straight down the yard for a stoning.'

I pulled my head away and made no comment, watching as Samson stepped back up onto his chair, throwing down the sheet of paper and encouraging us all to sing along with his finale. The whole room wishing to be *freaks like me*. As Samson finished, our rhythmic clapping hastened to hard applause. He took a bow and climbed down.

'Fucking brilliant, marra,' Bert said, slapping Samson's back as he rushed over to apologise to the manager.

'Let's have another hand for him, lads,' Bert said, rousing us to our feet.

The moment felt significant. As the team cheered and gathered around him, reaching over each other to pat at his shoulder, Samson must have known that he'd won everyone over, that he'd successfully staked his claim to my shirt, that he'd laid the foundations for all that was to follow.

A short while later, I excused myself to bed, and found myself alone with Samson in the foyer, waiting for the lift.

'Long day,' I said dumbly, filling the silence between us.

'Yes,' Samson said soberly. 'Long, but good. I enjoy your company.'

'Oh – yeah, same. I mean, I enjoyed yours too. And you were great tonight. Really great.'

'Thanks,' Samson said, pressing again on the already illuminated *up* arrow.

'I bet you'll go viral. Your dancing.'

'Ah, but I made them clap,' Samson said, tapping his temple. 'When you clap, you cannot record so well.'

'Very clever,' I said, unable to recall whether anyone had actually persisted with the filming. 'It'll be good – this season. I promise.'

'You promise?' he said, turning to face me, meeting my eyes. 'Okay then, I hold you to this. You make it good for us both.'

The lift arrived with a sharp ping and we stepped inside, standing with our backs pressed to opposite walls of the box.

'I call my mama now,' Samson said, pulling out his phone. 'She worries.'

'Oh, cool. Is she still in Monaco?'

'No, no. She lives in Paris.' He paused, examining my face for recognition. 'France, you know?'

'Oh, yeah. Of course.'

The lift pinged again, arriving at my floor.

'This is me. I'm in room fifty-three. Just so you know.'

'Okay, *bon soir.* Dream well.'

'Yeah. Night, mate.'

Swaddled in the dark of my bed, I allowed thoughts of him to consume me. The flex and pulse of his body. The harsh edge of his smile. The promise I had committed to. Desire throbbed in my groin like a disease I might succumb to. I lay there and held myself, commencing the telltale rustle of starched hotel sheets, gripping and stroking until I found relief, suddenly alone and wet with fresh shame.

9

I'd had these feelings before. But less defined, more abstract forms of want. Kissing Kyle had just been experimentation. Easier to deny, to dismiss as confusion. Bodies want bodies. Skin wants skin. We want what we know, and I only knew football – the white concrete walls of our changing rooms, the low stuccoed ceilings, the *clap-clap* of muddy boots, air diffused with the tart aroma of male effort. I knew of their bodies in the showers, washed clean of the winter sod, the scrub and blush of tired limbs. Bodies exhausted by a shared triumph, strengthened in spirit by a narrow defeat.

I put no name to those feelings, that frantic, carnal energy. I subsumed it all into my play, into what mattered, what would define and save me.

At training the following morning, *L'oracolo* announced his line-up for the exhibition match. Samson had been placed straight into the first eleven. I had a spot on the bench.

I had come to the session intending to keep a distance from Samson, wary of his allure, eager to focus and desperate to make a bid for my place. I would need to reprogramme myself – to think of him as competition, to perceive him as a threat.

After the warm-ups, we were split into opposing teams – first teamers and bench fodder. Bibs and shirts, seven a side, fifteen-minute halves. That was my first time seeing him in our proper kit. He wore our colours so effortlessly, unburdened from the heavy hopes of fans, unencumbered by the weight of our history.

The good will Samson had garnered through his vocal performance did not translate into leniency on the pitch. Attempting to nullify his pace, we challenged him hard, forcing his side into a patient approach.

Samson showed no signs of frustration. He played with an uncommon flourish, embracing the role of diversion. In devoting our focus to Samson, we exposed ourselves, opening up room for Mario to find the net with an angled finish past Kyle's near post.

'Lazy, lazy,' Jean-Claude scolded from the sidelines, hustling us. 'Give him more cover – track back, track back.'

At the restart, Kyle lobbed the ball long. I watched it over my shoulder, running on, taking one touch, and dinking it neatly over Theo, our first-choice keeper.

'Very nice,' called Jean-Claude, 'Good energy. Nice recovery.'

In a rest between games, I busied myself with a ball, dancing through my repertoire of tricks, peripherally aware of Samson's gaze.

'How did you do that?' Samson approached to ask.

'Do what?' I said coolly, aware of exactly what he'd meant. The move had been my signature trick for years – it was one I'd stolen from *FIFA* aged twelve. I'd practised the trick for hours in my garden every evening.

'Show me again,' Samson commanded.

'This?' I said, stepping back and repeating the trick. 'It's just a heel-flick-turn. You have to step on the ball with your right, kick it out from under with the inside of your left, then control at a diagonal with your right, and shift positions. Easy.'

I passed Samson the ball and watched, as within three attempts, he was able to pull off the move, then again, managing it even more slickly than I was capable of.

'Nice,' I said, my voice catching on the word. 'Good job.'

'When I do this in the match, I think of you,' Samson said, backing away, still practising.

I felt a slurry of fury and fear. Overwhelming inadequacy. From that point onwards, it would no longer be possible to fool myself. I accepted then that he was on a different level. That his talent was incomparable to mine – to any of us in the squad.

'Half-time,' the manager told me as we left the field, finally done for the day. 'I will bring you on at half-time.'

'Whatever you decide, boss,' I said, pulling off my bib.

'You're a good boy,' he said, raising an affectionate fist to my chin. 'You know how much I need you this season, yes? You know how important you are to this team?'

'Yes, boss.'

'Good boy. Go get some rest.'

10

The stadium was at the centre of the capital. We were bussed over from the resort under an armed police escort, sweltering in our match-day suits. Our owner had elected to join us for the short journey, leading to a muted atmosphere on board. The manager sat by his side and attempted to fill the silence by exuberantly commenting on the phenomenal architecture en route – the alien verticality of their edifices, modern totems sprung from oil.

'So tall!' *L'oracolo* pointed, uncharacteristically animated. 'Incredible, no?'

'How you feeling?' Kyle whispered from beside me.

'Yeah, all right.'

'Don't you think it's odd though, football without a crowd? Makes you feel like a plaything. A toy for some spoiled brat.'

'I haven't really thought about it, to be honest.'

'Well, you should. We're only here because that daft git's trying to flog the club to the Qataris. I don't know how well it'll go down with these big-boy Arabs if we go out there and humiliate the locals eight–nil.'

At the stadium, a beautiful woman in a hijab escorted us from the entrance to our dressing room, leading us on a scenic route that highlighted the ground's numerous features and amenities: a capacity of thirteen thousand, floodlights, covered terraces and an on-site mosque.

'And I understand you have just hosted Dortmund,' the manager said enthusiastically, loud enough for the entire team to hear.

Before kick-off, both squads lined out on the pitch, facing our owner and the honoured guests. I watched from the bench as the opposition players sang along to the Qatari national anthem with exaggerated passion, arms draped around each other's shoulders in either comradeship or fear.

From kick-off, it was immediately apparent that the Qataris were rank amateurs in comparison to our regular opponents. They had set up in a tight formation, clearly intent on damage limitation, planning to attack on the counter, despite lacking the pace.

We caressed the ball around the pitch casually, playing it out the back, keeping our passes low to the ground, dominating possession. Of our eleven starters, only two had been with the club for more than three seasons. It was vital for us to feel out a natural rhythm of play, for adjusting wavelengths and connections.

Samson seemed to be enjoying himself. He played with a broad smile, anticipating space, darting instinctively between players, running off the ball and calling for pass after pass with a relentless, bounding energy. I watched him drift wide, dragging out his marker, then with a flick and a swivel, cut back inside, leaving the defender in his wake, challenging shadows.

Once I began watching him, I found it impossible to look

away. There was a hypnotic, brute beauty to his movement. With his back to his marker, Samson dropped his shoulder. Then came the feather touch, hover and pivot, and finally the strike – twisting and reaching, the ball low and unstoppable, shaving the grass into the right corner of the goal.

A rising cheer from everyone around me, a hand on my shoulder, shaking me from my stupor.

'Bloody hell,' fawned Kyle. 'How'd he find the space for that?'

In the stands above us, moderate applause from the dignitaries.

Samson freed himself from the mob of celebrating bodies, raising one arm towards the royals in thanks, then running back to the centre circle. The Qatari players squabbled among themselves, pointing and accusing, unable to hold their shape in the face of real class.

Before half-time, he'd scored another: a bullet header at the far post, rising high and picking his spot, the keeper flapping comically. The manager allowed himself a small fist pump, then resumed writing furiously into his notepad. With a click of his pen, *L'oracolo* turned to me. 'Get ready,' he said, 'You're coming on, remember?'

I pulled on my bib and shuffled up the dugout, stepping over legs, into the sunshine. I ran up and down the touchline, my attention divided, endeavouring to watch, to follow the play, to appreciate Samson's magic. I found myself wondering whether I was being subbed on to actively limit our goals, as Kyle had speculated.

In the VIP area, many of the royals were occupied with their phones, seemingly having grown weary of the one-sided match.

At the referee's whistle, I jogged to the dugout, filing behind the others into the dressing room. Some players excused themselves to the urinals, while others snatched greedily from a table of fruit, snacks and sports drinks.

'Okay, okay,' the manager said, stepping into the centre of the room, clapping and whistling, ushering everyone to benches mounted around the walls.

'Good half, boys – good half. But this is the minimum we expect – you hear? The absolute minimum. Two goals, this does not flatter us. Imagine we lose the focus, give up a goal. Imagine, boys! One lapse and we concede? This is unforgivable. Just stay focused and be patient – these men, they are full of mistakes. One pass, two pass, we cut them apart, just as I said.'

Around me, players chewed on bananas, listening attentively. The manager's team talks always found a good balance between motivation and tactics. He had the charisma to hold the room, commanding the space, walking back and forth in calculated strides, doling out intense stares. He possessed the subtle genius of finding new ways to say the same old things.

'We do not need any stupid challenges – you hear me, Bert? No needless injuries, please. To us or them.

'Mario, I want you to stay closer to the number eight. All their play goes through him.

'Samson, very good. Excellent strikes. You will rest for the second half.'

'But gaffer,' Kyle objected, 'It's his debut. He's on for a perfect hat-trick.'

The manager spun on his heel to face Kyle, his expression severe.

'Did I ask you? Did anyone ask you? Who the fuck are you? Who the fuck are you to say this? I decide when a player comes off – do you understand?'

'Yes, gaffer,' Kyle said, looking down at his boots, humbled.

'What else?' *L'oracolo* said, waiting expectantly.

'Sorry, gaffer.'

'Anyone else got an opinion on how to do my job?'

Heads shook or dropped, hidden behind bottles.

'Okay then, good. See you back out there.'

I changed into my shirt and began my pre-game routine, relacing my boots – always the right shoe first. Having a ritual helped me settle mentally, quell the nerves, calm the hollow thrum at the bottom of my gut.

'Come on then, boys,' Bert cried, 'Let's fucking stick it up 'em.'

Lining up for kick-off, I enjoyed knowing that Samson was watching me. His attention charged my every touch with added drama. My body and skill, presented for his judgement, inviting voyeurism.

I played with extra zeal, trying to replicate the tenor of Samson's movement, his hurtling runs, his springing leaps. I completely abandoned the thought that this was a friendly match, launching myself after every loose ball, every errant pass.

'Relax, relax!' called the manager's voice from the touch-line, directed to me as I sprinted past.

I had a hand in our third goal on the hour mark, taking a shot from range that the keeper fumbled, allowing Mario to smash the rebound into the roof of the net.

A comfortable three–nil victory. We shook hands with the

opposition players and waved to acknowledge the royals, who remained seated.

Back in the changing room, *L'oracolo* made his way around, congratulating each player.

'Good work,' he said, ruffling my hair like a coddled infant.

'Thanks, boss.'

'You raised your game today. Feeling strong, yes?'

'Pretty good, thanks, boss.'

He stepped away to grab a topless Samson and led him over to where I was sat, still removing my shoes.

'Fighting for a place – it makes us all better. Stronger in mind and heart. You will be a good influence on each other, I hope.'

'I hope so too,' Samson said, meeting my eye and smiling.

I did not look away.

11

Following games, I retreated into myself. I'd fulfil any media duties as required, then put on my headphones and avoid conversation, rushing back to my car, or straight to the team bus. I liked to imagine this self-imposed isolation was akin to meditation – a healthy, mental retreat, enabling me to recentre my focus and properly process the result. But sometimes, the routine engendered the opposite effect, forcing me to dwell on what could have been, privately obsessing over missed chances, shanked shots, unjust refereeing decisions. In the wake of bad results, I'd developed a compulsion for self-flagellation, searching the internet for mentions of my name – checking to see what anonymous commenters and armchair pundits had to say about my performance, scrolling through an endless stream of amateur analysis and barbed insults, spread across a dozen languages.

I only used social media from nameless, private accounts. Dad had arranged for my verified platforms to be outsourced to an agency who tweeted and posted on my behalf, curating a voice far wittier and more palatable than my own, fulfilling all the contractual obligations to my small selection of sponsorships.

When news of our three–nil scoreline leaked through to the public, the online buzz around Samson was fevered. Our new loan signing had scored twice in a forty-five-minute debut. Some were prematurely calling him our saviour. Others wrote off the result as meaningless – putting three past a bunch of farmers and sheep-herders meant nothing in the grand scheme of things.

If Samson was aware of the hype and debate, he showed no evidence of being affected. For the rest of the pre-season tour, he applied himself exclusively to football and the team: to learning *L'oracolo*'s patterns of play, our set piece routines, our strengths and our weaknesses as a squad.

Once I'd seen him naked in the showers, an element of mystery to my lust was lost. I grew less bashful in his company, more capable of proper conversation. I no longer had to covertly scan his shorts for the outline of his cock. I could just sense it, visualise it while lying in bed, thinking only of him.

For much of the trip, I stuck by his side, under the ruse of nurturing some blossoming synergy between us. We sat together on flights and at dinners. We spoke about his mother's escape from Rwanda in the aftermath of the genocide: her months in a refugee camp in Zaire, her asylum in Paris.

'Some day, I will visit my mama's country.'

'Oh, wow. I didn't realise you'd never been there.'

Samson scratched at his neck, seemingly embarrassed. It was the first time I'd ever seen his mask of confidence slip.

'In Paris, the rents are very high,' he said. 'Mama, she had to budget. Priorities, you know? And now – with this life – when is there time? With this life, when can there be a chance to make this trip?'

'I guess so. I bet it is amazing there though.'

'Yes,' Samson said. 'The land of a thousand hills. My mama has great affection for her country. She is loyal. Mama always says there is much so much beauty. We are both proud to be Rwandan.'

'Spending a lot of time with him, aren't ya?' Kyle observed one afternoon, a touch of jealousy in his voice.

'I guess so.'

'Popular lad, isn't he? Settled in real nice.'

'Seems that way.'

At mealtimes, Bert and I helped to build Samson's vernacular, delivering a crash course in the local dialect. Howay the lads and the reet canny lasses. The radgie fellas, clamming for some scran. We emphasised that language was essential to survival – the passcode to the city and our fans' hearts.

I spoke with him about the British climate. I warned him of our winters – the frozen turf and the dawn's dewy glaze. The endless canopy of rolling grey. I presented myself as his guide, his light through the northern murk.

In Dubai, I took him shopping for thermal clothes – gloves and base-layer tights, cashmere scarves and woollen fleeces: clothing that had no rightful place in the middle of the desert. Samson proved a willing model, insisting on photos for his Instagram, posing with that inscrutable smile.

Occasionally, he would seem to offer me a sign, suggesting some recognition of my desires. A returned gaze, held for just a beat too long. A flex of his arms while he knew I was looking.

Though I dreamed and longed for frankness, I feared the reality. I knew that I'd deny everything, attempt to dissuade him, cut off the connection between us, everything we had forged. It was safer living with a fantasy that could never be – accepting the consolation of his friendship.

But I could not monopolise his attention. For some matters, Samson looked elsewhere. I stayed on the periphery as he discussed women with Dami, our London-born midfielder. Sat in an airport's first-class lounge, hunched over Dami's phone, they flicked through photo after photo of their conquests, hooting and yapping like wild animals.

'I swear, bruv,' Dami said, slapping his own knee, 'the girls in the city are crazy for it. Gagging, you get me? They ain't like the London galdem. Up North, the ladies, they all love Dami. We'll smash the town and I'll show you the way.'

'Sounds good, my brother,' Samson said, taking his hand, pulling together.

In that moment, I hated them and I hated myself. I hated him for being so basic. So ordinary in his desires. Most of all, I hated their performative, primal appetite for curves and softness – things I could never offer him. I hated that there would be no reason for me to hope.

'You're kidding yourself, Dami,' I heard myself saying, looking up from my own phone. 'None of those girls are crazy for you.'

'Because you've had better?' Dami said, scoffing.

I shrugged my shoulders. 'Maybe. But either way, those women are real people, you know? They're not just objects for you to ogle.'

Dami got to his feet and loomed over me, all muscle and menace.

'Go fuck yourself, eh?'

'Hey, hey,' Samson interjected, standing and coming between us, his hands raised in a placating gesture towards Dami. 'There's no need. Calm down, eh?'

'Calm *doon*,' I corrected, trying to sound relaxed.

'I'll say what I want,' Dami said, returning to his seat. 'Fucking wasteman teacher's pet.'

12

Across the remaining three games of the tour, Samson found the net another four times, playing in front of a few hundred devoted fans who had made the trip out to the Middle East to support us. Hype around Samson was reaching a crescendo, and the broader media had started paying attention. I was a footnote to most conversations about him; an afterthought on how our abilities might complement each other.

Four straight wins and only one goal conceded. *L'oracolo* was pleased and the owner was delighted. It seemed there was a real possibility the club would be sold to an equally problematic but cash-rich buyer.

On our final afternoon in the United Arab Emirates, a few hours prior to our return to England, Bert decided it was time to give Samson a proper initiation. Bert firmly believed that pranks and banter are the lifeblood of morale in a football squad. The significance of morale cannot be overestimated. A positive atmosphere can caulk most faults.

As we rested by a hotel pool, Bert swapped out Samson's sun cream for a tube of our physio's Deep Heat lotion – a therapy product intended for localised pain relief, causing penetrating warmth. Emerging from a swim, Samson covered himself before feeling the effects and registering why everyone was laughing. Moments later, he was screaming and vowing revenge. He threw himself back into the water, calling for ice in three different languages.

I had to excuse myself. The sight and sound of him begging and writhing was too much for my cock to bear.

On the flight back to the UK, Samson sat next to me and slept, his head lolled to the side, presenting the taut muscle of his neck. In the din of the cabin, I tortured myself, inspecting his beautiful mouth, slack in a silent moan, the pink wetness of his lips and the brilliant white of his perfect teeth. I longed to taste the sleep on his lips, to sink my nails into his strong thighs, to brush myself against his skin, to grapple with his body and feel him grow in my hand, to drain him of his essence, to claim his talent as my own.

FIRST HALF

13

My mother had refused to send me any pictures of the on-going renovations to my new home, insisting that I must wait until my return from tour, until everything was ready, until everything was perfect. On my first night back, I stayed in my parents' house for what was supposed to be the final time. My old room was stripped bare of my possessions, just a shell with a single bed, a well-loved duvet in our team's strip.

My parents planned to convert the room into an office for my father. He had been taking his duties as my agent seriously, registering with all the correct authorities, keeping paper copies of contracts and negotiations, even travelling to London to attend conferences and forums with his new peers. He described it as 'the career he never knew he wanted'.

The following morning, my mother drove me to the new house, fretting out loud, defending her choices of colour, the carpet material, her arrangement of mirrors and sofas and tables. Nothing I said on that drive could have reassured her. Only my reaction could bring her relief: the reaction she'd imagined throughout those long months of bossing around builders, waiting for deliveries, measuring and re-measuring.

It was the thought of my reaction that would have sustained her.

The house was almost exactly equidistant from the stadium and the training ground. A twenty-minute drive in each direction, and just a half-hour walk away from my parents.

When we arrived, Mam insisting on recording the grand reveal on her phone, handing me the keys at the bottom of the driveway like the passing of a torch. It was a pressure distinct from anything I'd felt on the pitch. My mother's expectations were matched only by the size of her love.

My face was already drawn in shocked delight before the door was fully open. In the video, I walk from room to room, hands on my head, saying 'wow' and 'thank you', complimenting her every choice, every feature, patiently indulging her as she points out minor embellishments in every room, the little touches that she had obsessed over: the indents on the mantel, the handles on the dresser, a custom-built cupboard for the boiler.

'And this here's a spider plant, love,' she said, turning the camera to a pot on the kitchen counter, overflowing with ribbons of olive-green and bone-white leaves. 'Just like the one your auntie's got, remember? They're dead easy to take care of. A drop of water now and then. Brings a bit of life to the place, doesn't it? A bit of air for your soul.'

The video ends with me hugging my mother in the master bedroom, her phone pressed into my back, muffling the audio – on the recording, you can just about distinguish the word 'love' from both of us.

Still holding my body, Mam looked at me with a soft,

concerned expression. She reached for my fringe and adjusted my hair.

'You'll be okay here, won't you?' she said, more statement that question.

Mam stayed until lunch, then left me alone in the house. That huge, empty space. All mine. Just me and my imagination, my racing thoughts and awful desires, the caustic smell of fresh paint.

That first night, I lay in bed, on edge. My ears perked at every noise: the unfamiliar creaks and groans of a settling house, the whistle of the wind in the trees outside, casting long shadows against the curtains.

I rolled onto my front and fanned out my legs, straining for rest. Under the sheets, tossing and brooding, thinking of him, only him, counting minutes until they became hours, until there was sun.

Just once. That's what I told myself. Once to be satisfied. Once chance to feel the heat of his lips on my neck, his hand on my thigh, his flex of his fingers in my hair. Just once and the need would be met. Once and I'd want no more.

14

On the morning of our return to training, I was first to the ground. I planned to exhaust myself: to push as hard as possible and find rest. It had been three days since I'd moved in, and I still wasn't sleeping well.

As the squad arrived, we greeted each other like long-missed brothers – lots of grabbing and shoving, playful and boisterous. After weeks of being around each other constantly, just a few days apart had felt like an eternity. Samson was among the last to arrive to the pitch, emerging with a gaggle of staff who had just led him on a guided tour of our facilities.

'So what do you think?' Bert asked, grabbing Samson by the shoulder.

'Good,' Samson said, bobbing his head, giving nothing away. 'Very nice.'

'*Nice?*' Bert said, sneering affectionately. 'We know it ain't Monaco, but don't fuck us about with *nice*, ya cheeky wee bastard.'

The manager arrived five minutes later, notebook in hand and a smile on his face.

'Good morning, good morning,' he clamoured, calling our

attention, his voice loud and firm. 'Welcome to our new boys. Welcome to our home, eh? Are you ready for the *baptism of fire?*'

Our first match of the campaign was at home, versus Manchester City, the reigning league champions. We were expecting a capacity crowd. It was a game that we weren't expected to win. Last season, they had thrashed us at home and away en route to the title, winning by an aggregate score-line of nine–one.

'In this game,' *L'oracolo* roused us, 'there is no pressure for us, hmm? We can play with freedom. We play with ex-pression. We enjoy ourselves, yes? Focus on the basics, eh? Simple football – pass and move, pass and move. Simple, solid football. Tight at the back, hit on the break. Just how we like it, eh? Shut them out and we claim a point. Every point matters, eh?'

He paused, waiting for a response.

'That's right, boss,' Bert said, taking the initiative, applaud-ing aggressively.

'You all know why you are here,' the manager continued, 'We come here to train. We train to play. We play to survive in this league. We train as a team and we fight as a team. This season, we will be proud – proud like lions.'

With that, the manager brought his hands together in a single, firm clap. Rolling back on his heels, his expression softened.

'So let's get started, hmm?'

15

In the lead-up to that first game, we were subjected to a near constant stream of media duties, sponsor obligations and photo shoots. Every day at the training ground, there'd be a troop of marketing professionals and journalists, queuing to hold interviews, to pose and dress us like dolls.

The weight of responsibility is distributed unevenly across the team, with the biggest stars carrying the largest burdens. As a relative unknown, I had escaped mostly unused, until our press department called to verify their notes from the previous campaign, which suggested that Tommy and I were the squad's most dedicated gamers. They were nominating me for a video promoting the FIFA video game series as their sole remaining option. The format of the video would require me to make guesses at my in-game stats, then act incredulous when the actual numbers were revealed. I agreed to the video, on the provision that I could do it with one of my teammates, rather than the smarmy looking YouTuber they'd lined up to host.

'Who would you be most comfortable with?' asked the video producer.

'I dunno,' I said, wincing as a young girl fluttered a make-up brush over my forehead. 'Either Kyle or maybe Samson, I guess.'

'Not Kyle,' interjected a man with a clipboard. 'No one's going to click on a video starring the reserve keeper.'

I have never been comfortable on camera. With so much to hide, I had a tendency to become withdrawn and dreary, which put me at risk of coming across as either uninterested or arrogant. Fortunately, interviews are always held under supervision – members of the club's marketing and legal teams hovered, vetting my answers, shaping the narrative, stage-managing everything to present me and the club in the best possible light.

Ten minutes later, Samson had been dragged out of the gym and mic'd up. I watched as he charmed the production crew, introducing himself to everyone, shaking hands and apologising for being 'a little stinky'. He seemed completely assured and unfazed by the cameras.

'Thanks for saving me, mate,' I said. 'I hate these things.'

'*Pas de problème*,' Samson said.

'Hah,' I said, fidgeting. 'Nice one.'

'Right,' Samson said, taking the seat beside me and slapping his thighs. 'What is it we do?'

A young, pretty member of the production crew briefed us on broadly what to say, directing most of her attention to Samson; blushing a little when he complimented her outfit. A pang of jealousy shot through me. My whole body tensed up – jaw locked, face severe.

'Relax, bro,' Samson said intuitively, leaning across, putting his hand on my knee, 'This too is a game, no? We pretend they are not here.'

'Okay,' I said, spellbound by his touch.

The video began with us introducing ourselves and talking about how much we played the game. After a few takes, I managed not to sound utterly robotic.

'Okay, we go,' Samson said, eager to proceed. He was handed a large cardboard cut-out of my in-game player card, detailing all my key stats, the back of the card facing me. 'Last year, they say your pace is seventy-four.'

'I know,' I said, 'And that was a joke. That should have been at least five points higher. Did you see my goal against Brighton?'

'This is what you guess? Five points better? Seventy-nine?'

'Yeah, go on then.'

'Final answer?'

'Yes! Don't mug me off, please.'

He tutted. '*Ooh la la*. You will not like – they say you are seventy-six.'

'Rubbish,' I said, pulling a disgusted face.

'Ah, but it is improvement, no?'

'Do you know what they've given you?'

'Can you check?' Samson asked, turning to the production crew.

'Give me a second,' the pretty lady mumbled, balancing a laptop on her arm. 'Samson, Samson – he's got eighty-six.'

'Eighty-six! Ten whole points faster?'

'Seventy-six, this is still pretty quick,' Samson said cheekily, producing that infectious smile.

'If we got out and race right now, do you really think you'd have that much of an edge?'

'I trust the experts!' Samson said, raising his hands like surrender, beaming a smile to the entire room.

'We ought to put you two together more often,' the marketing director told us afterwards. 'Great chemistry there, guys. You bring out the best in each other. I hope we get to see it on the pitch.'

'Me too,' I said.

'And if you actually decide to do a race, that'd be great content.'

'I will consider it,' Samson said, brushing down his shirt and heading off to speak to the pretty woman.

I unpinned my microphone and threw it to the floor.

16

Samson continued to settle in well. The club were paying for his suite in a fancy hotel just a ten-minute drive from our training ground. Without the enforced proximity of the tour, we were spending fewer hours together – our daily interactions being limited to time on the pitch and in the gym.

Stood in my hallway, watering the spider plant, I watched on Instagram as Samson gave the world a tour of his hotel room – moving from his walk-in wardrobe to his marble-countered bathroom, to his balcony overlooking the city: familiar spines and spires of factory chimneys and church steeples. The stadium's floodlights just visible to the north. And beyond the lights, the distant point where the city faded back to country: where motorways became roads, and roads became lanes.

I watched, suspicious of what Samson might be hiding, of what he didn't share. I hungered for signs that he was happy here – that he didn't resent his choice.

Sometimes, alone in my home, I felt myself altering my behaviour as though he were watching. I rehearsed conversations with him in the shower, on the drive to the training ground. In the hours we spent together, I posed him questions I'd already researched the answers to, casually mentioned music I knew he approved of, exaggerated the aspects of my personality that most closely mirrored his. I wanted to resemble the type of player and person that he'd truly respect. The excuse to be around Samson each day felt like a wonderful gift that I needed to continue proving myself worthy of.

The manager gave me the freedom to pick a new shirt number for myself from any of the vacant options. I consulted with Dad and ultimately selected number twenty-four – Mam's birthday, and the age that Dad planned for me to captain the side. When I texted Kyle to tell him the news, he sent a voice note reply, evidently in a huff.

'Oh, so you do still have my number?'

'Yeah, of course – why wouldn't I?' I replied in kind.

'Figured you'd pretty much forgotten me, what with your new best mate and all.'

'Ah, don't be daft, Kyle.'

'Proper chummy with the pretty boy, though, ain't ye?'

'We get on all right,' I said, trying not to sound too defensive. 'What's the problem with that?'

'No problem so long as you don't forget who your real mates are. The people who really know who you are and what you are.'

'What's that supposed to mean?'

'You know what it means. Mate.'

'Kyle – has something happened? Can you call me?'

Kyle scoffed as I answered.

'Figured you'd have heard by now. They're selling me, ain't they?'

'What? Are you serious?'

'Yeah. I'm probably gone by the City game.'

'Why didn't you say anything?'

'Why didn't you ask? Didn't you think to check where I've been?'

'I hadn't—'

'I ain't been in training all week. I fucking knew you hadn't noticed. Too busy with your new boyfriend, eh?'

'Don't say that.'

'I'll say it as I see it, mate,' Kyle hissed. 'I see the way you look at him.'

'I don't know what you want me to say. I obviously don't want you to go. Do you actually know where you're going? Going to get to use that Spanish?'

'As if you actually care,' he said.

'Kyle, please don't be like that. Of course I care.'

'I'm going wherever'll take me. Probably Watford, they reckon.'

'Watford's good!' I said, overly enthusiastic, 'Still in the Prem, right?'

'Yeah, I s'pose. So, what's this about your shirt number?'

'Oh,' I stumbled, 'It guess it doesn't matter really.'

'You're right. I guess it doesn't. See ye around, mate.'

'Kyle, wait—'

Kyle's transfer was confirmed the following day. Among our fans, reactions were muted. Theo was unquestionably a better keeper, and we'd finally managed to extract a decent fee for an academy player. On the other hand, we'd sold our second-choice keeper to one of our relegation rivals, with the transfer fee likely going straight into our owner's pockets.

Following Kyle's departure, I was the final home-grown player left in the squad.

'There is nothing sad about this,' Samson advised. 'We do not mourn the loss of cowards.'

17

The game against Manchester City established the tone for our season. We had everything to gain and nothing to lose. *L'oracolo* encouraged us to play with some joy, to embrace the occasion – another year at the pinnacle of football.

For Samson's competitive debut in the English game, he'd be facing down a three-man defence whose combined transfer value eclipsed our entire squad. I watched from the bench, basking in the balmy midsummer heat. The air smelled of lager and freshly clipped grass. In the stands, our fans wore short-sleeved kits, emblazoned with our sponsor's logo – living advertisements for another of the owner's struggling business ventures.

Around the twenty-minute mark, Theo made a long clearance, which was gathered well by Bert. With a quick twist and shift, Bert beat his marker and fed the ball to Samson, who found himself onside and clean through. One-on-one, Samson sent the keeper the wrong way, shooting emphatically into the corner of the net to put us one–nil up against the champions of England. Around me, the stadium erupted with brutish noise – a detonation of feeling as Samson ran to the stands in celebration, announcing his arrival.

I remained restrained. There were seventy minutes to play. Through years of hiding and ceaseless repression, I'd learned to audit and control my emotions. In the academy, they praised me for my restraint. They boasted that emotional discipline is a key component of athletic fortitude. In the eyes of my coaches, I possessed the steely focus of a born predator, an ideal striker's disposition. At nineteen, I had already forgone many joys in the name of stoicism and restraint.

Still leading at half-time, *L'oracolo* deployed military expressions to motivate us, referring to us as brothers-in-arms, urging us to fight, to defend, to work as a unit. Following Bert's lead, the squad barked back with intent, thumping each other roughly with bunched fists.

I found comfort in thinking and speaking of my teammates as brothers. Brotherhood meant a curious, boisterous bond. A connection that tempered affection with competition. Where we saw all of each other and would die for each other. Most important of all: you couldn't ever desire a brother. Your brother wasn't a sexual prospect.

Shortly after the restart, we conceded a penalty – handball from a close-range shot. From there, the game became a prolonged, nervous shudder. I watched as our defenders reverted to primitive tactics – punting the ball clear from danger, loading the box with bodies and praying for favourable deflections.

Since his goal, Samson had received limited service, only managing one other shot on target – a bobbling effort that was comfortably gathered by the City keeper. Recognising the situation, he had instinctually adjusted into the role of an agitator – dropping deep to support our midfielders, running the ball into the corners to waste time. It was unglamorous, necessary work – more evidence of Samson's maturity and selflessness.

Come full time, we'd held out for a well-deserved point against the title favourites and defending champions. In the terraces, our fans celebrated the result like a victory, singing the praises of our manager:

He sees what you don't
He sees what you don't
We've got the oracle
He sees what you don't

Stepping into the tunnel, I was surprised to spot my lurking father, proudly adorned in our full kit, the curve of his gut stretching the polyester.

'Dad, what are you doing here? You can't be down here.'

'No problem, is there? I just came to meet my new favourite player.'

'Yeah, but not now – Dad, stop, wait!'

Recognising Samson, my father launched himself into his path.

'Um, Samson, this is my dad.'

'Ah,' Samson said. '*Enchanté.*'

'Good to meet you, lad,' Dad said, grabbing Samson's hand and shaking it vigorously. 'Honestly, we're so glad to have you. We've been waiting for a player like you for a bloody long time.'

'So they say,' Samson said, smiling politely, wiping his free hand up and down his shirt.

'Proper man's performance out there today. Really good, tough stuff. Putting your body about a bit. That's all we ask for here. A proper bit of effort, you know?'

It occurred to me that my father would relay every detail of this interaction to his friends at the pub later that evening; that Samson's behaviour in this moment was as significant to my father as his performance on the pitch.

'What do you make of this one then?' Dad said, grabbing me by the arm. 'How's he coping in the man's game?'

'Ah, this is not mine to say. Your boy, he has many skills, but we play as a team, yes? Both of us, we rely on the good service.'

Samson flashed his eyes to the dressing room door and turned slightly towards me, his eyebrows raised, imploring me to help.

'Won't your mates be waiting, Dad?' I said, moving my body between them.

'Right, yeah,' Dad said, clearing his throat. 'I'll let you lads crack on. Ice baths and massages, all that good stuff.'

'Pleased to meet you,' Samson said, his voice rich and sincere.

'You too, lad. I'll see you about.'

In the dressing room, my nerves thawed, warmed by the good cheer of our squad and the earnest praises of *L'oracolo*.

'I am so proud, boys, so proud. Today, we show this league that we are here to stay.'

Despite not having played, I queued for a massage. I looked forward to these treatments. Strong, sexless hands that scoured my body for dormant, latent, lactic aches. The therapists thumbed intently across the map of my skin – at nodes and knots, the ridges and pockets of pain, kernels of cramp and buds of hurt.

Around me, older members of the squad stripped off, unwrapping themselves from braces and bindings – black strapping that looked like mourning. I watched as Bert received a cortisone shot into his knee. He insisted on receiving the injection in front of us, leading by example. A career-long cycle of receiving and recovering from countless minor injuries had inured Bert to the discomfort. He seemed to have made peace with the pain he would carry in his sinew throughout his impending retirement.

'Stings so sweet,' Bert growled, baring his teeth, fists clenched like fury as the long needle was pushed through dense, defiant flesh.

Among those who'd played, Samson's mood seemed to be the most tepid. He sat apart from the swaggering and jostling of our other players, calmly removing his boots.

'Aren't you happy?' I asked, stepping out of the queue to squat beside him. 'You've scored on your Premier League debut. Surely that's worth something?'

Samson shrugged his shoulders.

'We tie,' he said, now pulling off his shirt, flaunting his torso. 'I prefer that we win.'

'Right. Fair enough, I guess.'

'You look much like your father,' Samson said, now nude and standing before me.

'No I don't!' I responded, almost by instinct. 'I mean, obviously, but not really.'

'Of course you do. The nose, the shoulders. You must see this, no?'

'What? You're an idiot. I look nothing like him. He's about a foot shorter and he's huge.'

Even as I spoke, I felt surprised at myself, questioning where the reaction had come from.

'Deny if you must, my friend,' Samson said, shaking his head as he strutted to the shower. 'Whatever you say.'

18

Following the City game, Samson trained even more fiercely. It felt like he had taken it upon himself to inspire us, hoping that we might find ourselves caught in the tailwind of his energy. Samson ran and fought as though labour were its own pleasure.

I pushed my body hard, trying to keep pace, exerting myself, willing Samson to notice. But physically, I simply wasn't the same specimen. Compared to the rest of the squad, I was a boy.

For some time, our club dieticians had been emphasising that it was of critical importance for me to bulk up. It was in my interest to eat, to accumulate mass, to become a larger version of the same person. These analysts committed days and weeks of their professional lives to studying every aspect of my biology and genetic make-up; to honing and crafting a diet and exercise regime that would maximise my potential. They'd mapped out a future for me.

I forced down four large meals a day. Since moving out, Mam had retained responsibility for feeding me, keeping my fridge stocked with pre-prepared, nutritious dinners, flatly refusing my offers of payment for her efforts.

'It's good to have an excuse to pop over,' she justified her-self. 'Lots of little loose ends still to tie up around the place.'

By our next day off, I was as tired as I'd ever been. Tired from the head down, from shoulder to shin – my body heavy with its own resistance. A tiredness that spoke of perpetuity.

Wednesdays were our designated rest day. A chance to recover on our own terms. For most the squad, it was time to spend with their kids, to hang out with friends, to study English, or to manage their affairs. On Wednesdays, the team's group chat went mostly silent.

Football had denied me the ability to be spontaneous – to safely nip to the shops, to roam the city, to visit the coast. Without training, Wednesdays could be a long day to fill, locked away inside in my big, new, empty home. I struggled to sleep in – the rhythms and routines of a footballing life conditioned me to rise around seven, leaving me at the mercy of my thoughts for fifteen or so hours. Typically, I'd do some yoga, then torture myself with social media until around nine, before driving over to my parents' home for a second breakfast, disrupting Dad's work so that we could binge a series on Netflix.

That day, Dad had lined us up a well-reviewed Swedish crime drama.

'Fucking class, this,' he mumbled, as the autoplay ushered us mindlessly to the next episode.

It's easy to see how some players sink into their vices. Whether it be gambling, women or alcohol, I'm convinced that most habits begin as just another way to kill this exces-sive expanse of time. Time until the next day, the next game, the next season.

Samson had informed me of his intention to spend his days off back in the Île-de-France, taking the short flight home on a Tuesday afternoon, before returning late on a Wednesday evening, a taxi straight back to his hotel suite. Despite spending six days a week with Samson, I felt resentful at the prospect of sharing him, jealous of his family and childhood friends, these people who held a greater claim to his heart. We were one game into the season, and I'd already begun fostering a naive hope that Samson might stay with the club; that he might remain with me.

'Are you even watching?' Dad asked, snapping me out of a stupor.

'Sorry, Dad,' I said. 'Just distracted.'

'I've got a job to do, you know? If you're not in the mood, I'll crack on. You wouldn't believe the amount of nonsense I've got to deal with. There'll be another hundred emails waiting for me by now.'

'I know – sorry. I want to watch together. I'm enjoying. Go on, play the show.'

Returning home after dinner and a season's worth of Nordic gore, I climbed into bed and held myself, growing hard at the thought of Samson's head on my shoulder, his hand on my thigh. I craved small, impossible affections; kindnesses I'd never be worthy of. Many nights ended that way, gripping and tensing at the thought of him wanting me, needing me. But immediately after – the moment I had finished – cold reality leeched through: cool sheets and torrid remorse. A life unburdened from lust.

19

On Friday afternoon, our team coach departed the training ground, setting course for East Anglia for our first away fixture of the season – against Norwich. *L'oracolo* had stuck with the same eleven starters, keen to build on the foundations we'd set.

For our away games, it was the club's policy to travel the day before the match, staying overnight in a nearby hotel. No wives, no girlfriends – just the team. *L'oracolo* had paired me to share a room with Samson.

'You look after Samson, yes? Good discipline. Stay sensible, okay?'

'Yeah,' I said, 'No problem.'

'I rely on you,' *L'oracolo* said, 'my ambassador. For now, this is how you help the team.'

On the coach, Samson slumped himself into the window, his headphones in. Sat beside him, I could hear the tinny, ambient noise of French rap, feel the warmth that radiated from his body, smell the coconut cream he'd rubbed into his ashy joints. I busied myself with a game on my phone, but ten minutes into the journey, Samson interrupted me.

'This – what is this?' Samson asked, pulling out one headphone and grabbing my shoulder, pointing out of the window.

'Oh – that's the *Angel of the North*.'

As the coach turned onto the motorway, the statue seemed to hover. Both human and not: a great, ruddy edifice – its arms fixed against the wind, outstretched, spanning the horizon, rust on a field of sombre blue.

'This is a church?'

'No, I don't think so. It's a big steel sculpture. It's been there for ever – at least, since before I was born. My mam loves it; she brought us up there for a picnic once. It's built on an old mining hill, I think. Mam says it's like a big embrace – like a welcome to the proper North. It's sort of a boundary: old meets new, you know? Like for miles around, you can see it – you see it and you know you're almost home. And it looks like it's floating there, but it's actually fixed to the ground – tied to the land, I guess. Like it's a mark of the history of the space.'

'It is very beautiful,' Samson said, transfixed.

'I'm surprised you hadn't noticed it before. Have you not gone for a drive yet? Around the city?'

'No,' Samson said, curt.

'If you like, I could show you some stuff? Take you on a tour or something.'

Samson paused, turning back from the window, twisting the chain of his crucifix around his finger, pulling it taut, as though he were testing its strength.

'Okay,' Samson eventually said. 'On Monday, after training. We go.'

'Great. I'll have a think. Anything in particular you'd like to see?'

Samson wrinkled his nose. 'Surprise me.'

The hotel was a nondescript building, straight off the

motorway. We were half an hour from town, just beyond the reach of any temptations.

After eating as a group, we retired to our respective rooms for what the manager insisted should be an early night. Samson claimed his bed first, chucking down his suit carrier and roughly emptying his bag straight onto the hotel carpet.

'*Merde*,' he spat. 'Hey, you have the English charger?'

'Yeah,' I said, 'Hold on, I'll get mine for you.'

'*Merci*,' Samson said, throwing himself onto the bed, the springs groaning under his sudden weight.

For someone who could be so light on his feet, Samson had a habit of sitting heavily, flinging himself onto cushioned surfaces as though to assert his dominance.

'What time you like to sleep?' Samson asked, taking the charger from my hand.

'I'm pretty easy. Before eleven, I guess?'

'So now, what? We play *FIFA*?' Samson suggested, pointing to the console I'd brought with me.

'Yeah, that'd be great.'

'I am the one who plays as Barcelona,' Samson said, as if I might object.

'They're all yours.'

I linked up the console to the hotel television and within a few minutes, we were underway. Five-minute halves, with me playing as my custom-built team: a squad of European superstars and my own digital avatar in the number ten role. Samson played hunched forwards, perched at the edge of the bed. Deep in focus, he spoke mostly in French, narrating his own skills with a bawdy patois, kissing his teeth at unfavourable refereeing decisions.

With the score at two–one in my favour, my phone started

ringing. I knew it would be my father. He liked to check in with me before matches.

'Hang on,' I said, pausing the game. 'I should take this.'

'*Pas de problem*,' Samson said, flinging his controller towards the pillow, and excusing himself to the bathroom.

'Hey Dad,' I said, answering.

'Hello lad, how's it down in inbred country? Spotted any webbed fingers yet?'

'Dad – don't.'

'Aww now, since when did you go all woke on me?'

'Just, not now, okay?'

'They got you in some fancy hotel then?'

'It's pretty plain, actually,' I said, scanning the room. 'Nothing special. Just having a game with Samson and then an early night.'

Samson was now topless, brushing his teeth, leaned against the bathroom doorframe, not even attempting to disguise the fact he was listening in.

'Big game though. Winnable one, I'd say.'

'Yeah.'

'It'd be our best start to a season in eight years if you get the three points.'

'Oh, right.'

'All right, son, I can tell when I'm interrupting. I'll leave you to it. See you tomorrow, yeah? Your mam sends her love.'

'Yeah, okay, bye.'

Samson was still staring at me – his expression contorted by the force of his brushing. From the casual tilt of his posture, he seemed amused.

'Sorry about that,' I said, setting the phone face down behind me on the bed.

'Your father, he loves you,' Samson said, swallowing the froth and wiping his mouth with the back of his hand, a long smear of white against his skin.

'Yeah, I guess. He just likes to call before the games. To wish me luck. In case I come on, you know? And he's my agent, so I guess it's his way of staying involved.'

'Ah,' Samson said. 'This is a lot of trust you show. To make him your agent.'

'I guess,' I said. 'Don't you speak with your family before games?'

Samson sat back down on the bed, wearing only his underwear.

'Mama, tonight she is at the mass. It is the Feast of the Assumption.'

'Oh, is that like another Easter or something?'

Samson looked at me baffled. 'You are not taught this? You do not know the Blessed Mother?'

'I know who Mary is,' I said, 'But my family, they aren't super religious. Actually, my Auntie Grace is, but no one else, really.'

'The Assumption feast, it celebrates the ascension of the sacred mother into heaven.'

'What, so when Mary died?'

Samson laughed, walking back to the bed to retrieve his controller.

'The Blessed Mother never dies. We finish the game, okay? I beat you and then we sleep.'

'Fine,' I said. 'By the way, it's weird that you swallow. Most people spit out toothpaste in this country.'

'I am weird,' Samson replied, nudging me gently. 'And so are you. We can both be weird. Now come, we play.'

20

We won the match against Norwich. A comfortable two–nil victory, with Samson scoring for the second game in a row. I replaced him for the final eight minutes, with the game already decided.

At the full-time whistle, Samson was immediately dragged away for interviews by the media. Charging down the tunnel, into the dressing room, the rest of the squad went straight to their phones, checking their messages, their Fantasy teams and the other results from the 3 p.m. kick-offs.

For a club in our position, each victory was to be relished. *L'oracolo* encouraged it. Wins are good for business. There was once a time when phones were banned from the dressing room, but posting pictures and videos of the team celebrating was a guaranteed way to attract a lot of engagement on social media. Fans love to see us dance, love to see us sing, love to see us united.

As a junior member of the squad, I often found myself having phones forced into my hands, being instructed to record, to take the photos.

'Boys,' called *L'oracolo* over the music, 'coach leaves in twenty minutes. Get a move on now. Let's get home.'

Fresh from the shower, I sat down to towel off and check my phone, greeted by the usual message from Dad: *nice appearance son, proud of u xxx*

'Hey, big man,' Dami approached me, 'I beg you let me to use your flip-flops for the shower.'

'Where are yours?'

'Well they ain't here, are they? Don't be a waste man, just give them.'

'Fuck's sake,' I said, kicking off the flip-flops. 'Just give them straight back. I'm not taking a fine because of you.'

Since I rarely forgot my kit and never arrived late, it was exceptionally rare for me to be fined. I'd benefitted from being raised in and around our club culture. For as much as the football evolved and expectations rose as I grew through the ranks, the rules and procedures remained broadly consistent from manager to manager. From what I'd witnessed, foreign players received disproportionate punishment. Language barriers were perhaps partially to blame, but there was definitely a racial tint to Bert's arbitration. Fines went towards funding the squad Christmas party and other social team-bonding activities.

By the time Samson had finished his media duties and rejoined us in the dressing room, most the squad were already dressed and eager to leave.

'You ain't holding up the coach, son,' Bert told him. 'Change your shoes and come as you are.'

On the journey home, we sat together again. On Twitter, I watched his post-match interview. His boasting was so matter of fact that it sounded almost like modesty. And that smile – that glorious smile.

As he slept, exhausted by his industry, I luxuriated in Samson's unwashed aroma, breathing in the tang of his sweat, the musk of his body. I would have stayed in that seat for ever.

21

Then came the day.

On a drizzly Monday afternoon, Samson and I left the training ground in my car to explore the city. Samson had decided he wished to pick out a local church, somewhere he could attend mass on Sundays. Driving those familiar streets, my senses felt heightened by his presence: the greens of the hedgerows more verdant, the smell of the rain piquant and crisp. I pointed out landmarks as if their significance were self-evident – the surviving segments of the Roman wall; the newly renovated castle keep; the coal tunnels that had doubled as air raid shelters during the Second World War.

Samson reacted to my commentary but did not meaningfully respond.

'Are you okay?' I asked.

'Yes, okay.'

'You're being very quiet.'

He paused, tugged at his seatbelt. 'This city, this country, you love your ruins. You live so much in your past.'

I felt my enthusiasm falter. Oxygenated by Samson's apathy, I was suddenly conscious of my blind affection for this place, the only city I'd ever known. The crumbling, faltering architecture, cenotaphs and statues, all analogues of empire. The city's narrow streets, named after slavers and barons. The rows and rows of dreary, monotone terraces.

'You don't want to stop and go inside any of the churches?'

'Sure, we can stop.'

'Okay – St Mark's is just up here. It's one of the best ones, I think. Two minutes.'

The church was imposing to me. Gothic sandstone and tapering peaks, stained glass obscured behind mesh grating. Inside, we found the space almost empty, just a few elderly people in raincoats, spaced disparately among the pews, their hunched outlines lit by flickering candlelight. The smell was redolent of Christmas. Dusty radiators, spice and incense. I followed behind Samson, once again imitating his movements. I copied as he daubed himself with water from a font, kneeled in the centre of the aisle, bowing his head to the altar.

We wandered up the aisle, hands behind our backs. Samson turned to me.

'Where are the pitches?' he whispered.

'The pitches?'

'Yes – in this city. Where do the children play football?'

'Oh, well, we don't have many proper pitches. Kids mostly just have to play in parks and in fields. Not today, obviously, because of the rain. I guess there's a few AstroTurf pitches in the sports centre.'

'This is crazy, no?' Samson said, 'How do you make footballers with no pitches?'

'I've never really thought about it.'

'Look!' he said, swooping his arm back towards the entrance. 'No pitches, no games! In Paris, in Versailles, in

Normandy, there is a pitch everywhere. On every estate, they play. We name each cage: San Siro, Anfield, Camp Nou. On my mama, I swear it is true!'

I raised a finger to my lips in an insipid gesture to hush him. But Samson continued, barely modulating his voice.

'All night, you hear the fences – how you say? *Reverb*? No, *clatter*! Balls clatter and vibrate off the fences – that is the sound of my hood. Football is there at the heart, you see? The elders and the youths, all come together and play. Blacks and Asians and whites. All are welcome. Football is free and free for all. All these styles and influences, melting together. Competing together.'

It was the most impassioned I'd heard him. I looked over my shoulder, raising placating hands of apology to the stares we were garnering.

'And you must understand – in Paris, when we play, we play to ruin each other. Not just to win, but to embarrass. Beat your man and sit him down. We must play a beautiful football – the world around us is so ugly, but here, with just a ball, we can make a beautiful thing, no?'

'I guess,' I whispered.

'We grow up on these small pitches – very small – so we learn the close control, we learn skills – this is our focus. First touch, fake out, flip-flap. Every day, I spend on these pitches. Every day, you know? The men, I am eight when they scout me, take me away to the academy, to Normandy, away from my mama.'

Samson stared ahead to the altar, pausing for a moment, playing with the crucifix round his neck. He cleared his throat.

'In Paris, they call me *Megs*. I nutmeg all these little boys in my sleep. This is how they know me, eh? In the hood, football keeps the respect. The rudeboys, they see me and they recognise, they say, leave him, that is Megs, that is Samson of Grigny, you should see him play!'

From behind us, a firm shush. Samson slipped into a pew, pulling me beside him, leaning into my ear. I felt my hair stand.

'And in Île-de-France, we are the best – *incontestable* – the best footballers in all of France. Because this is all we do, no? It is all we know. When you live and sleep this game, you improve and improve, every day. Among this talent, it is so hard to stand out. Most of those boys, they never make it. Too short. Too weak. So here, I take my opportunities. I take nothing as given. I play not just for God and myself, but for all of them. All the boys still out there, *sur le bitume.*'

With that, Samson leaned away from me and slipped forward, kneeling on a padded cushion attached to the pew before us. With his eyes gently shut and his fingers meshed, Samson's lips moved in a silent prayer. I felt an overwhelming compulsion to kiss his neck, just above where his necklace lay. The thought kept me frozen still until Samson retook his seat.

'Anyway, forget it. This church, I like it. Very good. This will do. Thank you.'

22

Following the tour, Samson agreed to come back to my new home for dinner. As the rain stopped, the sun was setting. The tan light promised an imminent autumn, dappling the road with rainbows splashes of colour, oil patches shimmering like bruises – spilled spots of hurt.

Walking up my driveway, Samson moved so purposefully, all limb and length, as though his body were set to a beat. Guiding him into my home, I punched in the code to kill the alarm and locked the door behind us.

'It's a nice place,' Samson said, kicking off his shoes, then walking down the corridor, stretching out his arms in a cartoon yawn.

'Thanks,' I said, placing down my keys. 'It's all right, I guess. Better than the hotels, for sure.'

'Definitely,' he said, now assessing the living room.

'Want to have a look around? Or are you sick of tours for the day?'

'*Non*,' Samson said, scratching softly under his waistband. '*C'est bon*. Lead on.'

Once I'd put on some music, I escorted him from room to room, feeling as though I were imitating my mother, highlighting the same ignoble features that she had, the little marks of her devotion.

'It is large,' Samson commented. 'High ceilings.'

'Yeah, pretty big space for one person. But it was a good time to buy, apparently. And it's an investment I suppose. It commits me to the club for a few years, at least.'

'How so?' Samson asked, trailing his fingers over a table.

'I mean, a lot of my money is tied up here now. That's all.'

Samson sniffed philosophically. 'Money comes, money goes. Better to be happy. Better to play and to win.'

Now ahead of me, Samson strode down my corridor, leaving damp footprints on the freshly lacquered oak flooring. I walked in his steps.

'I guess there are positives to the hotel. Having people around you and stuff,' I said pointlessly.

'*Oui*,' he said, 'Sometimes, I guess so. You are lonely here?'

'Um,' I hesitated, unsure of his tone. 'It's just – different. I only just moved in. I'm still getting used to it.'

As we headed upstairs, towards my bedroom, the music faded and the air seemed to contract. I could feel the silence between us, a static purr, gathering edges.

Mam had complained that the trophy room was by far the most complicated part of the renovation. It was the only space that I had a specific vision for. I wanted glass cabinets and subtle lighting, the signed, swapped shirts of my vanquished opposition framed and lining the walls. A space where fantasy became aspiration and aspiration led to reality. The room was a converted walk-in-wardrobe, positioned on the first floor, at the heart of the house. The difficulty came in rewiring the space, procuring quality shelving and plinths, then assembling everything within the cramped dimensions of the room.

'This,' I said, feeling dramatic as I opened the door, 'is my little indulgence.'

Boxed in on all sides and void of windows, the room's light was controlled by a dimmer, generating a subdued, museum-like ambience – top-lit glass cabinets, filled with labelled relics, the triumphs of my childhood.

'Aha,' Samson said, smiling, examining the space with a reverent look. '*Tres, tres bon.* May I?'

'Feel free,' I said, stepping aside, willing the room to speak for me, to make a case for my talent.

I watched in silence as he walked from cabinet to cabinet, hands behind his back, the same posture he'd adopted in the church – all respect and restraint. He leaned in, reading the plaques under each match ball and medal, each minor glory on the path that had led me here. To him.

The mementos were spread thinly across the room in order to fill out the space. Mam had padded out the cabinets with framed photographs of various landmarks in my career.

'This is you?' Samson said, pointing to a picture of me shaking hands with the owner, having just signed my first amateur contract. 'So little! How long ago?'

'I was twelve, I think. So seven-and-a-bit years?'

'*So little,*' he repeated, his voice twee and deliberately ugly.

I shrugged my shoulders. 'I grew quickly, I guess.'

'And the owner – he had more hair, eh?'

'Yeah,' I said, laughing timidly, hovering behind Samson like an anxious guard.

'You were always a striker?' he said, inspecting my match balls, awarded for scoring hat-tricks.

'Pretty much, yeah.'

'Me too. We share this, eh? This hunger.' He slapped at his torso for emphasis. That firm, chiselled strength.

'Sorry, I know there's nothing much to see. You probably have way more.'

'We are still young,' Samson said, his breath condensing on the glass. 'Soon enough, all this will be full.'

'Maybe.'

'Maybe? This is not a room built for maybes, my friend. Your Premier League winner's medal goes here, no? Your Champions League medal goes there. It is fated.'

'I'm not sure I believe in fate.'

'Okay then,' Samson rolled his eyes. 'So it must be earned. And you will earn it. You have this greatness inside of you.'

With this, he laid his hand on my chest.

My breath seized.

'We both know you're the one destined for greatness,' I told him.

'You must not say this,' Samson said, drawing closer. 'You must believe that you can achieve everything. Everything in this game can be yours. Believe me, you have this inside of you.'

I turned away from him, facing the cabinet before us. In the reflection of the glass, I met his eye and held his gaze, surrendering myself. My heart thumped like a last-minute penalty.

'I'm afraid of what's inside of me. The things I feel. The things I want. Not all this,' I said, gesturing to the room. 'The things I *really* want.'

My mouth was dry and the air was still. Fear thrummed in my ears. Turning back from the glass, I felt space blur and time clot. This rip tide of emotion, threatening to drag us both under. I was resigned to it, to the terror, beat by beat, committed to my fate. I dared myself to take a step. I would imitate him once more. I would be as bold as Samson.

'I'm not—' Samson said, suddenly vulnerable, aware of my intentions. 'I'm not like that, you know? I like girls.'

'Me too. I just . . .'

I took his wrist and directed his arm towards my crotch. His hand came willingly, resting flatly against me, finding the shape of my want.

A moment of terrible quiet stretched between us.

'I would never do anything to risk this,' I said, still gripping his arm, keeping hold. 'You know I would never risk this. For either of us. I know what it means. What it takes to get here.'

The way he looked at me then – it was a countenance I hadn't seen in him before, hesitant but curious.

'Stay,' Samson instructed, pulling his hand away and backing away to the other side of the room in three long, deliberate steps.

With my back to the cabinet, I slid down the wall and watched as he removed his T-shirt, then his jeans and pants, setting them to the side, then lowered himself to the carpeted floor of my trophy room.

From the depths of my daze, I pledged to commit this image to memory, feeling sure it would never be repeated. I vowed to cherish the sight of him, just a few feet away, sat in the low, gentle light, his strong thighs spread, cock hardening in his hand, poised and waiting for me.

I didn't dare speak, for fear of breaking the spell he'd cast between us. I shuffled off my own underwear and mirrored his pose, my back pressed to the cool chill of the cabinet, our feet mere inches apart, straining towards each other, but not touching. Not quite.

In mutual silence, we watched each other and held ourselves. I fixated on the twitch of his forearm, the strain of the muscle, gripping and stroking, slow and firm, growing for me. It felt like a gift. The most wonderful kindness he could possibly grant me. The most precious trust I could ever imagine.

I watched the bounce, bounce, bounce of his crucifix as he found a rhythm, softly biting his lip. Closing his eyes and tipping his head back, he gathered pace, his jaw jutting forwards, eyes clenched, legs tensing, toes curling, body stiff and pressing back, back against the cabinets, pressing and pressing until he broke into a low, juddering groan, finishing over himself, up the dark skin of his perfect body.

He was so beautiful. The contented slump of him: heavy eyelids and puffed cheeks.

'Can you finish?' he asked timidly, looking away, arm slack by his side.

'I'm not sure,' I said, abruptly self-conscious, letting go and pulling my knees up and in, hiding myself from him.

'I'm going to clean up,' Samson said sheepishly, easing up on one foot, grabbing his clothes and shifting gingerly past me to the door.

I slipped back into my pants and cursed myself, feeling the shame swell, confusion and panic, a shiver of nausea that softened my want. I was overcome with a grim suspicion that he had been indulging me. That he had performed not out of kindness, but out of pity.

Gradually, my pulse settled. A haze descended and I stared into space – the space across from me – the space he'd just vacated. I listened to the toilet flush and the water run and tried to think through the fog. Think of what to say, of what I could possibly say to make it better, to take it all back.

Then the pad, pad of his footsteps down the stairs. His voice calling to me from the kitchen, 'Hey, I can have one of these apples?'

I cleared my throat. 'Help yourself,' I called, turning out the lights and closing the door, stepping back in reality, descending the stairs.

'It's a good apple,' Samson said, his back to the kitchen counter, T-shirt creased, mouth full.

'One of life's simple pleasures,' I said.

'Ah,' he said, still chewing. 'But no pleasure is simple.'

I shuddered. 'I didn't realise we'd left the music on. You can't hear it from upstairs.'

Samson made a vague *mhmm* sound, his focus on the fruit.

'I don't want to piss off my new neighbours straight away.'

'I'm sure they forgive you for this.'

'I dunno,' I said, keeping my distance. 'The people up here, they have long memories.'

'You okay?' Samson asked, surveying me, taking one last bite of the apple, then chucking the core in a perfect arc into the sink.

'Yeah, I'm good.'

'Okay then,' he said, swallowing hard. 'I'm pleased.'

'It doesn't have to change anything,' I said. 'We can pretend it didn't happen.'

'It happened,' Samson said, seemingly at ease, smoothing out his T-shirt, palms flat, fingers splayed.

'I'm not gay, you know. Not like, properly gay. It's just you. It's only you.'

I felt so childish. I had wanted the words to carry some heft, some definitive punch, but instead, they'd come out rushed, like an excuse. I stood there, before him, blushing and looking at my feet, all my cards played.

'Sorry, I'm an idiot, aren't I?'

'No, no,' Samson said, a crease in his voice. 'I am flattered. It's nice.'

I stepped away to the fridge.

'Do you still want to stay for dinner? I've got some pasta, I think.'

'It's okay,' Samson said, stepping away from the kitchen counter. 'I should go back to the hotel. Charge my phone.'

'Right, yeah. Of course.'

'But we will share a room for the Everton game, no?'

My heart seized.

'Yeah, I guess so.'

'Then I will see you there.'

Samson smiled again and let the silence speak for him.

'I'll book you an Uber,' I finally said, fumbling the words, pulling out my phone and facing away.

'Thanks,' he said. 'I go to find my shoes.'

Waiting for the taxi, we sat in my living room and chatted about training. About the squad. He laughed so naturally – so blasé, at ease in my company. Unperturbed by what we'd shared.

'Your car's outside,' I announced a few minutes later, swiping away the alert.

'Cool,' he said, standing and clapping his hands. 'Thanks for the tour. I am glad to find the church. And I enjoyed this.'

'Me too,' I said, 'I mean, obviously. I enjoyed.'

I followed him to the door, cursing the clumsiness of my words.

'See you on tomorrow then,' he said, hand on the latch, faltering.

'Yeah, see you,' I said, keeping a distance, my arms crossed, afraid to move, to let him leave.

From the doorway, I watched Samson climb into the back of the car and accelerate up the road, back to his hotel.

The rain had stopped. My life was changed.

23

According to the tabloids, Samson was being followed by scouts from major European sides. Record-breaking prices were quoted without hesitation. Among experts and amateurs alike, comparisons were being drawn between Samson and some of the greatest players of all time.

One paper quoted an *inside source*, who was confident that the owner would finally sell the club before the opening of the January transfer window. It was a ready-made deal, simply awaiting board approval. According to journalists, *L'oracolo* was desperate for the sale to be pushed through. He had supposedly determined that the squad would require a minimum of five additional signings in January to ensure our survival.

Outside the stadium, a group of masked fans strapped an effigy of the owner to the club gates, dousing the dummy with oil. They chanted our songs as they watched him burn. The acrid smoke could be smelled for miles, social media aflame with low-resolution, candid videos. It was deemed a line too far.

24

The hotel for our Everton fixture was in the heart of Liverpool. Our room overlooked the river Mersey, straight across the Royal Albert Dock. Twinkling lights illuminated the Friday-night drinkers lazing in the late summer warmth.

Through the week, Samson made no mention of what had happened in my trophy room. At the training ground, he showed no outward sign of resentment, no evidence of regret. For the second time in my life, there was a tacit oath of silence strung between me and a teammate.

Together and alone in the hotel room, we played our games of *FIFA*. Samson was magnanimous in his victories and tortured in his defeats. The evening would only end when he had finished on top.

With the lights out and the curtains drawn, Samson emerged from the bathroom freshly showered, moving through the dark towards my bed. Sitting there, he ran his hand up the outline of my body, the firm geometry of my willing frame. I remained still as he pulled back my sheets, removed my underwear and flipped me onto my front.

'Wait – are you sure?'

'Do not speak.'

There was no nuance to his desire – none of the elegance I knew he was capable of. Samson spread my legs and spat into his hand, pushing himself straight into me, fucking me in the same way he threw himself down onto surfaces: heavy and unsympathetic.

The pain shocked through me in waves. Samson was bigger than anything I'd experimented with. I bit my pillow, muffling the sounds that fed through him, into me. Samson fucked me like he was making a point, asserting control. It was as though he was forcing something out of himself, channelled through my flesh. I felt certain he was imagining someone else – that he was using my body as a convenient, compliant stand-in – an outlet for his real desires.

That first time, there was only pain. My mind was overwhelmed with the urge to pull away. I fidgeted and writhed under the weight and want of him; my body tensed – a snarl of passive acceptance. It was both everything I wanted, and not at all what I had imagined.

After he finished, he lay there on top of me, shrinking inside. The sweat between my thighs grew cold, and I felt afraid. I resolved to remain still, to not disturb him, the now spent beast. In that moment, cramped and tense, I was sure I would never let it happen again. I would not let him use me in this way.

Eventually, Samson pulled out and rolled away, excusing himself back to the bathroom, silently cleansing himself of my innocence and effluence. I pulled the covers back over my body, tucked them tight between my legs, relieved by the gentle pressure. My arsehole stung. Rolling onto my side, I felt his cum seep out of me, onto the sheets.

Returning to his bed, Samson fell swiftly into a heavy sleep. I listened to the steady surges of his breath: the contented rise and fall of his mighty lungs.

Across the river, Scousers drank and sang. The summer was waning, but the night was still young.

25

Upon the first bleep of his alarm, Samson bounded out of bed, prayed, stretched, pissed, washed and dressed, dashing down to breakfast before I had a chance to catch him, to confront him. It was match day, and he was all business.

Everton played a heavy, lumbering game, misplacing simple passes and wasting opportunities through hesitation and poor link-up play. Samson found the net just before half-time with a stooping header from an inswinging corner. It was his third goal in three games; a play straight from our training pitch, a move we'd rehearsed dozens of times throughout the week.

The opponents' frustration was apparent. They started playing more aggressively, leaning into challenges, pulling shirts and picking up needless yellow cards. By the time I came on to replace Samson in the seventy-third minute, we'd scored a second, and were in full game-management mode. I pressed myself through the lingering discomfort from the night before. There was a slight twinge to my movements – a cramped feeling of trapped air. My job was to draw challenges, hold up the play, track back and chase any loose long balls that were punted forward. We closed out the game convincingly, but I had no meaningful chance to impress.

As our victory playlist filled the dressing room, I pulled off my kit and headed straight to the showers. I scrubbed myself hard, desperate to purge the feeling of dirtiness, the mordant, bilious taste that coated my mouth. As I washed, the music changed. A slow, fuzzy, string-led instrumental, accompanied by Nat King Cole's distinctive, soft voice. 'Unforgettable'.

Returning, I saw our Ukrainian left back, Milo, in the centre of the room, still in his kit, dancing a stilted waltz, counting out the steps in time with the song's faint, regular drum beat, moving in three-stride circles, his arms in a fixed position, holding an invisible partner, studs clicking on the tiles.

'One, two, three, one, two, three,' he said to himself, neck down, examining his feet with a look of absolute focus.

Across the room, Samson sat topless, a towel draped over his head. He fiddled busily with his phone, perhaps recording the dance, glancing up occasionally to offer Milo an encouraging smile as he completed a rotation of the room.

I hovered by the showers, wary of intruding on the newly christened dance floor, but also attempting to attract Samson's eye. Through all my confusion, I still craved his gaze. I wanted him to observe me as I leaned coquettishly against the partition wall, fresh from the shower, wrapped in only a towel, the steam rising off my body, bathed in the warmth of light jazz.

As the song ended, the changing room applauded with hands and boots, perhaps slightly too enthusiastically. I gave up on catching Samson's gaze and took the opportunity to shuffle back to my seat and slip on my boxers.

'Milo's learning for his wedding, ain't he?' Bert explained. 'Good to make an effort for the missus.'

'So,' Milo said, walking over to us, his arms now dropped, 'What you all think? How is posture?'

'Hard to say, ain't it?' Bert answered, 'Without a partner, difficult to tell, to be honest with you. Very different game when you're doing it proper, like.'

'Okay then,' Milo said, stamping his foot as though accepting a challenge. 'Who will be partner?'

A nervous laughter rippled through the room. Sideways glances and defensive postures.

'Come *onnnn*, boys,' Milo pleaded, arms open, back straight, a bright, Slavic smile.

'Here's your man,' Bert said, shoving me upright, back to my feet.

'Get fucked,' I said, twisting back, attempting to sit down, to force away Bert's powerful arm, now blocking my spot.

'Go on, son,' cheered the room, as the music restarted.

'Come,' Milo said, beckoning me softly, 'I not bite.'

'What do you need me to do?' I asked, stealing a glance over at Samson, still tapping away at his phone.

'Just follow lead,' Milo said, taking my right hand, raising it full stretch. 'Feet go like little box, yes? Forward left, side with right, close together. Up and down, up and down. I count for you.'

'I'm not sure counting's going to help much. I really can't dance.'

'If you shoot the goal, you can move your feet, yes? It is just moving feet. You see?'

Milo stepped forwards, his hand tucked round, behind my shoulder, leveraging me back.

'Oneeee, twoooo, threeee,' he counted, slowly dragging me through the simple movements.

'Get closer to him, you sissy,' Bert jeered.

'Fuck off,' I shouted, aware of my defensive tone. Facing Bert, I almost tripped over Milo's leg.

'Count with me,' Milo said, 'It help. One, two, three, one, two, three.'

'One, two, three,' I repeated back, just about easing into his sway. 'One, two, three.'

'There ye go lads,' Bert hooted over the music. 'Naturals, the pair of yous.'

As Milo gathered pace, I briefly closed my eyes and tried to listen to the music, to really listen: to catch the rhythm, will the flow through my legs, down to my bare feet. My precious, essential feet, exposed and vulnerable, just inches away from the clack of Milo's boots.

'You much taller than Tijana,' Milo said, still looking down through the gap between us, shifting me through a rotation, 'Much more muscle, you know? She is so light, so danceful.'

'I bet,' I said, pulling away, hyper conscious of my toes. 'I think that'll be enough for them to judge you.'

'Applause for beautiful assistant,' Milo said, stepping back and gesturing to me.

There were a few wolf-whistles. I considered bowing, but thought better of it, returning meekly to my seat. Samson clapped for our performance with an open palm to his bare chest, phone still gripped tight in his other hand.

As the song started to repeat for a third time, someone cut off the sound abruptly, switching back to popular rap.

'So you now tell me,' Milo said, facing Bert. 'How is posture?'

'Not a fucking clue, marra,' Bert laughed, pulling off his shirt, spitting on the floor and heading to the shower.

26

Our team spirit was good – as good as I'd ever experienced. From the management team, to the cleaners, to the lunch ladies, everyone at the training ground preferred it when we were winning. Our success was what kept them in employment. It was important to enjoy these times, to appreciate what we'd achieved so far. We needed to keep building, to not let things slip.

During his midweek reprieve, Samson had flown home to France and returned with a new haircut. His fresh trim transitioned from a close fade into a sharp, etched line that ran from temple to collar. Above the cut, a flare of royal blue.

On social media, fans speculated the blue was for Barcelona, a coded message of intent ahead of an inevitable summer transfer. Others argued that it was a clear demonstration of his national fidelity – the blue of France, definitively selected ahead of the Rwandan football team, who were very publicly staking a claim to Samson's international future.

Samson had played a handful of games for France's junior squads, but was yet to be selected by the senior side. Until that call-up came, under FIFA rules, his allegiance wouldn't be set. Much of the French media's focus was on whether the national coach would give Samson a chance in the forthcoming October friendlies.

Thanks to my compulsive stalking, I'd seen Samson's new hair within ten minutes of him updating his Instagram story, but for the majority of our squad, their first impression came when he arrived at the training ground on Friday morning.

'Man thinks he's a model now, ye?' Dami said, grabbing Samson by the arm as he entered the gym, pulling him in for a closer inspection.

Samson kissed his teeth, pulling free dramatically. 'No touching, eh?'

'Or what?' Dami postured, smirking.

'Or I fuck your mother,' Samson said, sounding remarkably childish.

'Hi,' I said, noting Dami's tensed muscles and stepping between them. 'I like it. It looks clean.'

'Clean?' Samson said.

'You know, clean. Crisp. It looks good. It suits you.'

'Thanks,' Samson said, stepping past me to the dumbbells.

I loved spending time in the gym. The delicious, savoury smells of male sweat: all musk and funk and effort. The gym was one of the few places we actually got to chat, to mix among each other. There's something socially accelerating about the tedium of shared, repetitive movements. Out on the pitch, we're all breathing too heavily to force conversation, too focused on cardio, on intricate drills. In the dining hall, players silo off into cliques, segregate by race and language. Samson often ate with Baba, speaking in pattered French, beating the table as they laughed ferociously, trading memes and girls on their phones.

Samson finished one final set on the medicine balls and

excused himself to the sauna. Following shortly after, I could see the outline of Samson's body through the frosted door – sat alone, his legs up in a perfect triangle, soles flat, his back and bare arse pressed against the cedar wood.

As I stepped inside, he flashed his eyes open to acknowledge me.

'*Ça va?*' he grunted.

'Hi,' I said, sitting down and mirroring his posture at the opposite end of the space, putting as much distance between our bodies as possible.

'Good session?' he asked, his eyes softly shut.

'Yeah. Not bad.'

'Good,' Samson murmured, beads of sweat forming and gliding over his shoulder, careening down the skin of his arm and dripping sensually from his fingers onto the floor. More than anything, I wanted his fingers in my mouth, his sweat on my lips. I felt myself starting to get hard.

'Have you decided yet?' I asked, shifting my focus. 'Between France and Rwanda?'

Samson's brow furrowed.

'Today, there is no choice. No choice until France makes the ask.'

'Yeah,' I said, inhaling the humidity. 'But we both know it's coming. You must have thought about it.'

'It is you who does all this thinking, my friend. You love to think and to talk.'

'Yeah, but—'

'No more talking in here,' Samson said. 'Another time. We talk another time.'

'Sure,' I said. 'Of course.'

27

Without any spoken agreement between us, a routine was established for our away games, based on the precedent set in Liverpool. He'd shower first, stripping in front of me, but not for me. When he returned, wrapped in a towel, fresh and gleaming, I'd have the console set up, ready to play. Best of three, five-minute halves. No extra time, straight to penalties. Samson celebrated and protested, always unashamedly vocal, no matter the hour, no matter the thickness of the hotel walls. While he cawed and mewled, I bit my tongue with absolute focus, tightly gripping the controller, my hands sweating, body tensing, each digital kick desperate and essential, a battle for dominance.

There were no stakes to these games. The virtual football had become our foreplay. Facing the same direction, together but apart, close but not touching. This is how we mentally prepared – filled the dead space between the spoken and unspoken, the imagined and the real.

I took responsibility for shutting down the game, then immediately excused myself to the bathroom. Upon my return, the lights were out. Abandoning my previous disavowals, I moved through the quiet, wanting him. I perched on the edge of his bed, waiting for him to pull back the covers, just slightly, in invitation.

Samson only ever fucked me in the dark, preferring his own bed, my body hidden under the covers. He positioned me face down, arse up. We stuck to that one position. I was at peace with the fact it allowed him to disassociate from the body beneath him, to imagine a person I was not, the curves I could never offer. I didn't dare to question any of it, never risked disrupting the sanctity of our nascent routine with my stupid, blunt words.

Even with my face smothered, I could sense every part of him, heavy and trembling, his hands desperate, frisking my body for purchase, for give. I pressed back into him, assuring him I welcomed it all, that I would accept everything and anything he offered me.

Expecting the discomfort made it more tolerable. I learned how to control my breathing, as though swimming through the feeling, rising above the surface with each stroke. Samson fucked with long, purposeful thrusts, using my body as though I were another piece of equipment in his personal gym, a resistance exercise, slicked with his sweat and spit. Once I managed to relax and accept him, waves of warm, glowing pleasure shocked through me. I never reached round to touch myself, but sometimes I came anyway – heavily and with minimal warning. It felt like magic.

Once finished, Samson would roll off and away, spreading out his legs, filling the space, muscling me to the very edge of his mattress. I'd concede and retreat, waddling clenched to the bathroom, cleaning myself, then returning to the cool sheets of my own bed, together but apart, curled foetal and still, still filled with the hollow ache of him.

When morning came, our game was over. On and off, clean as a switch. In the stark light of day, we were professionals. Colleagues. Brothers in arms.

28

As our form slipped and we dropped down the table, Samson began to treat me differently. It was a slight, but noticeable shift. It seemed there was no longer any occasion for us to talk. Samson had made it clear that we would speak on his terms. At the training ground, he distanced himself – preferring the company of Baba. Beyond congenial exchanges on the pitch and in the gym, we could go a full week without a meaningful interaction.

I had no grounds to resent his actions. Samson was free to do as he pleased, to speak with whom he chose. I recognised that there must be some comfort in surrounding himself with more familiar voices – voices that sounded of home. But as the weeks rolled on, the experience became torturous. I carried around the secret of us like a pulled muscle – slowing me, restricting me.

It was the sheer proximity that tormented me most. I was afraid when I could see him and afraid when I couldn't. My eagerness frightened me, my complete willingness to excuse his behaviour. Just a smile could abate me for an entire day.

Thoughts of Samson consumed me. His Instagram captions began to read like coded messages. His failure to pass me the ball in a practice game was confirmation of his resentment. I woke up to the thought of him, began measuring time in relation to our away games: the desperate wait until I could be with him again, until my fears could be relieved.

I vowed that so long as the routine persisted, so long as he remained mine, he could treat me how he liked.

29

I played for the final twenty minutes of our away game against Manchester United, providing an assist as Dami scored to earn us a late draw and an unlikely point, breaking our recent losing run. After eight games, we'd slipped to fourteenth in the table.

As I came off the field, *L'oracolo* embraced me, ruffling my hair.

'Good job,' he said. 'I will see you inside.'

I felt elated. It was the first time in the season that I'd directly contributed towards our fight for survival. I knew that I'd played well, that Dad would boast to his friends. I knew that I'd completely concealed the discomfort inside me; Samson thrummed through me with every step.

But this thrill was cut short. Stepping into the tunnel, I was informed that I'd been randomly selected for a drug test, and led down a series of corridors to a sterile room in the bowels of Old Trafford. The walk had the timbre of a punishment. I felt panicked without cause.

Once I was seated, the doping agent unwrapped a fresh needle and proceeded to draw blood from my arm.

In his team talks, Bert often spoke of blood. He considered

bleeding to be heroic and valorous and uniquely British. Sometimes, he would slap at the tattoos on his arms – the names of his daughters, twisting in a dark, cursive font. He demanded that we fucking well remember who all our blood, sweat and tears were for.

I looked up and away as the agent drew back the plunger. Staring into the corner, I clenched my jaw and considered what secrets my blood might betray. I wondered how much of me could be known through this sacrifice. A metallic tang swelled in my spit.

The agent pressed a cotton ball on my arm and attached a plaster.

'That it?' I asked.

'Not quite,' he said, handing me a sample bottle.

With a neutral expression and a bowed head, the anti-doping agent watched as I pulled out my penis, inserting myself into the moulded plastic. Despite years of being nude around other men, this experience felt like a violation.

'Do you have to look? Because I don't think I can go if you're looking.'

'It's policy. I need to see.'

I closed my eyes and tried to disassociate. I thought about the match. My cut inside, the one-two with Baba, my pass across the box for Dami to stick the ball home. I thought of the roar from our fans, the weight of Bert launching himself onto my back in celebration. I thought of Samson, applauding from the bench. I thought of Samson. I thought of Samson.

'All done?' the agent asked, pinging a purple latex-glove over his wrist.

'Yeah,' I said, handing him the warm plastic.

'Okay, that'll be all then. You can go now.'

'So did I pass?' I said, jokingly.

The agent screwed a cap onto the bottle, his face a mask of solemnity. 'That'll be all. Thanks for your cooperation.'

30

It was October. On my drive to the training ground, the roads were dense with fallen leaves; copses of hawthorn and ash, shedding themselves of the dying summer, spindly bird's nests suddenly exposed. Above me, the sky was smudged and grey. Clouds loomed like omens.

Talking to my father on speaker-phone, I previewed our forthcoming game against Southampton.

'The manager keeps saying that he wants us to be *warriors*. He reckons they'll try to play down the channels and swing in lots of crosses.'

'Makes sense,' Dad said. 'They're fucking massive, those lads. Squad full of giants.'

'I really feel like I could do something in this game, Dad. The centre of the park is going to be wide open. The game's screaming out for two strikers. Can you have a word? Message Jean-Claude or something. I need to be starting games.'

'A good warrior knows when to use his head, son,' Dad counselled. 'Your bosses have better heads than either of us. Especially when it comes to tactics and stuff. Let's hold off on meddling for now. Show them some trust.'

Come Saturday, I watched from the bench as my

teammates dutifully executed the *L'oracolo* plan. The whole squad moved in a combative stance – squared shoulders and pursed lips. Dami and Baba played much deeper than usual, regularly shifting low balls along the grass, inside to Bert. We kept the pace slow, drawing fouls, frustrating them.

At the half hour mark, Milo won a free kick around twenty-five yards out from goal – an awkward distance, given the height imbalance. As Dami stepped up to take the free kick, I watched Samson size up to the Saints' captain at the edge of the box. They grappled, all leaning and defiance – the brawling confidence of drunks at a bar, matching weights, pound for pound, pint for pint.

As the ball was lofted into the box, Bert threw a hard shoulder and broke free from his own marker, finding space at the near post to head the ball powerfully down and into the net for his first goal of the season. Bert raced to the away stand, kissing his daughters' names on his arms, punching the air in unrestrained joy. There at the centre of the celebrations was my father, his hands aloft, dancing, happiness radiating in every direction.

Amid the commotion, a few critical seconds passed before anyone noticed a young woman skip over the hoardings, running onto the field. A band of men in luminescent yellow chased after her, grabbing wildly as she zipped and twisted over the grass, bearing down on Samson.

Alert to the intruder, Samson shifted into a posture of counterbalance, one knee forwards, anticipating the collision. The girl flung herself at his feet, embracing his legs, as though he were her nominated protector – her personal warrior. As the men closed in, she clung to him like ballast. Samson made no attempt to shake the girl loose. He rested a hand on her head, bent down to her level, eased her to her feet and into the arms of the stewards.

Bawling, the girl was paraded around the edge of the pitch, behind the benches and down the tunnel, into the hands of the police. As she passed us, I could just about make what she was saying through her staccato, choking tears.

'*He. Knows. Who. I. Am. He. Knows. Who. I. Ammmm.*'

In the space of three months, this was the manic, crazed devotion that Samson had already managed to inspire. The desire to be seen by him, to just exist in his world. As her cries receded into the distance, I felt great empathy for that girl.

31

When I typed *S* into my phone, autofill suggested him. The algorithms knew me better than anyone. Searching his name had become a muscle memory, a reflex – like taking the ball down on your chest, or exhaling as he entered.

My stalking was producing diminishing returns. By November, I'd uncovered every available photograph from Samson's youth career, every video from his time at Monaco.

Samson's follower count on Instagram had grown to over a million. Fan pages had been created for him, attracting tens of thousands of likes on reposted photos of his smile, short clips of his skills. I came to recognise the avatars of some of these fans – these strangers around the globe, as obsessed with him as I had become.

Mam framed the back page of a newspaper featuring Samson and me roaring like warriors, celebrating his latest goal, his sixth of the season.

SAMSON'S LAST-MINUTE HEROICS SECURE VITAL POINT IN BATTLE FOR SURVIVAL.

Without requesting my permission, Mam hung the cutting in my trophy room.

After four months, my house had finally begun to feel like

a home. I'd mastered using the washing machine and the thermostat. I had even bled a radiator. Dad boasted in our family group chat.

Nineteen years old and already a proper man. Proud of you son.

At work, Samson continued to snub me. After training, he swiftly returned to his hotel, or rushed away for English lessons he scarcely needed. Samson's command over the language was proficient enough to curate ambiguities, to leave himself open to interpretation, carving out gaps for me to fill with my imagination and insecurity. Ten minutes in conversation with Samson could fuel an entire week of obsessive thinking.

I was doing yoga in the living room when he texted me. It was the first direct message he'd sent me in nearly two months. Apparently, Samson's agent was keen to meet me. He thought I had great potential and wished to take us both to dinner. His name was Sebastian.

32

Sebastian represented a stable of thoroughbred footballers at every stage of the career cycle. I knew that Samson respected his opinion. It had been Sebastian who engineered the move to our club, who championed our manager as a tactical genius.

Up to that point, I had only seen Sebastian from a distance. I knew he was a slim, attractive man with an Iberian complexion and appealingly sharp stubble. His hair and outfits had a designed, sculpted shape – elegant, with crisp edges. He was how I imagined Monaco to look.

'He looks after me,' Samson had told me. 'Sebastian knows what is good in this world. He likes the best things.'

I agreed to dinner, travelling with Samson by taxi to a small French restaurant around an hour outside of the city. A quick search revealed that TripAdvisor graded the restaurant 4.5 stars across 316 reviews.

'Sebastian prefers privacy,' Samson explained. 'No cameras, you know?'

I'd dressed up for the evening. A white shirt and smart trousers. Assessing myself in my bathroom mirror, I felt as though I was dressed for either an interview or a trial. I had consciously omitted telling my parents about the dinner.

In the taxi, Samson buried his head in his phone.

'This country,' he grumbled, 'Are there no straight lines here? Must every journey make you sick?'

We were heading into a picturesque part of the county – a part I associated with landed estates and honeymoons, with old money and cricket, where my accent and ignorance of fish knives and soup spoons would betray me as thoroughly working class.

'Welcome, my good friends,' Sebastian said, standing to greet us, as we were led to the back of the small, low-lit, bare-brick restaurant.

'What do you think? Very nice place, yes? A good find? I do the research and pick out the finest French restaurant in a hundred miles, just for you.'

'Looks good,' Samson said, nodding, his face unmoved. 'I brought him, like you wanted.'

'Hi,' I said, stepping forwards, extending my hand, 'Pleased to meet you.'

'So polite, this one,' Sebastian said, taking my hand and pulling me in for a hug. Then over my shoulder, to Samson: 'You could learn lots from him, eh?'

Samson took a seat in the corner and slumped against the wall in a juvenile huff.

'How long will you be in town?' I asked.

'Not long, not long. Just enough time to do a little business. To shake a few hands, you know? But this evening is not about me, my friend – this evening is about you – you both! We are celebrating your success! Your new partnership and your brilliant manager. There is much to smile about, yes? Shall we drink?'

'Well, we're not supposed to, really,' I said.

'Ah, a real professional. A rare thing, you know? I will not try to tempt you.'

'I want a drink,' Samson said with the candour of a spoiled child. 'You've brought me all the way here. I want a little wine with my food.'

'These are the choices you make,' Sebastian said warmly. Then to me: 'My clients, they make their own choices, and I stand by them. Only you know your body. Only you make the choices that decide your fate.'

'Right,' I said, somehow blushing, flushed with his attention.

'So,' Sebastian said, 'No business tonight. For these evenings, I prefer to enjoy the food and the company.'

With this, he placed his phone face-down at the centre of the table. It felt implied that I should do the same, though it hardly seemed a proportional inconvenience. There was no one I needed to speak with. Once I set my phone down beside Sebastian's, Samson followed suit, a petulant, accusatory look on his face, directed towards me.

On Sebastian's suggestion, I ordered the *saumon à l'oiseille* – a fillet of line caught fish, served in a creamy lemon and shallot sauce. Both protein and flavour-rich, he advised.

While we waited for our food, Sebastian held court, sharing gossip and controversies from across the European game. As he spoke, he ate crusty French bread, ripping and dipping it into a generous dish of oil and balsamic vinegar. He was completely at ease with his convictions. Everything Sebastian said felt weighted and considered. He was irresistibly warm and bright, in the manner that only exceptional people can be. My initial nervousness waned. Occasionally, Sebastian paused his monologue to solicit our input. Samson refused to comment on most matters, feigning ignorance. While I offered only vague and clumsy answers, Sebastian treated each of my contributions as though they were revelatory and insightful.

'Very clever, this one! A true student of the game.'

Opposite me, Samson sipped at his wine and drummed on the table with his fingers in an idle beat. At one impasse in the conversation, Samson reached for his phone. In a sudden, darting movement, Sebastian leaned across his body and slapped his hand firmly.

'*Ayyye,*' Samson exclaimed, snatching his hand to his chest.

'Stop this,' Sebastian said, stern and terse. 'What is wrong? This is the way you choose to behave? This is how your mother raised you? Is this because you are jealous? Not the centre of attention and you become jealous?'

'I'm not jealous.'

'Then you will apologise for behaving this way.'

'I didn't even do anything!'

'You know what you are doing. You know *exactly* what you do.'

For a while, they switched to French, bickering back and forward in rushed imperatives until Sebastian grabbed Samson by the arm and pulled him out of the booth, hustling him towards the restaurant door.

While waiting for them to return, I restrained from reaching for my own phone. The waiter approached with our meals, and finding me alone, served the food without comment, taking care to angle the plates so the restaurant's embossed logo faced the vacant seats. Steak and potatoes for Samson and a beef bourguignon for Sebastian.

The salmon smelled glorious – rich and citrusy, with sprigs of bright, fresh herbs. I picked up a fork, but second guessed myself, electing to wait.

I had no gauge on whether any of this was usual behaviour, whether the dynamic between Samson and Sebastian was typical for an agent and his charge. I'd seen Samson become stroppy and gauche a handful of times, but only when he was being denied something – when his penalties were saved in training, when he was kicked out of the sauna by our senior players.

'Samson has something he'd like to say,' Sebastian informed me, returning a few minutes later, presenting Samson like a scolded child.

'I'm sorry.'

'You are sorry for what?' Sebastian prompted, a hand on his shoulder.

'I'm sorry for being rude.'

'That's okay,' I said, hesitantly, sensing the eyes of the whole restaurant upon us.

'There,' Sebastian said, gesturing for Samson to sit. 'All friends again, yes? And doesn't this food look delicious?'

'It smells great,' I said, while trying to meet Samson's eye.

'So tell me, my friend,' Sebastian said, tucking a napkin into his collar, 'how much do you earn?'

'Me?' I said, shocked by his abrupt shift. 'Umm. Honestly, I'm not sure.'

'You are not sure?'

'I don't really pay attention to that stuff. I mean, I know it's a lot.'

'A lot? A lot what by standards?'

'I guess, by normal standards?'

'You English!' Sebastian laughed. 'You English and your *normal*! All these unspoken, nonsense *normals*. My friend, you are so far from normal! You are exceptional!'

Blushing, I fumbled my knife, dropping it to the floor, wincing as it clanged. Sebastian clicked his fingers to our waiter, gesturing to the knife before continuing uninhibited.

'Only in England is there this fear of discussing your wealth. In no other country is it like this – I tell you this. Only you English are so ashamed of your own success. The English and their precious classes. The English who love to keep the working-class man in his place. Your English media, always shaming footballers. Always saying this and that about what you earn, where you belong. Your English fans, the only fans in the world who love a tackle more than a goal. Who scream for you to shoot from forty metres out!'

A new knife was placed before me. Unsure of what to say, I looked to Samson for support. He seemed unmoved. Still sulking; his face down, focused on his plate, cutting diligently at his steak.

'I hear it is your father who represents you,' Sebastian said, his own knife now poised at a surgical angle.

'That's right.'

'And your father, he knows football?'

'Well, he didn't play. But he knows the club. He's supported the club his whole life. He used to work for my uncle, in construction.'

'But now this man negotiates your image rights? Your brand deals? Your sponsorships? He fights for you to gain more minutes on the pitch?'

'Yeah,' I said, swallowing hard.

'I see,' Sebastian said dubiously, bobbing his head. 'Good. Very good. He must be so proud.'

'He is. Or, at least, he says he is.'

Sebastian raised an eyebrow, dabbing the corner of his mouth with the napkin.

'Samson,' he said, 'How is your steak?'

'It's very rare.'

'Ah, but this is how it is meant to be. He has no taste, this one, you see?' Sebastian said, just a little too tart.

Samson sneered and continued to cut at his meat.

'Samson – he only knows the Paris cages – the concrete pitches. All his life – just football, football, football. When he signed with me, I ask him what he wants – I promise him whatever he wants – he tells me he just wants the football. He just wants to play.'

'I understand that,' I said, carefully assembling another forkful of food, making an effort to avoid consuming the modest portion of salmon too quickly.

'And now he wishes to play for his adopted country. Isn't that right, Monsieur Kabarebe?'

Samson scowled, tightening his grip on the steak knife.

'Above all, our Samson desires to win, so he must play for *Les Bleus*. He must ignore the preference of his mama; must choose to serve this nation who brutalises his motherland, who is complicit in permitting the most terrible atrocities. Quite the conflict, no?'

Slamming down his cutlery, Samson rose to his feet.

'I am going to the toilet,' he stated, shoving his chair back.

Sebastian was unmoved, reaching for a sip of wine.

'You know, it was my suggestion to call him Samson. Much more marketable. Much better branding that *Kabarebe*, don't you agree?'

'Yeah,' I said, 'I suppose so.'

'And you my friend?' Sebastian said, setting down his empty glass. 'What is it you want? What do you desire?'

A waiter tucked Samson's chair back in place. I looked in the direction of the bathroom.

'I guess – I guess I want the same as him,' I said. 'Just to play and be part of a good team. To win things, you know?'

'And your father? This is what he wants also?'

'I guess so. My dad just loves our club.'

'So much guessing! None of this is for guessing, my friend – this is your life! This is your whole life that you are deciding upon! These are the years that will make you. This is the most important decision you will ever make, and you guess?'

'I don't know,' I said. 'I suppose I need to think more about it.'

'The truth,' Sebastian said, raising the almost-empty carafe, 'is that you are fluid. At this point in your career, you are still liquid. Like the wine, you see?'

He swilled the carafe like evidence.

'You will fill any container that you are poured into. Any club, any colour of shirt. The shape of the container does not change you. You are your name and your body and your mind. That is all you trade upon. When I work for you, my job is not to find the most beautiful container – my job is to help the wine breathe. To help the flavour mature under the correct conditions. The optimal conditions. You and our petulant friend – you are born from a vintage year. We drink to this, yes?'

'Cheers,' I said, raising my water to clink Sebastian's refilled glass, feeling a little ridiculous.

'Promise me that you will think on this, okay?' Sebastian said, picking my phone up from the table and typing in his number. 'Tomorrow, next week, whenever you are ready. You will call me and we will talk about your representation. I have seen your situation before – many, many times before. There are solutions to this, okay? You call me and we will talk about the opportunities there are for you – for a boy of your talent.'

'So, you want to represent me?'

'But of course!' Sebastian said, laughing, setting my phone down and reaching across the table to grab my hand. 'My good friend, it would be my honour to work with you. But as I say, this is your choice. Everything in this life, these are the choices you make.'

Samson returned from the bathroom, we finished our meal and Sebastian settled the bill. At the door, he drew Samson in for an aggressively determined hug. Samson allowed himself to be embraced, his eyes open, lips puckered.

'The things I do for this boy,' Sebastian joked, his hand in Samson's hair. 'He is my goat you know? My *Greatest of All Time*. He is worth all the trouble.'

Our taxi driver had waited outside the restaurant for the duration of our dinner. On Samson's command, we took a slightly longer route home, sticking to the motorways – the straighter roads. Twenty minutes into the journey, I gathered the courage to speak.

'I didn't realise; about Rwanda, about your mam, the pressure. That must be really hard. We can talk about it if you want.'

Samson scoffed. 'Talking, this changes nothing.'

'Right,' I said, scratching at my jaw, 'Fair enough. But is Sebastian always like that with you?'

'Like what?'

'You know – like, so direct. So strict.'

'This man is not my father.'

'I know, but—'

Samson interrupted, turning to me. 'So Sebastian has offered to represent you, yes?'

'Yeah, how did you know?'

He emitted a small, mean laugh.

'This is why you were brought here. This is why he steals this evening from us both. Right now, I could be back in France, with my mama.'

'Samson, I'm sorry. I didn't mean to—'

'It doesn't matter. Forget it. I am tired. I just want to rest.'

'But – what do you think I should do? Should I sign with Sebastian?'

'You can do what you please.'

Outside, the *Angel of the North* crested the horizon, wings spread wide in sacrificial love.

'Right, okay. But – like – if I did sign with him, would it be okay with you? Would you be even more annoyed at me?'

'Who says I am annoyed at you?'

'Well – it's just – you seem annoyed right now. With me. With everything.'

'There is more in my life than you,' Samson said, toying with his crucifix. 'You may do what you please. I couldn't give a fuck.'

'Okay,' I said. 'I guess I'll think about it. I'll let you know.'

'See that you do,' Samson said, angling himself away, staring out to the rolling dark.

33

It's true what Sebastian said that evening. Football in England remains a working-class sport with working-class fans. The media in this country love a humble footballer. A loyal footballer. A footballer who knows his roots and knows his place. The media loves a footballer who never demands too much, who's grateful for what he gets. The media will never let you forget that in this sport, you'll always be working-class – no matter what you achieve or where you go, you'll always owe it all to the fans. The fans are a living history of their clubs. They are the curators of an endless well of legacy and expectation and suspicion.

It was nearly December, and I was yet to start a game all season. When I called my father to inform him of my spot on the bench against Chelsea, Sebastian's words played on my mind. I questioned if my dad would ever dare to complain on my behalf. Whether he'd ever be prepared to stand up and fight for my professional interests. I was yet to tell him about Sebastian's offer of representation.

Over the phone, Dad expressed his standard set of platitudes, empty reassurances about how my time would come, how I needed to be patient, how I needed to trust the genius of our manager.

'You're still getting good minutes, son. Think back to this time last year – think how pleased you'd have been for those run-outs.'

'But it's not last year, Dad. I'm better. I'm stronger. Every week, I'm doing everything they ask for me, and it's still not enough.'

'It's enough for me, son. I couldn't be more proud.'

Since my dinner with Sebastian, I had been imagining what life would be like under his stewardship: courting the biggest clubs in the world, being wined and dined across Europe, heralded and praised as Samson's equal – as his spiritual counterpart, our destinies inseparably and eternally tied under the guiding influence of a handsome, charismatic mentor and friend.

For every minute in this fantasy, I spent two considering the consequences. I dreaded the extra attention that a potential transfer could bring. I feared the inherent risks of joining a new club, a new environment; the increased likelihood of finding myself exposed. In a world of social media, of endorsements and appearances, how long could I realistically remain single? How long before Sebastian insisted I needed a girlfriend?

When I visualised Dad's reaction to being usurped, dropped as my agent, it felt more hypothetical, more manageable. He would be devastated, for sure – but in time, he'd come to understand. He'd eventually recognise that the decision was in the interest of the family, our collective financial security.

We lost the Chelsea game three–nil, with Samson lucky not to be sent off for a senseless, lunging challenge in the dying minutes. His frustration was palpable. It had been a fixture he had looked forward to – these were the games that had drawn him to England.

In the dressing room, *L'oracolo* raged at us.

'We expect this, no? All week I tell you boys – this is what happens against top, top sides. Drop the focus, and *pop* – there's a goal. Focus dips again, and *pop* – another goal. So if we expect this, why these faces? Why all this pity for ourselves? Are we not to blame?'

In his post-match interview, the manager evaded questions about our tactics, about the frailties of our back line. Instead, he congratulated Chelsea, redirected the conversation to our next game against Liverpool, spoke about the importance of the week ahead. Our chance to bounce back.

But the Liverpool match followed a near identical script. A four–nil battering in freezing conditions, with few redeeming positives. Conceding seven goals in two games without reply was relegation form, no matter the quality of the opposition.

In the dressing room at Anfield, a fight broke out between Dami and Mario.

'He's a lazy fucking faggot,' Dami spat, heaving dramatically forwards as Bert struggled to restrain him. 'That's three goals he's cost us today. Useless fucking cunt amateur!'

'You look at yourself!' Mario countered, brandishing a boot above his head. 'Maybe look at yourself for once, no? Mister so-perfect. You can fuck yourself and your mother.'

'Don't you fucking mention my mum!'

'Fuck your whore mother!'

Amid the commotion, the manager charged into the room.

'CESSARE!' he yelled. 'Stop this at once.'

Immediately, both Dami and Mario backed down, slouching timidly to their seats.

'Just now, I am interviewing again to spare you all. I speak so none of you have to speak. I am out there taking all your blame. And I am forced to abandon during the interview, and for this? And now they will fine me, I am sure. We lose the game, and now I am in trouble with BBC also. This is what you want? You want me in trouble? You want me paying fines?'

The room hung silent.

'It is good to care. This is what we need, yes? We need a squad who care. We care because this hurts. Losing and losing. It hurts. But sometimes we must lose. Sometimes, they are better. On this day, Liverpool, they are better. And so what? And so we fight ourselves? So now we disrespect? This is not good, boys. This is not how we play. None of you is perfect. Mistakes, they happen. We do not learn from perfect. We do not survive alone. We win together. Okay? Now, Mario, Dami, you must shake. Go now, shake hands. Good. And now we are better. No more of this, you hear? It is over now. *Finito.* Everyone get changed. Monday, we go again.'

We were seventeenth in the table, only one point clear of relegation.

34

Through the winter months, our schedule was unrelenting. We were set to play eleven matches over the next eight weeks. The manager insisted that everyone would play a part, get a chance to prove their worth.

What is it you want? What do you desire?

For weeks, I had been turning over Sebastian's questions in my head. Repetition had rendered them rhythmic and clean: a pebble rolled smooth by the tide. My wants and desires had become a mantra. An affirmation.

I wanted to seize this chance. I desired vindication. I wanted more than what Samson was prepared to offer.

On Tuesday morning, Bert gathered us at the training ground. He had been tasked with raising morale, getting us back on course. *L'oracolo* emphasised that it was essential that spirits were buoyed during this critical period. In his infinite wisdom, Bert had decided that the best way to motivate us was to start planning the Christmas party.

'Now, I don't want none of yous calling us a tyrant,' Bert said, 'So if you've got any bright ideas about what to do and where to go, I'm happy to listen. We've got about twelve grand in the kitty from fines, so hit me with some suggestions. I'm all ears, boys.'

'I'm not fucking dressing up again,' Theo said, his arms crossed.

'I'm fine with whatever,' Dami said, 'So long as we don't end up back at that strip club.'

'Ah, don't tell us that wasn't a proper laugh.'

'No mate, it's fucking grim. And the birds are all mingers anyways.'

While Bert debated with Baba over the best casino in the city, I shuffled to the back of the group, happy for others to lead the discussion. My only previous night out with the squad came after we secured survival. I'd found the experience exhausting and exposing. I had a low tolerance for alcohol and didn't know how to speak to women.

What do you desire? What is it you want?

Since signing my professional contract, I'd barely ventured into town. It was safer and easier to shop online – to stick to home-cooked meals and the direct path from the training ground to my new house. The club met all my social needs, and I had no private life to speak of.

'How about that brand new place?' Mario suggested. 'The one just off Central Street.'

'Bit studenty, ain't it?'

'Couldn't tell you,' Mario said. 'Haven't been yet.'

There had been a period in my early teens where the city centre represented the whole world to me. It contained every possibility. Every luxury and freedom I could conceive of was there, price tagged and available. On the few days I wasn't playing football, I'd catch the bus to town and loiter with my school friends until dark, seeking mischief. We pushed each other in the fountains by town hall. We snuck into betting shops to check the machines for forgotten change. We had a regular booth in McDonald's, sharing a small Coke between five people to keep our seats and pass the day.

Just as the fortune of our club declined under the owner's mismanagement, the city had visibly changed. Along the high street, every third shop front was boarded over with flimsy MDF, adorned with sloppy, rushed graffiti. Even the grand, Gothic spires of the cathedral were obscured under layers of scaffolding.

And yet, the fans remained. Hope persisted.

'All right then,' Bert said, clapping his hands, as though to break a trance. 'I guess we'll have to do some research on this new gaff. Due diligence, you know? When we go out, all those promoter cunts are out of a fucking job, because the whole city will be queuing to get in there with us. Mario, this one's your suggestion so you're definitely in. Who else's up for joining?'

'When you got in mind?' Theo asked.

'What's wrong with tonight? Day off tomorrow – no excuses.'

'It is a school night,' Baba said, 'I have to put my kids to bed.'

'Aye, fair dos – then I guess it's us and the young ones, Mario. Samson, lad – you jetting off to *gay Paris* tonight?'

'No, but—'

'Well, about time you get to see what this brilliant city has to offer, eh? So you're fucking coming.'

Samson kissed his teeth. 'Fine,' he said.

'And the youngest handles the whip,' Bert said, pointing at me through the crowd.

'What?' I said, 'That's bullshit.'

'Them's the rules, sonny.'

'I thought you just claimed you weren't a tyrant?'

'Changed me mind, didn't I? And you'll have the lovely Samson here for company.'

Samson met my eye, pursed his lips.

Who do you desire? Who is it you want?

'Well I'm not drinking,' I stated flatly.

35

I took my time getting ready, attempting to determine a suitable outfit. I had no idea what people wore to go clubbing. My wardrobe prioritised comfort over style, practicality over statement. I feared that Samson had already seen every outfit I owned. Perhaps he'd grown bored of me. A one club, one town boy; a bench warmer who just laid there timidly and took it. No surprises left and nothing more to offer.

Bert had assured me via WhatsApp that he'd undertaken some reconnaissance. He'd made some calls and we'd be able to walk straight into the club – a private area would be cordoned off and waiting for us.

I was the last to arrive, stepping out of my taxi at the nightclub entrance. I saw my teammates at the top of the stairs, loitering in a dimly lit foyer. Samson was wearing an oversized designer sweatshirt, hood pulled up to hide his face. Bert and Mario stood by him, adorned in understated blazers. They were arguing.

'It's a Tuesday, what did you expect?' Mario blared.

'I expect you to take responsibility for a shite suggestion.'

'What's wrong?' I asked.

'It's dead in there,' Bert said. 'Bunch of toddlers, cracking on to some ancient pop.'

'So, can we go home?'

'Fuck that. We'll hit the Roxy instead. I'll give my guy a call now.'

We stepped outside for better internet reception so that Bert could request an Uber.

'You okay?' I asked Samson.

'Yes. Why?'

'Just asking. That looks warm.'

'Yes,' he said, drawing the hoodie tighter round his neck. 'This country – it is very cold.'

A group of university-aged girls rushed through the lobby in tiny dresses, hurrying down the stairs, their heels clacking like studs, a wake of steam pouring from their mouths into the bitter winter air.

'Your women,' Samson said, 'the way they dress, they are crazy, no? They must freeze.'

'Made of different stuff up here, son,' Bert said, shoving him. 'Come on you cunts, ride's here.'

36

Observing the town from the taxi window, I wondered whether I might bump into any of my old school friends, whether I'd still recognise them.

I once had a group of friends I imagined I'd keep for ever – the group who'd be my champions, my support network. They were supposed to stand by my side through the years, to tell the public that fame hadn't changed me, that I was still the same boy, the same bloke, the same man.

The shift happened gradually. Their requests began small and reasonable, but grew proportionally with my compliance. It became expected that I'd pass on my spare boots. Provide free tickets to matches. Source autographs from our star players so that they could sell them on eBay. Soon enough, every meal was on me – an unofficial celebration of the success I'd yet to really achieve. I had to retweet their bands from my verified account, to champion their little brothers for an easy route into our academy. I was the ambassador for their parents' shops, the star customer at their mams' salons. I was clout incarnate. A magnet for likes.

On the increasingly rare occasions we met up, I was blamed for killing the vibe – labelled a *buzzkill* for turning down photos, for refusing their booze, their weed, their laughing gas. Eventually, I stopped going out entirely. Once I signed my professional contract, I had colleagues, not friends. I had a career, not a life.

Occasionally, Mam would enquire about one of my old mates. I'd give her some vague reply about them being fine, alluding to jobs and universities, the basics I'd gathered from social media. She'd nod, sensing what I didn't say – what I couldn't know.

In time, she learned not to ask.

37

Arriving at the Roxy, the host greeted Bert like an old friend, pulling him in for a big bear hug and slapping his back aggressively.

'Boys,' Bert said, yanking himself away, 'This is my man Jamal, but yous can call him JJ.'

'Only to friends, innit,' JJ said, issuing each of us a fist bump. 'Follow me, boys, I've got a nice private spot waiting for you.'

In single file, we walked through the club to a roped-off area, guarded by a bald man in a tank top, who nodded to JJ and raised the velvet.

'You lot prefer Moët or Dom?' JJ asked, directing the question to Bert.

'What we saying, lads?'

'Dom, always,' Mario said, sliding into the black leather booth.

'I'm not drinking,' Samson called over the music.

'Yeah, me neither,' I said, shifting up the seat, next to him.

'Haddaway, lads!' Bert said, exasperated. 'Yous know how it works. Minimum spends on a private table.'

'We can split the bill,' I said, almost shouting, 'But honestly, I did tell you earlier, I'm not drinking.'

Samson took a second, then nodded in support.

'You're gobshite bairns, the both of yous. Why come down toon then?'

'You made us!' Samson yelled over the pulsing music. 'You said this was research!'

'We'll get three bottles of Dom and some juices, please, JJ, marra,' Bert said, 'But you'll have to get us some lassies over. Mario and me will get mortal if it's just the two of us on the bevs.'

From the raised height of our booth, we could survey most of the nightclub. While Bert and Mario judged the girls and Samson tapped at his phone, I quietly observed the order of the space – the behaviours and customs that the room seemed to abide by. Everything seemed to revolve around the women, grouped together at the centre of the dance floor, gripping clutch bags and shimmying, faced inwards in clusters, their glasses lofted high each time the beat dropped. Around them, the men orbited, with their small, measured movements – just enough to constitute dancing. In turn, they'd make their moves – a tap of the shoulder, a brush of the hip, light appeals for attention, for legitimacy.

JJ returned with our drinks ten minutes later, accompanied by three girls.

'Boys, let me introduce you to Imogen, Holly and Eliza – Imogen and Holly have recently appeared on a certain TV show you might be aware of.'

'Oh aye,' Bert said, patting the empty space beside him. 'I recognise yous. Just as pretty in real life, ain't you?'

'Awww, thank you,' Imogen said, sitting down clumsily, constricted by the tightness of her dress.

'Three girls for four guys?' Mario said, brazenly. 'Do you expect us to share, JJ lad?'

'We'll see how you get on, yeah?' JJ said, winking and slipping back under the rope.

'Nice to meet you,' I said, reaching out from the booth to offer Holly my hand.

'Look at you!' she squealed. 'Proper gentleman, aren't you? I don't do handshakes, babes. Give us a kiss.'

Leaning in, Holly kissed both my cheeks and shuffled in beside me. I resisted the urge to wipe off the tacky smear left by her lipstick.

'And who's your mate here?'

'This is Samson,' I said, tapping his shoulder, prompting him to glance up from his phone.

'Hello,' Samson said, nodding nonchalantly before looking back to his screen.

'Bit rude,' Holly scoffed. 'Thinks he's a man of mystery, yeah? Here, let's get between you.'

Without waiting for permission, Holly slid over my lap, inserting herself into the sliver of space between me and Samson.

'How many of you are married?' Eliza asked, projecting over the music. ''Cos I don't fuck with married men any more.'

'I'm taken, love,' Bert said. 'But the rest of 'em are fair game. Is it hunting season for yous lot then?'

'Something like that,' Eliza said, giggling, adjusting her cleavage.

'Here gorgeous, get a picture of us,' Holly said, passing me her phone – sheathed in a pink silicone case with bunny ears.

Wrapping her arms around Samson's neck, Holly leaned

back, pointing one leg in the air, her stiletto trembling with the effort of the angle.

'Say cheese,' I said.

'*CHEEEESSSSE!*' Holly shouted, sticking out a pierced tongue.

I snapped four photos in quick succession. Somehow, despite my amateur composition, Samson looked impossibly handsome – brooding and sultry, his eyebrow lifted knowingly.

'Ain't you drinking, boys?' Imogen asked.

'Nah,' I said, trying to sound casual. 'Not during the season.'

'That's so shit,' Imogen said, topping up her glass. 'I think I'd die. Like actually die.'

Holly was yet to release her hands from round Samson's neck. I watched as she draped her once extended leg over his knee, turning to look him in the eye. Samson was permitting it – perhaps even enjoying it. He smiled, pocketed his phone, leaned in as Holly spoke into his ear.

Imogen seemed determined to retain my attention.

'So did you watch us? On telly?'

'No, sorry. I think I missed it.'

'Honestly, it was like the best experience of my life. I know everyone says it's all fake, but actually, only little bits are. Like the producers will suggest some things, but they won't *make* you do anything, you know?'

Seeing them together, seeing Samson's hand on Holly's leg, her lips brushing his ear, his cheek – the chemistry I'd imagined between us became farcical. I could not compete. I was nothing in the face of actual biological desire.

'Like, I told them, I am *not* wearing anything yellow. It just doesn't suit me. It makes me look like a proper actual lemon, you know?'

'Right,' I muttered.

On the other side of the booth, Bert and Mario seemed unfazed by Samson's flirtations – they were busy playing some sort of betting game with Eliza, where the loser of each round had to take a swig of champagne.

'Three in a row!' Bert yelled at Mario, 'Down it, down it, down it!'

'So what position do you play?' Imogen asked me.

'I'm a forward,' I said. 'Striker.'

'Yeah, I know what a forward is.' She irked. 'And you're allowed to ask me things too, you know?'

'Sorry,' I said, pulling my gaze away from Samson, resigned to the inevitable. 'So, Imogen, where are you from?'

Later, when Samson excused himself to the toilet, Holly slid up the booth, pressing into my side.

'Be honest with me,' she slurred, 'is he nice though?'

'What?'

'Your mate, Samson,' Holly said. 'You've got to tell me if he's just another arsehole.'

Looking at Holly, I considered my options. I weighed the temptation for sabotage – composed a sentence that might dissuade her.

'Samson's the best,' I heard myself say. 'A really good guy.'

'So I should definitely fuck him, yeah?'

'Uh – whatever you like.'

'Okay,' Holly said, still suspicious. 'But I'm blaming you if he's a dickhead.'

'That doesn't seem fair,' I said, attempting a smile.

'I just love the Black ones, you know?'

My body tensed.

'What was that?'

'Nothing bad,' Holly sniffed. 'Nothing racist, like. I just really fancy Black boys. Proper Black, like him, you know?'

In the distance, I saw Samson re-approaching the booth.

'Don't tell him I said that, will you?'

'Right.'

'You could come too, you know,' Holly said, now placing her hand on my thigh. 'If you like . . .'

Taking a long sip of my juice, I momentarily pictured the scene. A threesome with Samson. A chance to witness him honestly – his true, uninhibited want. I was capable of sharing him, I told myself. I was prepared to accept that reality. And more than that: I could be desirable in my own right.

Somehow, without a sip of alcohol, I felt woozy. Time had slowed, grown textured. The air was full and silky, charged with yearning.

Before I could answer Holly, Samson stepped over the velvet rope and stood by us, one knee tucked up onto the leather of the sofa – a stance of impatience.

'Okay, now we go,' he said, beckoning Holly.

'You're leaving already?' I said.

'Yes,' Samson replied, looking over his shoulder, scouting a path to the exit.

'And you're taking her home? To the hotel?'

'Of course,' Samson said, as if the decision were obvious.

'I was telling your mate that he could join us,' Holly said, her palm now placed possessively against Samson's abs. 'What do you think, sexy? Shall we bring this one with us?'

Samson paused – met my eye.

'He makes his own choices,' Samson said.

Is this what you desire?

Is this what you want?

'I'm all right,' I said, forcing out the words. 'You two have a good night.'

Samson's nostrils flared, breathing out slowly – clearly relieved.

'*Bon soir,*' he said, raising his chin to me before turning away.

Imogen had abandoned me to join the others in their drinking game, which showed no sign of slowing. I stayed, watching on for another ten minutes, before settling my part of the bill. JJ shepherded me outside, straight into a waiting taxi.

In the car home, I found the girls on Instagram. Holly had already shared the photo I'd taken of her and Samson to her 1.6 million followers, captioning the picture: *FRESH CATCH.*

38

Doctor Léonie arrived at the club in December. Though a press release was issued to the media, her appointment barely registered. The practice of appointing a dedicated sports psychologist had become reasonably commonplace at the top level of the game. During our hectic winter schedule, player welfare was the club's top priority.

The first we heard of our new appointment was at the training ground on a bitterly cold Friday morning. The kind of weather only athletes and dogs willingly suffer.

'Boys, *now*,' *L'oracolo* called, pinching his thumb and forefinger into his mouth and producing a harsh, quivering whistle to summon the whole squad away from our shuttle runs. On Fridays, the manager always attended training. These sessions were his chance to assess the squad for himself, ahead of finalising his team for the weekend.

'In a minute, I introduce a new staff. She joins us from Geneva – Doctor Léonie Roth. Okay? She comes to us as club sports psychologist, working with medical staff and our performance team. Over these next weeks, Doctor Léonie will be meeting you all for conversations.'

An unfamiliar terror moved through me like a rolling wave,

seizing up from my legs through my chest, pushing my heart into my throat and ears.

'Just conversations, yes? No need for all these scared faces! Conversations are one to one. The doctor is great asset for this club. This is all your health too, up here.'

The manager tapped at his temple benignly.

'Believe me, winning comes from up here. Doctor Léonie helps you to better understand your game – she comes here to equip you with new tools. Mental strength, boys! In Christmas, these fixtures come so many, so fast. So demanding on everyone. One loss and we slip our confidence. We find fear in our heads, our hearts. Doctor Léonie, she helps you with strength to be winning every time, every game. To keep the winning thoughts. Understood? Any questions?'

We stood in a unified front of crossed arms and silent reflection.

'Okay, very well. Trust, she takes time. Please, stay around here, I will bring Doctor Léonie to you.'

My understanding of psychology was informed entirely by Hollywood. It involved plush leather couches and bearded judge-like men who asked leading questions, intended to expose you, to uncover your secrets.

'I don't know nothing about no therapy,' came Bert's voice, 'But I can do without more meetings, I'll tell you that.'

'I already know how to win,' Milo boasted. 'In Holland, I win three league titles.'

'Fucking shit league though. Counts for nothing.'

'Ajax have won four Champions Leagues. Ajax are responsible for the basis of the modern game. There is no football without Ajax and Cruyff.'

Bert guffawed. 'Farmer's league. Living on past glories.'

'It is more that you will ever win.'

'Get fucked you filthy poof.'

Heart pounding, I instinctively looked around for Samson. He had separated himself from the group, occupying himself with a ball; keepie-uppies, arms crossed tight over his chest, braced against the cold.

As I broke off from the group to approach him, he brought the ball under control and looked at me intensely.

'What do you think?' I asked him, my voice low and clandestine.

'I don't think anything,' he said sharply, rolling the ball back and forth under his studs. 'I am here to play and to win.'

'Oh,' I said, scratching under my chin. 'I thought—'

'You are afraid?'

'No,' I said, suddenly smaller, more slouched. 'It's just new to me.'

'Everything is new to you,' Samson said smugly. With this, he booted away the ball, turning from me to watch it spin away.

It would have been ridiculous to hit him, hard and straight in his beautiful face. But surely he was inviting it? Surely he was attempting to provoke me? *Everything is new to you.* His words seared.

As I moved to return to the squad, Samson grabbed my shoulder, pulling me towards his body, levelling his lips to my ear.

'You will say nothing to this woman,' he breathed. 'Nothing of us. Understood?'

'Yes,' I muttered, dropping my shoulder and pulling away. 'Obviously.'

Doctor Léonie didn't look intimidating. She was dressed in

a club tracksuit, moving towards us at an easy pace, stride for stride with the manager, looking attentively in the directions he gestured: towards the gym, the youth pitches and kitchen facilities beyond. Doctor Léonie had dark, curly hair, cut to the shoulder, framing a soft, round face. Up close, I could see she was a similar age to the manager. She didn't seem to be wearing any make-up.

Somehow, I'd found myself at the front of the group, under her direct scrutiny.

'Boys, meet Doctor Léonie, as we discuss. I am sure you will be grateful and welcome.'

'My pleasure to meet you all,' Doctor Léonie said, opening out her palms and smiling sedately, her accent prim and taut, as though each word were a delicate thing, to be handled respectfully. 'I will speak with your manager here about scheduling in some time with each of you very soon. It would be lovely to get to know you all a little better. Has anyone here met with a sports psychologist previously?'

Beside me, Samson raised his hand. I restrained myself from turning to see who else had.

'Wonderful, a few of you,' Doctor Léonie said, scanning over us, meeting my eyes for the first time. Her smile was so austere that I managed to return her gaze quite naturally. 'My first priority will be with supporting your teammates who are recovering from injury. I am sure you are all very sympathetic to how challenging it can be to cope with pain.'

'A great resource for us, yes?' the manager said sternly, looking at us over his glasses. 'We do not just train our bodies. We train our minds. All this pressure you face, that you keep for yourselves, you will not cope alone. I promise you this.'

Above the tree line, two kestrels hovered, circling each other, their wings barely moving, floating on the air.

'This is a family club, yes? We care like a family. I defend you all like my family. *My boys*. There are some things you talk with me, there are some things you prefer to talk with the doctor. So you treat our good doctor here with this respect. There are fines for missing sessions with Doctor Léonie – same fines as missing physio, same fines as missing training.'

In a flash, one of the kestrels broke off, darting downwards into the canopy. With no tail to follow, the second bird now seemed attuned to gravity. It hung for a moment longer, flapped resignedly, then angled itself westward, catching up to the wind.

The manager and Doctor Léonie left the field together. The training session continued until the sun began to set. I paired up with Samson for our cool-down stretches, bolstering each other for balance as we swung our legs in perfect rhythm – our matching heights and matching frames.

'I didn't know you'd had therapy.'

'As I say, there is much you don't know.'

'Was it at Monaco then?'

'*Oui*. They insist. Sports psychology. This is not therapy. There is difference. *Big* difference.'

'Was it good though? Did it help?'

'Maybe. Maybe not. Who can say?'

As the rest of the squad jogged back inside to the warm, Samson lingered, lining up balls along the eighteen-yard line.

'Are you just going to keep going?' I said, allowing my teeth to chatter theatrically, gloved hands tucked under my armpits.

'Yes – for a bit.'

'How long is a bit though?'

'As long as I feel like it.'

I kept back a few feet, reverently aware of the space required for his craft. Watching him line up a ball, I stamped the feeling back into my toes.

'We've been out here hours. Don't you ever get tired of it? Bored?'

'Never,' Samson said, rotating the top seam to face him.

'Never?'

'It is all I know,' he said, stepping back with a sharp exhale, then lashing the wand of his right foot forward as steamy breath rose above his head, a puff of magician's smoke. We both watched as the ball pinged off the underside of the bar, bouncing back fiercely into the top of the net.

'This is home for me,' Samson said, stepping across to retrieve and adjust the next ball.

'Not Monaco? Paris? France?'

'*Oui, bien sûr.* But the pitch,' Samson said, bending down to pat a gloved hand on the grass, 'She is my real home. This is my joy.'

'No pleasure is simple, right?'

'Right,' Samson smiled.

For another two hours, as the night drew in and the floodlights beamed, we remained out there, taking shots on goal, modifying angles, alternating feet. Studying him up close, I discovered more of his idiosyncrasies. The way his chin jutted forward as he sniffed, the wince of his lips as he searched for the correct English word. Outside of the sanctuary of our hotel room, this was the most time I'd spent with Samson one-on-one since our taxi back from the restaurant. No depth of cold could drive me away from this privilege.

'Have you spoken with Holly?' I asked, trying to sound unbothered. 'Since Wednesday, I mean.'

'*Oui*,' Samson said. 'You are jealous of this?'

I spat on the floor. 'I mean, you can do what you like.'

'But you prefer that I do not like?'

'I – I just know – I thought—'

'My friend – this girl, whatever I do with her, she means nothing to me,' Samson said, calmly rolling out another ball.

'Right,' I said, suppressing my relief. 'Okay then. Cool.'

'But what about your decision?' he asked, 'You are yet to decide? About Sebastian?'

'I'm still thinking. It's a big decision.'

'Sebastian, he only waits for so long.'

'Oh – I didn't realise.'

'Each time I speak with Sebastian, he asks me: where is the decision, when is his decision?'

'Okay,' I said, 'Sorry. I promise, I'll let him know by Christmas.'

'*Bon*,' Samson said, smoothing down his shirt, striking the ball.

In the distance, the kestrels circled once more.

When we parted that evening in the players' car park, we clapped hands like usual, but Samson pulled me in close for a hug. As we embraced, his fingertips brushed the back of my neck, sending a shiver straight through me. I felt him notice and attempted to style out the stiffening rush as simple wind chill, jerking away and pulling my coat tight, then hastily unlocking my car, where I sat, waiting for my heart to slow back down.

39

When Dad called before games, I had begun letting my phone ring through to voicemail. There was nothing to be said that hadn't been spoken a hundred times before. I had incrementally convinced myself there was very little left that Dad could offer me. I texted to say I couldn't speak and forwarded him an email containing his complimentary tickets to the Sheffield United fixture.

'Love you, son,' he said to my voicemail. 'Come on and smash it.'

Ahead of our away games, I'd begun preparing my body for Samson. I wasn't the hairiest teenager, but I groomed myself fastidiously, trimming until I might look appetising, but not fully shaven so as to attract suspicion.

Advice on the internet was conflicted regarding whether to use enemas or not, with some articles deeming them essential, and others warning of various grisly health risks. I decided that a shower would be adequate, scrubbing between my cheeks with militant thoroughness. All the other advice was centred around using condoms, stressing the importance of copious lube. These were requests I couldn't possibly imagine imposing on Samson; these were requirements not written for our circumstances.

It had occurred to me that if Samson caught any STDs from Holly, then I was certain to receive them from him.

Come Friday, there he was, slumbering peacefully beside me on the coach, his headphones with their tinny echo, his hood pulled up and over his beautiful face. There he was at dinner in the hotel, sat apart from me, chatting in an animated rush with Baba. There he was, in our hotel room, claiming a bed, kicking off his shoes. And there he was, when the lights went off, pulling back my covers, relieving my fears.

It was on that trip to Sheffield that I first attempted to kiss him. Rallying all my courage, I leaned through the dark, towards his face, emboldened by his recent warmth and encouragement. But somehow, Samson managed to evade my lips, ducking back, as though it were all some terrible misunderstanding – as though I'd confused the entire nature of our arrangement.

Still, I let him have me.

In our short time together, I'd mastered a new range of skills: the ability to be discreet; the rhythm of pushing back in time with his cock; the talent of reducing myself – of becoming someone else – whoever he needed me to be. In bed, we were joined as one. True teammates. The sheer, physical mass of two athletic bodies, gloriously entangled; low, throttled sounds that bled from us in a single language.

For all the imbalance of our arrangement, I took great pleasure from the undeniable facts of our sex. I knew with certainty that I possessed the power to entice him, to corrupt and pervert him, to tempt and turn him. No matter what he pretended while he was inside me, no matter what he told himself or who he imagined me to be, it was still my body below him – my tight, boyish body; my welcoming, eager hole. Through it all, it was me who felt the force of his want, the damp slap of his flesh, the percolating desire that thundered up and through him, boiling over, shuddering deep into me. It was me who slipped away from under the spent weight of him, who tiptoed to the bathroom, who discreetly cleaned and removed the evidence. It was me who slept soundly on the mess we'd left behind.

40

My first session with Doctor Léonie was arranged for a Tuesday afternoon, straight after training. I walked to her office fresh from the showers, Samson's instructions in my head.

Everything is new to you.

You will say nothing.

Based on some research, I knew that Doctor Léonie had qualified as psychologist in France before doing another degree in America, specialising in sport psychology. According to her LinkedIn page, she'd relocated to the UK in the early 2010s, and had since worked with a number of sports teams, including Bath Rugby and the England women's cricket team.

Throughout my time in the youth ranks, the playing staff were exclusively male. Every authority figure I'd ever known had been a man. Doctor Léonie would be the first woman I had worked with. She would also be the first person more concerned with my mind than with my body.

Her office was in a corner of the training complex that I'd never visited before, tucked away in a remote corridor by the server room and the staff lounge. The high-pitched hum of machines seemed to be in dialogue with the rumbling of the kettle. The space smelled of dust.

I knocked, feeling like a schoolboy.

'Come in,' her voice came.

Inside, Doctor Léonie sat behind a white, medical desk, clearly too large for the space. The room had the dimensions of a shed – spanning no more than my outstretched arms. On the floor, two neatly stacked piles of books. Her computer screen was angled out, just enough to be visible from where I stood – a desktop image of a chubby, smiling baby.

'Hi,' I said, hovering by the doorway. 'I think it's my turn?'

'It certainly is,' Doctor Léonie said warmly. 'Please, come inside, sit.'

'Is the baby yours?' I said, nodding towards the screen.

'She is. Maud – she's two on Saturday.'

'Oh, cool. Tell her happy birthday from me.'

'You know, you're the only person to ask,' Doctor Léonie commented. 'So far, anyway.'

'Oh, sorry.'

'No – there's no need to be sorry. It's just interesting.'

'Right,' I said, forcing a small, pallid laugh.

Removing her glasses, the doctor slid back in her chair.

'So tell me,' she said, 'how's the season been for you so far?'

'Yeah, we're doing well. We can't complain.'

'Forget the team for a minute,' Doctor Léonie said. 'Forget *we* – tell me about *you*. Has there been anything for *you* to complain about?'

'I dunno,' I said, hesitant of being negative, of seeming fractious.

'I understand you were upset about your shirt number?'

'Oh – I didn't think they'd have told you about that. It's fine. I'm over it now.'

'But at the time, it hurt you? Giving up your number to Samson. How did that make you feel?'

'Well, to be honest, I was bit annoyed, yeah. Because it was a big deal to me. And to my family.'

An image of my father flashed through my head. He stood adorned in our jersey, his fidelity and pride bared for all to see. It was the brazenness of his love that made him so guileless. With a shake of my head, I jolted the thought away.

'They'd already bought shirts, you know? All my family. With our name and the number. So that was a bit embarrassing.'

'Family's important to you,' Doctor Léonie said – not quite a question.

'Yeah, I guess. But isn't it for everyone?'

'Their families are important to them, but only yours is important to you.'

Doctor Léonie wasn't taking notes. She was just looking at me – a precise, piercing stare, directed just above eye level, as though she were attempting to see inside my head.

'In the dressing room,' I said, stuttering slightly, 'Bert always says it's important to remember who we're playing for.'

'He's right,' Doctor Léonie said, now leaning forward, her elbows perched on the desk. 'That Bert – he's an interesting man. You're quite a bunch.'

'Have you met Samson yet?' I asked.

'You wish to talk with me about Samson?'

'No – I mean – we can if you want, but I was just wondering, if Samson had said anything. About the shirt number. Because you brought it up.'

'It wouldn't be appropriate for me to discuss the content of my conversations with your teammates. This is a private place. For me to work with you and help you, you will have to trust me. And I don't think you'd trust me if I shared the details of my other conversations with you.'

'Okay,' I said. 'Got it. So what, do you want me to start telling you about my family?'

'Not today,' Doctor Léonie said, now reaching under her desk and pulling out a folder that had been labelled with my name. 'I want to speak about how we'll work together, and how I can help you develop your mindset into a winning attitude.'

'You think I need to change my mindset?'

'I didn't say change – I said develop.'

'What's the difference?'

'The difference is that I can't change you – any change has to come from inside of you. And the developments I can offer – they'll be small differences. Differences in the way you think about situations. The way you think about yourself.'

Returning the glasses to her face, Doctor Léonie seemed to hone in her gaze, her tone shifting.

'If you treat this as work, and you take it seriously, it will start to add up. Small changes add up to a big impact.'

From the corridor, the sound of the staff lounge bled through – the radio, playing bright, cheery pop songs. A microwave pinging insistently.

'This is a rough schedule that we're going to follow,' Doctor Léonie told me, opening the folder to the first page and sliding it across the desk. There was a ten-point index with bland chapter titles:

Know Your Triggers
Raise Your Game
Train Like a Winner

'We can adapt the schedule, depending on what you feel is and isn't useful to you. For today, I wanted to speak with you about scoring.'

'Okay, great,' I said, flicking through the folder.

'How do you feel when you score?'

'It depends, I guess. Most of the time it's great. But if it's like a consolation goal or something, or if it's like a tap in and I've stolen it from someone else . . .'

'What's a stolen goal? Why shouldn't that stolen goal be yours? When you've worked hard to get in the box? When there would have been no goal without your influence?'

'I guess,' I said, setting the folder down, picking at a corner of the plastic.

'How do you celebrate your goals?' Doctor Léonie asked, selecting a pen.

'I dunno,' I said. 'I never planned anything. I suppose I look for my dad?'

'Okay,' she said, now scribbling notes. 'And when you score, what do you say? Do you stay quiet, or do you make a sound?'

'I suppose I say something . . .'

'Like what? Show me now – show me what you say.'

I squirmed.

'Just like, normal stuff, you know? Like: "*Yeah!*" or "*Let's go!*"'

'Show me properly. Recreate it for me.'

I cleared my throat.

'*Wooo!*'

Doctor Léonie smiled, clicked her pen.

'Good. But I didn't believe you. I didn't believe that was a goal that won the game. Try again for me. But this time, really visualise that you're scoring for me. Take a second to close your eyes. Imagine that feeling – the feeling of scoring a match-winning goal.'

Sat with my eyes closed, I felt very vulnerable. Very observed.

'It's okay,' Doctor Léonie said, intuiting my discomfort. 'Just relax and take a second to conjure that picture.'

Obediently, I pictured shooting from thirty yards, a firm connection, straight on the laces, the ball whorling through the air in an impossible geometry, buckling and dipping, beating a faceless keeper's flailing arm.

'*WOOOO!*' I screamed, a little too aggressive.

'Good,' Doctor Léonie said after a pause. 'Stay there for just a moment longer. Really enjoy that feeling.'

My eyes still closed, it dawned on me – I was picturing myself as Samson. The goal was his. I'd pictured something that only he could accomplish.

'Okay,' came Doctor Léonie's voice. 'You can open your eyes. That was a much better sound. How did it feel?'

'Good,' I said. 'It felt good.'

'For the next time we meet, I want you to think of a celebration for me. Something you can do when you score.'

'Okay, sure. I can do that.'

'When we have a plan, we begin to expect that we will score. And when we expect to score, we push ourselves that little bit harder. The sound is just an anchor – we make sounds to assert and place the moment. To mark it in our memory, to recognise that this has happened, and it happened because of us – because of *me*. We anchor in this emotion and keep it with us. We allow that feeling to carry us for the rest of the game.'

'Does that really work?'

'It works if you allow it. I promise you, all of this works if you believe it and work hard.'

'Okay,' I said, pulling the folder to my lap.

41

The France squad was announced for December's international fixtures. Samson had been overlooked. In his press conference, the country's manager refused to comment on his omissions, beyond saying that he had been forced into making some challenging selections, emphasising that this difficulty was an inherently good problem for any nation to face. He stressed that it would be disrespectful to his chosen squad to publicly debate their merits with the media, reassuring the nation that he would continue to track the progress of the country's fine selection of young, developing talent.

For the first time since joining our club, Samson arrived late to training, stepping into the changing room as we were filing out to the pitches.

Bert confronted him first.

'Care to explain yourself?'

'No,' Samson said, barging past the captain and stomping to his locker.

'What the fuck do you mean, *no*? Who the fuck do you think you are?'

Samson shrugged, his face puckered, as though ready to spit.

'So I'll ask you again: do ye care to explain why you're late for training?'

'Now, I am here. *C'est bon, oui?*'

'No, it ain't *c'est bon*, sonny. You can be in a hump all you like for as long as you like, but you're here to work. You're at this club to work. Everything else in your life, all the bullshit and all your pride? That can get tae fuck. While you're here, you'll buck up your fucking attitude and fight for your place in this team.'

Samson snorted.

'Listen lad: clearly, you're not as good as you think you are. The Frenchies know it, and we all know it. There's talent here in this room that'll make your head spin. Lads that'll take your spot in a heartbeat.'

Bert had pointed over at me, like an accusation. For a moment, I met Samson's eye, before pulling away sharply, as though I'd been burned.

'You and me, son,' Bert continued, 'We'll have words after – you got that? Now hurry up and get your fucking boots on.'

When he eventually joined us on the training pitches, Samson played with a frenzied menace, exerting himself in the manner of a child, overly keen to impress: constantly calling for the ball, driving his body hard, sprinting with his chin up, arms pumping, mouth wide. After a single misplaced pass, he screamed with a wild pain, his face to the wind, involuntary and anguished, as though he'd been shot in the leg.

'Forget it,' called Jean-Claude. 'Back in position. Go, go, go.'

A number of our squad had switched to training in gloves

and extra layers: compression vests, Lycra tights. The turf was solid, seized up like a muscle. To remedy the cold, Jean-Claude insisted on breaking up the session with regular stretches: heel to calf, hold for ten. Lunge and leap, repeat five times. Fingers to toes, hold for twenty. Jean-Claude reminded us: 'Stretching keeps a body young.'

'Fucking paedo,' Dami said, just loud enough to solicit a laugh from the squad.

Among our squad, only six players had been called up for international duty by their respective nations. I envied them. I'd been raised with the understanding that playing for your country was the pinnacle of a footballing career, perhaps even your whole life. To me, playing football for England would be a duty equal to any military service, any noble vocation.

During this brief lull, the business of the club carried on. The commercial teams had coordinated a stacked calendar of corporate events. Later in the week, we were due to host Stonewall as part of their Rainbow Laces campaign. The goal of the project was to make sport and sporting events more inclusive and welcoming places for the lesbian, gay, bisexual and trans communities. For the past month, our pitch flags and advertising hoardings had been adorned with rainbows. Even Bert's captain's armband had fallen victim to what he referred to as *the gay agenda*.

Every member of the squad had been photographed for the club's Twitter page, instructed to smile, to hold a rainbow sign with the hashtag: #everyonesgame. The engagement on these posts was significantly below our usual numbers.

After training, Bert worked his way around the dressing room, allocating responsibilities for the various upcoming events. We were obliged to send at least two members of the senior squad to every fundraiser and corporate event hosted on club grounds. As punishment for his late arrival and run-in with Bert, Samson had been assigned to take a slot at the Stonewall evening. Unsurprisingly, no one had volunteered to join him.

To my knowledge, I had never met a gay person – at least, I'd never met anyone who openly identified as gay. As curious as I might be, I couldn't be seen to volunteer myself. I wasn't a fool.

'Here now,' Bert said, stooping over me, punching me in the arm. 'You'll keep our Samson company, won't you? You'll enjoy hanging out with all them poofters.'

'Like fuck will I.' I sniffed, pulling off a boot, swallowing hard.

'Come on, I'm only teasing. Just an hour or two and you're golden for months. I promise ye.'

'Fine, whatever.'

'There's a good lad. Now, just remember to clean out your arsehole for them. Even the fags have standards.'

42

The Stonewall event was held on Thursday afternoon. A black-tie buffet lunch, with a silent auction and speeches from various celebrities and club legends.

As a retired footballer, there's good money to be made in ambassadorial roles. Patrick O'Shea was our club's record goalscorer, and my dad's all-time footballing hero. Patrick was essentially a one-club man, arriving from Ireland in the mid-eighties, and seeing out his career as our number ten. He had spent a significant chunk of his retirement working as our regular compère for corporate events, mixing around the room like he owned the space.

Samson had suggested that we should arrive at the event together, meeting in the players' car park. It was a grey, thoroughly English afternoon – light drizzle and a canopy of threatening cloud, the fragrant, mineral smell of sod, of turned turf.

Pulling in, I spotted his car. Samson had given up on using taxis and had rented himself a matte black Mercedes Benz – just inconspicuous enough to not turn too many heads, but modern enough to make a statement.

I rapped gently on his window, causing him to start.

'Sorry,' I said, as he opened the door to step out from the car. 'I didn't mean to shock you.'

'It's fine,' he said, swiftly switching off the music he'd been listening to.

'Had you been waiting long?'

'No.'

'Everything okay?'

'It's fine. Come on, it rains.'

In the lift to the club's corporate lounge, I stood with my back against the wall, admiring him. Samson was wearing a navy suit, silk and beautifully cut.

'I think this is supposed to be over by five,' I said. 'But we might even be able to leave sooner. Sometimes they let you go sooner.'

'Good,' Samson said, repeatedly pressing the button for floor six.

'Is this your first thing?'

'What you mean?'

'I mean, your first corporate. Since you arrived.'

'Yes. First.'

'Cool, cool. They're really not that bad. Just answer their questions and smile.'

'Okay.'

'I'm sure they'll all be excited to meet you. You're probably the player they're most hoping for. If they could pick, I mean. They'd pick you.'

'Mmm,' Samson said, now checking his phone.

'Will you bother watching the match tonight? France–Holland?'

'Maybe. I don't know.'

'If you like, I could watch it with you. We could watch together.'

'You wish this?'

'I mean, I'll just be going home otherwise. Would probably end up watching it on my own. It'd be nice to have company.'

'Okay,' Samson said, fiddling with his collar, nonchalant. 'But not at yours. You come with me. To the hotel. We will watch there.'

'Oh,' I said, 'All right then. Whatever you prefer. Thanks.'

'At the hotel, there is food,' Samson said, ostensibly feeling the need to justify himself. 'I will need to eat.'

'Right. Got it.'

'And after the game, I will call my mama and go straight to sleep.'

'Sure.'

'Straight to sleep,' he repeated, turning away to jam at the button again.

The event was already underway. In the lobby, rainbow banners; an unmanned table of pins and postcards and stickers. As we stepped into the corporate lounge, the manager spotted us and walked straight over.

'Boys,' *L'oracolo* said, nodding to us, speaking softly. 'Very smart. It's good. You know about the charity, yes? The Stonewall?'

'Yeah, I think so,' I said, matching the manager's cadence, speaking on behalf of us both.

'And you know that we treat all people with respect? We accept people as they are.'

'Yes, boss.'

'Good,' he said, patting us both on the back. 'Respect, always, okay?'

'Yes, boss,' we synchronised.

'Good,' the manager said, pinching my cheek then winking, walking back across the room to rejoin the owner and a group of other men.

'We should probably split up,' I said to Samson.

'Split up?'

'Like, we should speak to different people. Around the room.'

'No, stay,' Samson said, grabbing at my shoulder, 'I need you. I need – your help, with the English.'

'But your English is—'

'Please,' Samson said, squeezing firmly, his eyes wide.

'Okay,' I said, a little disarmed, feeling the lingering warmth of his touch. 'Sure. Whatever you like.'

Together, we walked up to Patrick O'Shea.

'Good to see you, lads,' Patrick said. 'Oh so sorry to deprive you of another precious afternoon on the bloody Nintendo.'

For me, the once intoxicating thrill of being in the same room as Patrick had cooled to a strained tolerance. Though my dad wouldn't hear a word against him, among the squad and coaching staff, it was broadly accepted that Patrick did the club's reputation more harm than good.

'Good to see you too, Patrick,' I said. 'Keeping well?'

'Always well, me, laddy. Never had a day off sick in my life.'

'Great, yeah.'

'Not like you lot. Little cold and you're off for a week.'

'We just do what the medical team tell us, Patrick.'

Beside me, Samson fiddled more with his collar, clearly uncomfortable in his shirt.

'You don't know how easy you have it, you lot,' Patrick said, projecting his voice to no one in particular.

'Right, yeah.'

'I was scrubbing boots and cleaning out the gutters at your age. Proper man's work. That's what made me the man I am. Two hundred and four goals in three hundred and sixty games. You'll never see numbers like that again. Not here.'

'Do you know many of the people here then, Patrick?' I said, pointing past him to some of the clusters of people. 'The Rainbow Laces people?'

'Everyone else knows me and that's good enough. Keep a good attitude, and some day everyone will know your name too!'

'Could you maybe introduce us to some people?' I suggested more firmly.

'I can do better than that,' Patrick boasted, 'I'll bring them to you!'

With a purposeful skip, Patrick turned heel, setting off towards a vibrantly dressed group in the corner.

'I have the thirst,' Samson said, looking over at the drinks table.

'Just hold on for a second. Wait until Patrick's back.'

'You want water?' Samson said, ignoring me, already moving away.

'Hey, what happened to staying together?'

Stood alone, I sized up the room. Judging purely by appearance, it didn't seem apparent who was gay and who wasn't. It was just a room of smartly dressed people, casually chatting, politely sipping from fluted glasses.

I was conscious that a number of men had turned to look at me. I wondered whether they recognised me, or whether they desired me.

'Here,' Samson said, pushing a water bottle into my hand.

'Thanks,' I said.

'The wine, it looked bad.'

'What did you expect?' I said, nodding towards the owner, stood with his arm possessively slung around the manager's shoulders. 'It's always going to be cheap.'

'I expect nothing from this country.'

'You can't let me do all the talking,' I said. 'When Patrick comes back, you have to ask some questions.'

'But you love to talk,' Samson said, facing me, raising a cheeky eyebrow. 'You always wish to talk.'

'Yeah, but not here. I don't know what to say to these people.'

'*These* people?' Samson teased.

'Please,' I muttered. 'Don't.'

'Okay, okay, I talk. But if I make the error, you must correct, okay?'

'Yeah, no problem.'

'The English teacher, she says that we learn from making the error.'

'Right,' I said, watching as Patrick shepherded a man towards us. The man appeared to be in his sixties – thinning white hair, his neck slack with skin. He wore a lilac shirt with an open collar and up close, smelled faintly of cologne – a warm, sandalwood aroma.

'Nigel, let me introduce you to some of our players. Boys, this is Nigel.'

'Pleased to meet you,' Samson said, his English over-pronounced and deliberate, clearly a phrase he'd recently practised.

'Nigel is on the board for Stonewall.'

'You're all so tall in real life!' Nigel said, shaking our hands. 'I'm always so surprised by how tall you boys are.'

'This one reckons he's a threat to my crown,' Patrick said, jabbing his finger at me. 'Only another two hundred odd goals to go, eh laddy?'

'Thanks, Patrick,' I nodded.

'Ah, it's only a laugh,' Patrick said, pounding me on the back. 'We do like a laugh. I'll leave you boys be.'

Nigel grinned awkwardly, a sheen of sweat glazing his forehead.

'I'm very grateful you both came to support the campaign,' he told us. 'It means a lot to so many people.'

'It seems like a good cause,' I said, gripping my water bottle tightly, thankful to have something to do with my hands.

For the next ten minutes, I spoke with Nigel about generic football matters. He was a Crystal Palace season ticket holder, with the sincere belief that his club had the best fans in the country. As we spoke, Samson stood in silence, shifting his weight from foot to foot.

We were mid-conversation when Samson interjected, unprompted.

'You are a gay?'

Nigel flustered, his expression frozen agape.

'Just gay,' I corrected, permitting Nigel some time to process.

'Are you gay?' Samson modified.

Nigel cleared his throat. 'As it happens, I identify as bisexual. In fact, my wife is over there. She's in the green dress.'

'Ah, very nice,' Samson said, turning as directed. 'A beautiful woman. I am sorry. My English is not so good.'

'He's being modest,' I said. 'He's already pretty much fluent.'

'Well, I think you're very brave to come here,' Nigel said. 'A different country. A different language. It's very impressive.'

'Ah,' Samson said, 'It's okay. Good team. Good teachers.'

'If I might ask,' Nigel said, leaning in, his tone shifting into something more furtive, 'have you encountered any abuse here so far? Any racist abuse in England?'

'*Oui*,' Samson said, '*Bien sûr.*'

'He says yes,' I translated.

'Yes, I got that, thanks,' Nigel said to me, a little snappy. 'Well, I'm very sorry. I'm so very sorry you've had to experience that – as a guest in our country. I mean, not guest, but as a person – just, I understand that you're on loan here and – well, you know what I mean.'

Samson took a sip of his water before replying.

'The idiots,' he said, 'They are everywhere. *Tout les mondes*. But you English, you are special. You never let the Black man forget: he is a slave. He is a thug, a brute. You call your Black players "beast" and "dog". This is no coincidence, eh?'

Nigel laughed nervously.

'But, we're not as bad as France, though, right?'

'If you say so,' Samson said.

'Well, I hope so! I really do!'

Nigel's laugh grew louder, as though he were compensating, balancing for Samson's indifference.

'Anyway!' Nigel said, 'It's so good of you both to come along. Support from players means everything to us. It makes such a big difference to the cause to have strong ambassadors.'

'No problem,' I said, leaning forwards to shake his hand. 'Glad to be here.'

'I'll leave you be now,' Nigel said, backing away, still smiling. 'Promise to go easy on us when you visit Selhurst Park!'

'*Salut*,' Samson said, raising his water.

We watched as Nigel walked off, promptly ingratiating himself into another group. Another conversation about good intentions and simple solutions.

'He meant well,' I said, rapping the now empty water bottle against my knuckles.

'These people,' Samson sneered, fiddling with his crucifix, 'They disgust me.'

'What people?'

'You know. These people. Their kind.'

'You don't mean that.'

'Yes, I do.'

'But they're just trying to help.'

'No,' Samson said, now sneering, 'They ask too much. It is too much. It is disgusting.'

I felt like he'd slapped me. Dazed, my eyes swollen with tears, I made my way to the men's toilets, mercifully finding the room empty. At a sink, I ran cold water over my wrists and cuffs, taking in shallow, gasping breaths, crying in ugly, messy bursts. I was disgusting. I disgusted him.

Inside me, a frantic, directionless anger – I felt it swell in my shoulders and back, a spring-loaded tension. Anger at myself. Anger at Samson. Anger at everything that made me disgusting.

How dare he? How could he be so abjectly cruel? With no warning, no build up? How could he be so deluded? So virulently in denial?

Stepping away from the sink, I paced about, sniffing, huffing. I considered punching the wall, smashing the mirror. In that moment, I swore again that this was the end of it. If I disgusted him so much, then I'd distance myself. I'd speak to the manager about switching roommates. I'd remove the temptation from us both.

Hearing footsteps, I swiftly locked myself in a stall, sitting, hanging my head between my knees, choking on the air. It took fifteen minutes before I could control my breathing, before the fury had dissipated.

Stepping back into the conference room, red eyed and sullen, I found Samson by the buffet, holding a plate full of cured meats and cheese.

'You are okay?' he asked, his mouth partially full.

'No, I'm not fucking okay.'

'The manager,' Samson said, 'he asked where you were.'

'There was a queue.'

'A queue?'

'Yes, a fucking queue,' I said, shoving my arm past him to grab a fresh bottle of water. 'We do that in this awful, shitty country that you hate so much.'

Samson looked at me blithely, popping an olive in his mouth.

'The manager, I mention to him about the France game. He says we can go after the speech.'

'You seriously still think we are doing that?'

'*Oui*, why not?'

'You're a psycho,' I spat, turning away. I watched as Nigel kissed his wife on the cheek, softly squeezing her around the hip. The room started to applaud as he stepped on stage.

In his speech, Nigel spoke about the importance of football to the Rainbow Laces campaign, describing the sport as the *very marrow of our national identity*, and a *key means of connecting with the average working man and woman*. Nigel spoke of breakthroughs and victories, of small triumphs and shifting attitudes. He emphasised how much work there was yet to be done.

'Listen,' Samson whispered. 'I am sorry. Please – we go. I want you to come.'

'Not too disgusting for you?'

'No,' he said. 'Never you.'

I set down my water bottle, freeing my hands to clap for Nigel, to briskly wipe away more tears.

'Have you really been racially abused here?' I asked, my voice cracking, masked by the applause.

'Every day,' Samson said flatly, spitting an olive pip onto his plate.

'What? Every day?'

'With this body, the racism, she never stops.'

43

Samson's suite was on the fourteenth floor, overlooking the hotel's car park. In the distance, you could see the lights and spires of the city centre: Victorian steeples and turrets, hidden amid a skyline of stationary cranes and high-rise, glass-fronted luxury redevelopments. The grey of the afternoon had matured into coarse darkness. Rain swept across the double-glazing in shuddering waves: a light, insulated, pattering sound.

'It's nice,' I said, stepping away from the window. 'Good view.'

'It's okay,' Samson said, stepping out of the bathroom and throwing his silk suit jacket on the floor by the bed.

'You still don't fancy renting a place? Getting a bit more space?'

'Why I bother? This is fine. There is food. There is bed, television, laundry. There is swim.'

'Swimming pool. There's a swimming pool.'

'There's a swimming pool,' Samson corrected himself, blessing me with a small, grateful smile.

'But it's not yours, is it? It's not private.'

'As I say: I sleep, I train, I eat. What more do I want?'

'I dunno. I guess, perhaps just to feel a bit more connected? To feel like you're part of the city?'

'I am not part of this city.' He laughed, as though the concept were absurd.

'Well, there are plenty of our fans who would disagree.'

'So, they can disagree,' Samson said, throwing himself onto the bed and switching on the TV. 'Sit here,' he beckoned, patting the space beside him, as though he were inviting a pet. 'Come on, the match, she starts.'

France were fielding a full-strength eleven. On paper, it was a match worthy of a final. One of the pundits mentioned that the combined value of the players on the pitch was close to a billion pounds.

'Want to predict a score?' I asked, copying Samson's posture: legs extended, propped up by a fort of firm pillows.

'Why?'

'I dunno, for fun! Stop being so bloody serious all the time.'

'Okay, for fun, *oui*? I predict ten–nothing to the Dutch. I predict this idiot manager's head to roll. This makes you happy?'

'Well, I predict a comfortable France win. Two–nil to Lez Blues.'

'*Les Bleus*,' Samson corrected me, nudging me softly with his elbow.

'*Les Bleus*.' I smiled back, sitting on my hands.

The match started slowly. France worked the ball up and down their own half, controlling the centre of the pitch, patiently waiting for an opportunity that didn't seem likely to come. Occasionally, the cameras panned to the French manager, stood sternly on the touchline, holding his broad, Gallic chin.

'*Connard!*' Samson spat upon seeing him, swatting his hand through the air, as though to swipe off him off from the screen.

Despite our bet, it was evident Samson was rooting for his own nation. I listened to his frustrated protests, his appeals to the referee when a decision went against France's favour.

I wondered who else had been in the room with him – what women he might have secretly brought back, the things he might have done to them on that bed. I wondered whether he had ever laid here and thought of me.

At half-time, the Netherlands were a goal up. A fine set piece that left the French keeper out of position and helpless as the ball swung into the top left corner. As the players filed off the pitch, Samson sniggered to himself, tapping furiously at his phone.

'Who you talking to?' I asked.

'No one.'

'No one?'

'No one you know. *Mes amis.*'

'In Paris?'

'*Oui.*'

'Do you think they'd like me?'

'Sure.' Samson yawned. 'They are – how you say? *Trop génial* – easy, very easy boys.'

'Do you think they'll visit you? Come see you play while you're here?'

'They work,' Samson said, still typing away, his phone buzzing incessantly. 'They watch on the television. It's enough.'

'Right,' I said, checking my own phone, my empty inbox.

The game ended as a draw. One all. A penalty to France

to equalise with ten minutes remaining. Overall, it had been a poor exhibition of the talent on display. Both sides seemed content with the result, lingering on the pitch afterwards, hugging and swapping shirts. No major incidents and no injuries could be considered a relative success.

'I guess you didn't miss much there,' I said. 'Not a great game to debut in.'

Samson scoffed. 'If I play in this game, I promise you we win. I promise you this. All these players – they are, how you say? *Laissez-faire.* So complacent. They do not care. It does not matter to them.'

'You can talk to me, you know,' I said. 'When you're feeling frustrated, like this. I'll always listen. Even if I don't fully understand.'

'Okay,' Samson said. 'Thank you.'

'You can trust me. With everything.'

'I know.'

'Samson?' I said, gulping.

'*Oui?*'

'Do I actually disgust you?'

Samson hesitated.

'No,' he said, sniffing. 'I don't think so.'

Without thinking, I slipped my hand into his. Side by side, facing forwards, we sat with our legs extended, our hands together, gently meshed in the lightest of grips. We sat, and he allowed it to happen. I held my breath and stared ardently forwards, watching the screen. He was permitting this, I told myself. Samson was allowing this to happen. For a moment, two moments, I held him and he held me. But as I drew breath, he pulled loose, shifting his hand slowly away.

For what seemed an age, I remained still.

'I should go,' I managed to say, shuffling off the bed, my mouth dry. I wiped my clammy hand on my suit trousers. 'I'll go and let you call your mam.'

'Okay,' Samson said, adjusting his position, sliding back up against the backboard.

'Thanks for inviting me though. For allowing me to watch with you.'

'It is not a problem.'

'I'll let myself out. See you tomorrow, yeah?'

'Okay,' Samson said, reaching for his phone from the side table. 'À demain.'

In the quiet of the lift, I selected *ground* and adjusted my cock, still hard, slipping it under the waistband of my underwear. I tapped my foot, fraught with the thrill of him, of the moment he'd permitted me. Leaning forwards, I pressed the button again.

44

For the squad Christmas party, we were going back to the Roxy, via the casino. It was important to stay in our own city, Bert claimed. Coming up to the halfway point of the season, we were sixteenth in the table. We were surviving, not thriving. It was appropriate to stay local, to keep things low-key. For our night out, we would be accompanied by a battalion of five security guards and sixteen Instagram models – girls that Bert had personally scouted.

'Only the very finest snatch for my boys,' he boasted.

For anyone who chose not to head home after the club, two whole floors at the most discreet five-star hotel in the city were booked out just for us. The casino had waived all their typical booking fees, upon the understanding that we'd let loose in the high rollers' lounge.

'So no skimping, all right?' Bert commanded.

Our evening started in the casino's gourmet restaurant. Endless magnums of champagne, served alongside a three-course spread of prohibited gastronomical pleasures: seared honey duck, butter-basted steaks, lobster macaroni cheese, tiered chocolate fondant.

I used my napkin as a bib, conscious of getting food on my

outfit. Under instruction to dress smart, I'd worn the light grey suit from our pre-season tour – the only suit that had been tailored to my exact shape.

My body had changed since our summer in the Middle East – in the space of four months, I'd filled out notably. The suit felt tight in places I couldn't have expected – my deltoids, my thighs, my glutes.

Samson looked incredibly handsome. He was dressed in an Italian three-piece: navy and tweed – a texture that seemed to invite touch. He sat on the opposite side of the table to me, feasting on the lobster, his posture that of a reclining medieval king.

After months on a restricted diet of lean meats, grains and fresh vegetables, the food proved too rich for many of us, and much went uneaten, shoved to the middle of the table to prioritise valuable real estate for the copious amounts of alcohol that remained.

'So when do these girls get here?' Mario demanded, as the staff cleared the plates. 'Not sure if I trust your taste, Bert, given the state of your missus.'

'I'll let that slide,' Bert barked, 'But only 'cos it's Christmas.'

'Quit waffling,' Dami said, swigging straight from the bottle. 'What about the birds?'

'The ladies will be meeting us at the club from eleven,' Bert said. 'I thought it was best that they see you lot in the dark.'

It was almost eight by the time we'd finished. Between us, we'd made it through a dozen magnums. Among the group, only Baba was excused from drinking, on religious grounds. I attempted to pace myself, refusing refills. And yet I was already feeling the effects of the booze.

Though the expense of the meal, club and hotel had all been covered from our pot of fines, I'd been delegated responsibility for the whip: I was expected to tip the waiting staff, the girls, the security, the club hosts.

Before we left the restaurant, Bert shoved an unmarked envelope into my chest with no further instructions – seemingly assuming that I'd know what to do – that I'd be able to apportion the cash in appropriate amounts.

Sequestering myself to a quiet corner, I counted out three thousand pounds in fifties.

'Thanks,' I said, hastily handing a clump of notes to the nearest waiter, hoping that it would be adequate.

Under casino rules, Samson and I were obliged to wear wristbands, indicating that we were over eighteen, but under twenty-one.

'Means they won't ID you every ten minutes,' Bert explained.

'This is bullshit,' Samson said, inspecting the wristband as though it were a shackle.

'Aye,' Bert said, 'But bullshit's the name of the game.'

The high rollers' lounge smelled of leather and polish. Within twenty minutes at the blackjack table, I had blown through five hundred pounds. It was the maximum amount my card would let me withdraw in a single day.

Time seemed to come and go, ebbing like a tide. Drinks made their way into my hands. All around me, the purr of shuffling machines, the arrhythmic clack of chips, the dealers and croupiers with their tight black outfits, manicured nails and their scripted, steady language.

No more bets please.

Twenty-four and bust. House wins.

Change only. Change only.

Cheers erupted sporadically from every corner of the room. Yelps of carnal excitement.

I began to trail Samson around the room, hovering behind him at a roulette table with a fifty-pound minimum bet.

'Are you up?' I asked him.

'*What?*' he blared.

'Up – are you up or down?'

By way of reply, Samson held out a fistful of chips.

'I have this many,' he slurred.

Standing there, my hand resting on Samson's back, I watched as my teammates effortlessly riffled the colourful stacks of chips, confidently betting on zones and spreads of numbers.

'Why fifteen?' I asked Milo, as he slid a stack of chips onto the same number for the third time in a row.

'Why not?' he replied. 'You've got to pick something and stick to it.'

45

By the time we reached the Roxy, I was the drunkest I'd ever been. At some point, the girls had joined us. There could have been sixteen or there could have been four. I was too drunk to tell. Under the club lights, they looked like a palette swap of each other. The women shared a single body shape: steep curves, enhanced by sparkly dresses that dazzled invitingly. Their features seemed consciously obscured, hidden under tans, lashes and extended hair.

Without quite enough women to go around, I felt excused from making any meaningful effort to flirt with them, but Samson found himself quickly surrounded – it was him who they seemed to recognise. It was him they wanted to talk to, to be pictured with.

'Aren't you with that Holly girl?' one asked.

'Don't believe everything you read, eh?' Samson said, throwing his arm around her shoulder.

For his part, Samson seemed to enjoy the attention, graciously pouring out drinks, dancing in place, his glass elevated in an indiscriminate toast.

Though I was aware that my teammates cheated on their partners, I hadn't expected them to be so brazen. I watched on as our group migrated to the dance floor – one gyrating, grinding mass, Samson somewhere in the centre, the pivot around which everything rotated. Only Bert stayed alongside me, maintaining his distance, remaining loyal, refusing the girls' advances.

'You're all right, love,' he told one. 'Go have fun.'

Another drink was forced into my hand. We had switched to beer and the bitterness wasn't sitting well with me. I held each sip in my mouth until the fizz flattened, wincing through every swallow.

I'd only drunk past the point of being tipsy a handful of times in my life. The experience felt novel and scary. I pressed my back against the leather of the booth and slotted the cool glass bottle between my legs. Somewhere to my right, a girl rubbed powder into her gums. For a moment – just a moment – I allowed myself to close my eyes, exploring the contours of these feelings. Around me, voices swam. The high pitch of the girls – their squealing, shrieking laughter. I felt hazily aware of certain words, perking up at each mention of my own name. Their laughter and the music blended into a sticky, sweet glut of noise.

'Oi,' came Bert's voice, jolting straight through me, a hand on my shoulder. 'Don't fall asleep on us you silly cunt. They'll boot us all out.'

'Sorry,' I said, opening my eyes and squinting to find focus, to make him out.

'If you're done, get yourself home, lad.'

'Home?'

'Yes, home! That place where you wank yourself to sleep? Get home and get to bed before the paps can snap you looking mortal.'

'But – you said—'

'Forget anything I said. You've done well, son. You've done me proud. Held your own.'

'I did good?' I garbled.

'Yes, good. Very fucking good. Now let's get you up and out. Gi' us what's left of the whip, there's a good lad. Your taxi's on me.'

'Thanks, Bert. I love you, mate.'

With a firm hand against the small of my back, Bert eased me to my feet and out from the booth, manoeuvring me by the shoulders to the door of the club and safely into the dominion of a neckless, suited bouncer.

'Sort this one out with a cab, would you Pavel?' Bert said, deftly slipping a few notes into the man's hand.

'Not a problem, my friend.'

Bert grabbed me by the jaw and planted a soppy kiss on my cheek.

'Good night, yeah? Straight to bed when you get in, all right? No fucking about – you hear me? No booty calls, nothing. Good lad.'

With a gentle slap on the cheek he'd just kissed, Bert shoved me away and disappeared back into the club.

Outside, the night air felt like a blessing – a cool rush of relief and clarity. I patted down my pockets for my keys and wallet and phone, swallowing back the congealed spit that was coating my mouth. Out here, the thumping beat of the music sounded tame and manageable.

Once Pavel had shielded me past lurking paparazzi and into a taxi, I checked my phone. It was just gone one o'clock. We'd been drinking for a solid six hours. I rolled down the car window and angled my face into the wind.

In the team WhatsApp group, Bert had shared a dozen or so dimly lit pictures of us in the club. We were all smiling, raising bottles and glasses in receptive, uninhibited appreciation to the camera. Looking at the photos, it seemed suddenly alarming to me how noticeably young Samson and I were compared to the rest of the team. Removed from the collective identity of our kits, our teenage faces looked misplaced among the gruff beards and hardened jaws of our teammates.

I wondered if he'd even noticed me leaving. Samson, there in the pictures, sandwiched between two of the models, draping themselves over him, one leaning in to whisper vague nonsense into his ear, the other gripping his thigh with both hands, claiming him like a prize.

I scrolled through the journey, exhausting the vestiges of my phone's battery, until, miraculously, we were outside the gates to my home. I had no recollection of providing anyone with my address. The journey had sobered me up somewhat and I managed to make it inside without incident, heading straight to the kitchen for some ice-cold water and leftover pasta.

Lying in bed, naked and dizzy, I spread my legs to the corners of the mattress and ran my tongue over my teeth, furred and tacky from the alcohol.

Rolling over, I thought about what the rest of them would be doing now. I pictured them on the dance floor – all limbs and rhythm, pressed and blurred together under the strobing lights. The sweating, groping desperation of their movements, spellbound by the pulsing of the music.

In my mind, Samson was there in the centre of the huddle – the centrifugal force around which all other energy orbited. I imagined the girls with their hands in his hair, their nails down his back, stripping him with a frenzied fervour, fighting for an inch of his flesh. I imagined them on their knees, grabbing at his belt and fly, desperate to take him into their mouths, their tongues wet and eager, lapping at his sweat, his essence.

According to my digital alarm, it was 3.37 a.m. when my intercom rang, shrill through the thud in my brain. With a halting lurch, I got out of bed and pulled back the curtains, just in time to see a taxi pulling away. Downstairs, on the video monitor, I could tell it was Samson, leaning heavily against the gate.

'Samson?' I said through the intercom, my voice parched and groggy.

'Lemme in,' Samson slurred, his face pressed up to the microphone, oblivious to the camera.

'What are you doing here?'

'*Tais-toi!*' he said, wiping his nose on the inside of his arm. 'Let me in, okay?'

I buzzed him through the gate and stumbled into a pair of shorts.

I stood with the door open, watching him wobble up the gravel drive, like a marionette suspended by invisible strings. His shirt was untucked on one side and his head was hung low, seemingly focused on putting one foot in front of the other.

'What's happened? How much have you had?'

'I'm not even drunk,' Samson spat, squeezing past me, entering my home.

'You're fucking wasted. How did you even remember my address?'

'Doesn't-*hic*-matter. I'm here. You didn't answer. Your phone. You didn't—'

'Yeah, it's dead, but—'

'Made it here on my own. No one saw.'

In my addled stupor, it felt like I had somehow summoned him. As though my dream had sent out a beacon, bringing him to me.

'Come on, sit down here,' I said, switching on the lights and guiding him to the couch in the living room. 'I'll get you some water.'

'I'm not drunk,' Samson repeated, slouching into the fabric, his head lolled to the side.

'Okay, you're not drunk.'

'I can get it up.'

'What?' I said, seizing up, turning back from the kitchen.

'You know what I fuck-*hic*-fucking mean. Let's do it. Come on then, let's get it done.'

'That's what you've come here for?'

'I don't fucking know. But I am here now. And you want it. You always fucking want it.'

'But, the girls – the girls at the club . . . '

'Fucking bitches. I hate all of those dumb, racist bitches.'

'Samson – this isn't – I mean, I can't just—'

'They're all the same. Everyone here. Everyone's the same. Except you.'

'Samson, I really think you should just get some water and sleep.'

'Shut up,' he said, now rising to approach me. 'You don't reject me. You don't get to.'

Reaching me, Samson grabbed clumsily at my crotch, attempting to pull down my shorts.

'I don't want this,' I said, as firmly as I could manage, extending my arms.

'You do,' he growled, yanking me by the arm and pulling my body into his, swaying both of us off balance.

It was fear I felt in that moment. With his arms on me, grappling for purchase, forcing me backwards, we weren't footballers or teammates or lovers. We were reduced to our bodies. And Samson was strong – stronger than his frame suggested – stronger than I could confidently resist.

'Come on,' he barked, driving me backwards, towards the sofa.

'*I don't want this,*' I repeated, with my mouth and in my head, looping like an affirmation.

I adopted a wide, boxer-like stance, straining, my hands clenched, ready to strike.

'Fuck – Off – Get – Off – FUCK – *OFF!*'

My fist landed clean, catching him from the right, just below the temple, hollow and wooden like a mallet-blow. My arm followed through the motion, glancing up off his skull in a wide, unwieldy arc, twisting my body out and away.

The world lagged. As he fell backwards, I watched as the impact registered across Samson's face, processing the shock into pain, like a sudden surge of sense.

My immediate instinct was to say sorry. To bend down and tend to him. Suddenly so dazed and docile, sprawled there on my floor, his mouth open in a mute, breathless sigh.

'I'm going to get you some water,' I heard myself say, sniffing, adjusting my shorts.

Walking away, I felt the sting of his grip – my arms red and chafed from the force of his hands. My eyes flooded with tears – thick, hot tears, boiling up with each catching, gasping breath. I watched my hand unclench and shake, turn the tap, my words of defiance still ringing through the pulsing blood in my ears, cycling like trauma.

I don't want this. I don't want this. I don't want this.

Standing there, by the sink, the water now overflowing the glass, ice cold against my skin, I had no idea what I wanted. I wanted so many things at once. I wanted the warmth of my bed and the easy escape of sleep. I wanted the life of my teammates – their assured confidence, the convenience of their ordinary desires. I wanted my mam – her calm, soft voice, telling me it would all be okay, that everything would work out okay.

Despite it all, I wanted the Samson in front of me, slouched there on my floor, pathetic and rejected, and I wanted the Samson that existed only in my head – the one I'd spent months imagining, honing, cherishing – the person I'd somehow willed into existence and called through the night, the one who had abandoned the rest of them to be here, confronting me, wanting me.

'Here,' I said to him, setting down the glass at arm's length, 'Drink.'

With look of chastised compliance, Samson took the water and gulped it down, loud and thirsty.

'I'm sorry,' he said, coming up for air, his voice wavering, still holding the glass. 'I'm really sorry.'

'It's okay,' I said, inching closer, my palms raised like a truce. 'I'm sorry too.'

Samson stared at me as I approached, wounded and somehow small, curled into himself, breathing hard, knees to his chest like a panicked child.

I extended a hesitant hand, which he took, and pulled Samson up, up to his feet, up to eye level.

'I'm so sorry,' he sobbed, conceding his weight straight into me, burying his head into my shoulder.

'*Shhh, shhh,*' I cooed, stroking his back, feeling the familiar contours of his muscles.

Beneath the drink and the aggression and the passion, this was still Samson. The same Samson I'd already excused and forgiven a hundred times over.

Easing our bodies down onto the sofa, I laid him flat, on top of me, resting his head on my bare chest. I held him there, stroking his neck and back until the panic abated, until his breathing settled, until he became still.

'I'm so unhappy here,' he whispered. 'This city – this country – it's so—'

'It's okay,' I said, 'I understand. You don't need to explain.'

'The girls – those ignorant, greedy, racist bitches. I don't have to take it, you know? I shouldn't have to settle for this.'

'I know, I know.'

'You are the only one – the only one who – and I treat you this way? I'm sorry. You don't deserve this. I know how you feel – about this city. About the club. You don't want to hear this.'

'I understand,' I said, 'Just another few months. Just a few more games and you can be rid of us. You can pick any team you like. Every team in Europe wants you. You'll never have to come back.'

Lifting his head off my chest, Samson met the corner of my mouth with a kiss – a real kiss, one that left a softness.

'I'll go now,' he said, rolling off and sitting upright, smoothing down his shirt.

'You don't have to,' I stammered. 'I mean, not if you don't want. There's a spare room and bed.'

'No, I should go. It's better that I go.'

'All right then. Do you want me to sort an Uber or something?'

'Don't-*hic*-worry. I'll do it.'

Waiting, we sat in a tense silence. Samson sipped from his glass, touching tenderly at his cheek. A welt was forming where I'd stuck him.

I was still half-dressed. I felt cold.

Ten minutes later, as the taxi pulled up the gravel of my drive, Samson rose heavily to his feet, tucking in his shirt. He poured the remaining water from his glass into the pot of my emaciated spider plant.

'You should bring this to the light,' he recommended. 'Here, it suffers.'

'See you soon,' I said, opening the door.

'Yeah – soon.'

Outside, it had begun to snow.

HALF-TIME

HALF-TIME

46

On Christmas Day, the senior squad always visit a local children's hospital. No one is obliged. There's no press, no reward. But every year, a dozen or so players reliably volunteer. Parents and childless alike, gathered there at 10 a.m. sharp, standing in the winter chill, armed with a sack of presents.

'You can't cry,' Bert commanded us, his lip quivering. 'Not in front of 'em. No matter what, you don't cry in front of the kids. It's a happy day. You got that, boys? Now, switch your phones off and pull on these hats. Smile and be merry.'

Samson wasn't part of the group. He'd travelled back to France to celebrate Christmas, then his twentieth birthday, with his mother and friends. With the intense winter schedule, it would be his only chance to visit Paris until the start of February. With Samson out of the country and rested for our Boxing Day fixture, I was due to start in his place.

Within moments of waking, I'd texted him, simply wishing him a Happy Christmas. As we stepped into the hospital, he was yet to respond.

In the lobby, the head nurse issued blunt instructions.

'We've got about an hour and a half till we start preparing them for lunch, so we'll need to be brisk. Six wards today, three on second, two on third, one on fifth. If you get lost or left behind, step out into the corridor, find a member of staff, and someone will bleep me. If at any point you hear an alarm, you must immediately end any conversations and leave the ward. Okay – any questions?'

No one dared to ask what the alarm might signify.

'Good, then let's go.'

We fed into the first ward in a sombre single file, washing our hands by the door while a junior nurse supervised our technique.

'Good job,' she said to me, winking kindly. 'Someone's brought you up right.'

The ward was unseasonably warm, lit by strips of harsh, luminescent lighting. At the nurse's station, a radio played Wizzard with cheery determination, the music syncopated with ambient beeps and harsh medical tones. On the counter, a miniature plastic Christmas tree was perched atop a stack of disposable glove boxes.

We clustered by the door, awaiting instruction. I adjusted my Santa hat, reminded myself to smile.

'Okay, so there are twenty-four beds on this ward. If you'd all like to couple up and make your way round, four beds each.'

I found myself paired with Dami. Together, we worked through our first three allotted patients, introducing our-selves by our first names, shaking their small, frail hands. It all felt much too formal. I handed over pre-wrapped presents from our sack at random, sharing in the kids' surprise as they opened their Lego kit; a pencil set from the club shop; a copy of Scrabble.

'Wicked!' Dami said, 'I bet you'd batter me at that. I've always been better with my feet than with my words, you know?'

I hugged the parents who sat dutifully by, posing for their photos, smiling wide and breathing deeply. I asked no questions, afraid of the answers.

Our fourth child was rolled on his side, into the hospital bed railings. He was wearing our club kit, the shirt pulled up over most of his face, revealing only a tuft of messy, ginger hair.

'You okay there, mate?' I asked, squatting by his bed, employing my friendliest, brightest voice. 'I love your kit.'

'He's a little embarrassed,' his mother said, leaning in. 'You're his heroes, you know? He doesn't want you to see him sick. To think he's weak and that.'

'Right,' I said. 'No, we'd never think that, would we, Dami? You're the proper hero, mate. We just have to kick a ball about.'

The boy pulled the shirt higher still, burying himself in his pillow.

'Well, I hope you get lots of presents and have a really nice Christmas. It was great to meet you.'

'Ta, love,' the mother said, leaning in to kiss me on the cheek. 'Good luck with the game tomorrow.'

As we filed out to the next ward, I worried whether the kids had been given an option to meet us, or if we'd been forced upon them. It occurred to me that at least some of the families might resent us. In some abstract way, our presence could be perceived as cruel – our robust health and fitness, spitefully paraded across the path of their suffering.

Moving from floor to floor, bed to bed, I tried not to stare at the tubes that hung limply from their noses, their hands. I tried to relax and keep smiling, to follow Bert's lead, mirror his natural charm. Bert had strategically paired himself with Baba, the most taciturn member of our group.

'Who do you support then, big man?' Bert asked at the bed across from us, crouching to the eye level of a young boy in a wheelchair.

'Man United,' the kid said proudly, shuffling back in his seat.

'*Man United?*' Bert postured, his voice shrill and indignant. 'No presents for this one then, Baba. Definitely on the naughty list.'

The kid laughed giddily, snorting a little.

'Aye, I'm just teasing, son. Let's have a root around in here and see what we've got for you. Baba, pick us out a really big one.'

Selecting one of the larger packages from the bag, Bert helped the boy unwrap a remote-control car.

'Ooh, that's a proper good one that. Bet no United player got you oot!'

The boy laughed even more, flapping his arms in delight.

'All right then, give us a hug.'

Bert leaned in and embraced the boy warmly, unbothered by the slick of drool on his cheek.

'Thank you,' the boy blurted affectionately.

Walking through the hospital, I thought about the messages that were sent to my official Twitter every day – the direct, desperate appeals for help: families begging for money to help their sick mam, their unemployed son, their incarcerated husband. Endless requests to retweet links to fundraising pages, government petitions, community events. In the space of a year, I'd grown numb to these pleas. They were a mild annoyance, part of the noise of a footballing life – something to scroll past, to dismiss or delete, filter and forget.

The final part of our visit was the intensive care unit on the fifth floor at the top of the hospital. The floor with the longest way down, the most perilous path to recovery. On the fifth floor, we were introduced to the families of children in medically induced comas. That ward was different to any other hospital environment I'd ever known. There was no palpable smell of sickness – none of the sharp chemical freshness, the general rush and struggle. There was a composed, mechanical calm to the ward.

'You don't need to be so quiet, boys,' the head nurse instructed. 'It's good for them to hear your voices. Speak to them.'

We moved as a single group from bed to bed, while doctors and nurses stepped unobtrusively around us, occupied only with the patients and their machines. They effortlessly decoded ciphers and lights, proposing hypothetical adjustments should the patient fall short of certain signs of life.

'Merry Christmas, boss,' Dami said in the direction of one boy. 'I'm going to leave a present here for you, yeah? Looks like you're in proper good hands. These lot are working mad hard to help you get better. Luxury, five-star service, you get me?'

Another boy was covered from neck to ankle by a blue, alien technology. Under the respirator mask and the network of wires and tubes, I guessed him to be fifteen, perhaps

sixteen. There were certainly no more than five years between us.

'This is Spencer,' said a woman by his bed, clearly the boy's
mother. 'We're not supposed to touch him, I'm afraid. The
doctors say we should keep all contact to a minimum. They
reckon any movement could be detrimental to his chances
of recovery.'

The mother explained that Spencer had been stuck by
a van, and that the blue device was a sophisticated cooling blanket, which was supposed to maintain therapeutic
hypothermia by lowering his body temperature, thereby
minimising the swelling on his brain.

Her words were so objective and calm, so resigned to the
influence of others, the medical language heavy and precise
on her lips. Listening, I spotted her son's left hand hung out
towards me, lolling outside of the blanket, palm up, his fingers
curled, twitching.

'Spencer's a big fan of the club,' the mother said. 'He'd be
thrilled to know you came.'

She thanked us for the signed shirt, and I felt ridiculous
for offering something so small, so meagre in the wake of
her pain.

Soon enough, we were finished. We posed for more photos
with the staff and wished them all a Happy Christmas. Out
in the car park, I shivered – part from shock, part from the
cold. Bert reclaimed the hats and sacks, stuffing them hastily
into the boot of his Range Rover.

'Same time next year,' he said, back in character, his emotions masked by the usual bluster. 'Merry Christmas you
filthy animals. Now fuck off home to your ugly birds.'

47

Leaving the hospital, I decided to take a scenic route home. I told myself that a drive would clear my head; would purge those caustic images. Children with burned and blistered skin; small bodies knotted with pain, fretted with silver wires and hollow tubes; the wincing fortitude of those parents in their bedside vigils.

Driving those slow curving roads, I rolled down my window and enjoyed the ruddy musk of the Christmas air. I felt great affection for the tawny winter woods: green that sprung greener, mile by mile. In the distance, a blanket of low, tissued cloud, threatening to break.

It was gone midday when I arrived at Mam and Dad's home and Samson still hadn't replied to my text.

Though my new place was twice the size of my parents' house, Mam had insisted that she would remain host for our Christmas dinner.

I unloaded the presents I'd hidden in my boot and unlocked the door. Stepping inside, I found Dad in his armchair, sat in front of the television, idly flicking through channels, sipping from a glass of prosecco.

'That took a while,' he said, lowering the volume.

'Yeah, sorry.'

'How was it?'

'All right, I guess. Pretty draining.'

'Sure you won't have a glass of this?' he said, swilling the glass at me. 'It'll do you some good. Cut through the shock.'

'I shouldn't,' I said, my body jolting at the prospect of alcohol. 'Got to stay fresh for tomorrow.'

'Well, you'd better go help your mam then. Running about like a mad woman as usual.'

'Why can't you help her?'

'I just get in the way, apparently,' Dad said, re-raising the volume.

My mother was in the kitchen, hunched in front of the oven.

'Ah, here's the man of the hour,' she said, rising stiffly, then climbing to her tiptoes, straining to peck my cheek and adjust my hair.

'You're a good boy for doing that. Your nan was a nurse in that hospital, you know?'

'Oh?' I said. 'Really? I actually didn't know.'

'Yeah – a good ten years she spent there. It was under a different name in those days, though. Queen Mary's or Queen Anne's or something. And it wasn't just for the kids back then. She had all sorts in there. Crazies and poofters and every type of degenerate.'

'Right,' I said.

'And the hours that woman worked! You wouldn't believe it. That was before the unions came in, remember. They worked you to the bone and you couldn't bat a lash. Here, pass me those chestnuts.'

Even with just the three of us, my parents' home could feel cramped. Every surface was decorated with a lifetime's accumulation of possessions. Mam had curated her home like a museum – each trinket was laced with rich history and notable provenance. When she dusted, she did so with a quiet reverence, taking care not to disturb the delicate equilibrium of her own design.

Even once I could afford to move them to a larger home, I suspected Mam would always prefer to remain in that house, surrounded by the comfortable familiarity of a life well-lived.

As she did every year, Mam had wrapped the banisters in tinsel – crimson and gold, secured with tape that she tore with her teeth. An artificial tree was brought down from the attic and dusted in the yard. Mam would take responsibility for decorating, but always granted me the honour of placing the star.

There were to be seven of us: we'd be joined by Mam's sister, Grace, along with my dad's brother, his girlfriend and her son.

'It'll be so lovely to have little Jackie again,' Mam swooned, handing me a stack of plates. 'It's just not Christmas without a little one around, you know?'

'Yeah,' I said, repressing thoughts of the hospital.

'And he's growing up so fast. Nine already – only a few years left for him to really enjoy it all.'

'It'll be good.'

'And at this rate, I'll be waiting years yet before you have any children of your own!'

She laughed merrily, rummaging through the spice cupboard.

'Come here.' She beckoned. 'You might have to reach for me. The cloves are always buried at the back. That's the problem with cloves! You only ever use them come Christmas!'

In the living room, Dad hummed tonelessly along with the crooning voice of Dean Martin.

'Do you remember that Christmas when we got you the bike? Oh, your precious little face. Your eyes! You couldn't believe it.'

'Yeah, I remember.'

'I'm sure I've got a picture upstairs of you on that bike – hold on, I'll go see if I can find the picture.'

'Mam, don't worry, I remember.'

'Okay, well, you'll have to remind me later. I should dig it out for your Auntie Grace. She'd love to see that picture again.'

Aunt Grace lived about an hour outside the city – far enough away to modify her accent, to be *beyond the grasp of that bloody football club*. She worked in the head office of a fashion house and spent her disposable income on antiques, routinely calling in on Sundays to lecture Mam about how cultured life suddenly became if you were to just venture a few miles down the road.

I was on the toilet when the doorbell rang. I'd been sat there for half an hour, enjoying the privacy, scrolling through the team group chat on WhatsApp – videos of the players' kids opening extravagant presents. Pictures of gravy-laden roasts. A topless, smiling Bert carving a giant turkey.

'Love, come down now,' Mam called. 'Come give yer Auntie Grace a kiss.'

In the living room, Aunt Grace was stood, fanning herself dramatically with Dad's TV guide.

'Honestly, it's always so hot in this house. You really need to crack a window, Adrian.'

'I like my house warm in t'winter,' Dad said, still sat in his armchair, exaggerating his own accent, as though to offset Grace's pretention.

Aunt Grace was wearing four-inch heels and a green dress that hugged her body unflatteringly around the middle.

'Hello darling,' she said, planting a wet kiss on my jawline.

'How was mass?' I asked, taking her coat and bag.

'Oh, not bad, you know. Except we've been stuck with this Asian priest for six months odd now – very nice, you must say, very sweet with the little ones, but for the life of me, I can't understand a word he says. All gobbledygook, you know?'

'Right,' I said.

'Promise me you'll put that on a hanger, won't you love? That coat has to last me a good few years. We're not all on footballers' salaries, you know.'

'I will,' I said.

'Nick will be late as usual, I suppose?'

'He's a busy man,' Dad asserted.

Aunt Grace laughed. 'Who's busy on Christmas Day?'

'People with a hundred and twenty staff are.'

Uncle Nick owned the construction company that Dad had spent the previous decade working for, prior to becoming my agent. Three years ago, he'd been through a divorce that saw him lose his home but retain the business. Shortly after, he met Shelley, a freelance masseuse and single mother.

Dad's theory was that at fifty, Nick felt he'd missed the chance at having kids of his own, and little Jackie had become his way of compensating.

'But it'll never be the same as flesh and blood,' Dad had commented to me. 'He might have his precious business, but he'll never have you, will he?'

Not ten minutes later, the doorbell rang.

'Could you get that, love?' Mam called from the kitchen.

As I opened the door, Jackie persisted at pressing the button, his arm almost fully extended.

'Hi Jackie,' I said. 'Merry Christmas.'

'Nick said we could do presents straight away,' Jackie said, squeezing past me, into the hallway. He was dressed in a designer tracksuit that looked brand new.

'Is that right?'

'Yeah,' Jackie said, hyper. 'I'm getting a Switch.'

'Nice one,' I said, watching Uncle Nick unload his car.

'Bet you don't have one.'

'Actually, I do. Sometimes we play it when we travel to play other teams.'

'My friend Toby says that Ronaldo is better than you.'

'Toby's definitely right on that one.'

'Toby's Dad is a policeman.'

'Oh, cool.'

'Wanna see me floss now?' Jackie said, launching straight into a dance, swishing his arms back and forth, alternating from in front to behind his hips, hitting his bunched fists against our narrow corridor walls.

'Very impressive,' I said. 'Careful on the paint.'

'Bet you can't do it,' Jackie said, speeding up.

'I'll leave it to the master,' I said, 'I'm going to go help your dad out now.'

'Nick's not my dad,' Jackie said plainly, as though it were a clarification he'd made a hundred times before.

'Right, yeah,' I said, stepping through the door, onto the driveway.

Shelley was leaning against the bonnet of the car, talking on the phone, while Nick hefted two heavy-looking bags from the boot.

'Do you want any help there?' I asked.

'I'll be fine,' Uncle Nick said, shuffling up the driveway, his voice strained. 'Save your valuable hands – wouldn't want the blame for you getting injured.'

Shelley was wearing a summery yellow playsuit that bunched at the shoulders. She was at least fifteen years younger than Uncle Nick – she wouldn't have looked out of place among our players' wives.

'Merry Christmas, lad,' Nick said, setting down the bags by the door and catching his breath. 'Don't stare at my missus now.'

'I wasn't,' I said defensively.

'I'm just teasing. Where does your mam want all this crap?'

'Just in the living room – under the tree's fine, I think.'

'Good performances so far, by the way,' Nick said, shaking out his arms, then shuffling the bags into the living room. 'Impressive stuff. Think you'll get any more starts in the New Year?'

Dad interjected from his armchair, answering on my behalf: 'That'll be the manager's decision. He's the one who knows best.'

'Merry Christmas to you too, Adrian.'

Behind us, Jackie was already kneeling on the floor, scouring over Mam's carefully wrapped presents.

'We've got a real tree at home,' Jackie said, 'It goes to the ceiling and everything.'

'Well isn't that impressive!' Mam said dotingly.

'Yeah, and I ate all the chocolate decorations.'

'Oh my!'

Jackie laughed, relishing her attention.

Once Shelley had joined us and everyone had been poured a drink, we took turns opening presents, with Mam acting as photographer.

Jackie ripped through a pile of twenty parcels in ten minutes flat – tearing with a frenzied, feral appetite.

Under instruction, I'd kept my present to him small, simply buying Jackie a copy of *FIFA* for his new Nintendo Switch.

'We can have a game later, if you like,' I said, as he studied the box.

'You're not going to play as yourself are you?'

'I might! Who would you prefer me to play as?'

'A good team,' Jackie said.

'*Jackie,*' Shelley scolded, her legs crossed. 'That's very rude.'

'Sorry,' Jackie mumbled.

When it was Mam's time to open gifts, I was assigned camera duty. Dad had bought her a pair of slippers.

'Very imaginative, Adrian,' Mam said, smiling forlornly to the camera, holding up the slippers like pieces of evidence.

Dad sipped at his prosecco.

I had bought my parents a hot-air balloon ride over the

county. Opening the gift card, Mam cried – big, messy tears – burying her face in my shoulder.

'Oh, love,' she sobbed. 'You thoughtful angel. Thank you.'

For dinner, Mam sat me next to Jackie. 'The kids' side of the table,' she quipped. We pulled crackers, with Jackie claiming all the prizes.

'Everyone has to wear their hats,' Dad insisted. 'House rules.'

'Mam says I can be a footballer when I grow up too,' Jackie told me, spinning a cracker keyring around his finger.

'Yeah?' I said, smiling across the table at Shelley. 'If you work hard and practise every day, why not?'

'Either a footballer or a YouTuber. That's what I'm going to be. Or a policeman like Toby's dad.'

'Some good options there.'

As host, Mam insisted on serving the food herself, plating me up a modified version of everyone else's meal: boiled potatoes, unbuttered cabbage and a double helping of Brussels sprouts.

'Tuck in, tuck in,' Mam instructed.

While we ate, she roved backwards and forwards from the kitchen to the table, ferrying condiments and fresh glasses, removing the detritus of the crackers.

'Would you bloody well sit down and enjoy your own delicious food, Lolly?' Aunt Grace commanded.

'In a minute,' Mam said, 'I have to get my lovely boy's peaches out of the fridge, otherwise they'll still be chilly when we're done.'

'Honestly, it's fine, Mam,' I called.

'Here now, if my boy can't join us for a nice bit of proper pudding, then I'm not subjecting him to ice-cold peaches.'

Adjusting her paper hat, she rushed away, her new slippers flapping stiffly, clearly a size too large.

'I hope you appreciate all this,' Aunt Grace said. 'Your mam suffering through all this palaver twice over for your sake.'

'I do – I'm grateful.'

'Are you though? For all she's done for you. All she's still doing at that new house? I'm sure you don't realise the half of it. I don't know whether you've got any true sense of how much that poor woman does for your sake.'

'She's the best,' I said flatly.

'An angel,' Aunt Grace said. 'Always the martyr, my sister. She was born to suffer. It'll send her to an early grave. I know it will. She'll give herself an ulcer from the stress of all this. Same happened to our Aunt Nelly. Did your mam ever tell you about our Aunt Nelly?'

'Um, I'm not sure.'

'Oh, she must have done. You likely weren't listening. That's the trouble with your generation.'

'Can I play Switch now?' Jackie begged his mam, pushing a sprout dolefully around his plate.

'After dessert,' Shelley said sternly, without looking up.

'But I wanna go *nowwww*.'

'*I said no*,' Shelley snapped, reaching for more wine. 'Eat the lovely food, Jackie.'

Between courses, Uncle Nick steered the conversation to football. While Dad was a lifelong supporter of his local team, his brother had switched allegiances to Liverpool in the mid-eighties, during their reign of domestic dominance.

'Looking like you might go down then,' Uncle Nick said to me.

'Bit soon yet,' Dad replied on my behalf. 'It's a long season.'

'You'd get a pay cut in the Championship, I suppose?'

'Probably,' I said. 'We're staying positive though.'

'Aye,' Nick said, cracking open a can of beer. 'Makes sense. Proper good job getting that manager of yours in. If you stay up again, he'll have done bloody well. What's he like to play for?'

'Yeah, he's really good,' I said. 'He's got a really clever approach to planning and training.'

'Here though, bet you wouldn't mind that Samson getting injured for a few games, though?'

'I wouldn't want anyone to get injured,' I said, measuring my words.

'Ah, that boy's a different class though,' Dad said, sliding his paper hat back up his brow. 'Anyone can see it. Best we've had since Paddy O'Shea, I reckon.'

'Hear that?' Uncle Nick laughed to me. 'Hear what your old man reckons? Don't compliment your own son, whatever you do, Adrian.'

'He agrees!' Dad said. 'We think the same, you know.'

'You do talk a lot of bollocks,' Nick continued. 'Eight goals by Christmas and this kid's your new lord and saviour?'

'Samson's very good,' I said, gripping hard on my knife.

'I'm not disagreeing,' Uncle Nick said, gulping from his wine glass. 'He's just got that trace of African in him still, doesn't he?'

I clenched my jaw.

'I'm not sure I know what you mean.'

'Don't be daft, of course you do. Adrian'll tell ye. They all lose focus. Get lazy off the ball. They're all like it. You never want a pair of them in the same side, 'cos that only makes it worse.'

'Hmm,' I sounded out, impaling a Brussels sprout.

I hated myself for not pushing back. I hated myself for letting that idle, cosy bigotry go untested. I hated that Dad laughed along.

'How's the new house then, love?' Aunt Grace asked me.

'Yeah, good thanks.'

'But I hear your mam's doing all your cleaning?'

'Just for now,' Mam said. 'Once he's settled, we'll sort out a maid.'

'I'll never have a maid,' Uncle Nick said, his mouth full, 'Not as long as I live. Not even for free. It makes you go soft, all that posh stuff. Maids and cooks and the like. Bit of house-work keeps you honest.'

'Listen here,' Dad said, pointing his fork, 'My boy's not posh. He's a good, loyal, working-class lad.'

'Aye,' Nick said, as though I weren't there. 'For now he is.'

After dinner, we moved back to the living room. With Jackie upstairs, immersed in his new games, Mam suggested a game of Pictionary, reaching behind the sofa for a conveniently prepared stack of paper and pens.

Beside me, Dad was snugly drunk, his eyelids heavy – a bruised, purple hue.

'What are the teams then, love?' Dad said, unfastening his belt, letting his belly spill over his trousers.

'We'll have me and Grace; Nick and Shelley; and then you two,' she said, pointing to us.

'You can't put us two together,' Dad slurred. 'It wouldn't be a fair contest.'

'Why not?' Shelley asked.

'Because we think the same, him and me,' Dad reiterated, prodding me in the leg, just a little too hard. 'Always have done. Ain't that right, Lolly?'

Mam smiled, but didn't comment.

'Like father, like son,' Dad continued, toasting his glass spitefully towards Nick.

'Dad—'

'We're the same, us two. Two peas in a pod. Cut from the same cloth. Spitting images. Everyone says so. All the lads down the pub.'

'No one cares what your daft mates think, Adrian,' Nick said.

'Ah, don't be so fucking jealous, Nicky.'

'Adrian, stop,' Mam said, clutching at the stack of papers.

'I'm fine, Lolly,' Dad said, 'If I'd had your chances, son, who knows what I could have done.'

Sat there, listening to him, smelling him, a rage smouldered through me. I felt ashamed and angry. Ashamed for Mam, who had to endure this. Ashamed to be compared to a balding, drunken bigot. Angry at the idea that it was this man who represented me, that this man could profit off my hard work, could take undue credit for the sacrifices that I endured.

'Nick'll tell ye,' Dad went on, 'I was the best in all our school. They wanted to offer me trials at Aberdeen, you know? But you had to pay your own train fares in those days and it wasn't an option for us. Not as far as our mam was concerned.'

'Oh yeah,' I announced, scratching casually at my jaw. 'I've been meaning to tell you all – I think I'm probably going to sign with Samson's agent.'

I heard myself make the decision. Sat there, I felt like an actor delivering lines. I'd intended for the words to seem flippant, but they came out tart and pointed.

'He got in touch a while ago,' I continued to a stunned silence. 'We went for dinner and we got on well. His name's Sebastian. He thinks I can go really far.'

'Congratulations, lad,' Uncle Nick said, a cruel smile spread across his lips. 'That'll be your ticket out of here, then. Off to a proper team, no doubt.'

Beside me, Dad had gone pale.

'You didn't tell me this,' he said, his voice suddenly more sober. 'I didn't know you were meeting other agents.'

'I didn't plan to,' I said, still scratching. 'It just happened. I guess it hadn't seemed like an option. Before now, you know? But it feels like the right time. Sebastian says there's always lots of commercial opportunities in the New Year. Lots of money to be made, you know?'

Dad looked different from anything I'd anticipated. He was neither angry nor upset. He appeared broken.

'We can talk about it later,' Mam said, the paper crumpling in her grip, her tone a controlled, placid balm. 'Nothing's been decided yet.'

'Sure,' I said. 'We can talk if you like.'

Just then, Jackie ran into the room.

'Mam, where's the charger?'

I stayed seated as Dad lifted himself off the sofa, and without another word, moved slowly to the door, closing it softly behind him.

Later, once the house had emptied and the dishes were washed, I texted Sebastian, cementing my decision.

There hadn't been any further discussion. Since excusing himself, Dad had locked himself in the bedroom and not re-emerged. Mam explained to Jackie that Uncle Adrian was feeling a little worse for wear, that he wouldn't be coming back down to say goodbye.

'Don't feel bad, son,' Uncle Nick said, hugging me by the door. 'He'll get over it in time. There'll always be a job for him back on the yard.'

Mam persuaded me to stay over, to keep her company. Together, we watched television in a sombre hush.

'I wish you hadn't done that, love,' she said between shows. 'Your dad was really trying, you know. I know it wasn't perfect, but I'd never seen him try so hard.'

'I'm sorry, Mam. If it's about the money, I can still—'

'It'll never be about the money. You know that. But I think you've hurt him. Maybe it's best you give him some space. For a bit at least.'

'If you think that's best.'

48

At 8 a.m., my alarm bullied me out of bed. My childhood bed – somehow, still capable of accommodating the man I'd become.

According to WhatsApp, Sebastian was yet to read my message about representation. I couldn't picture who Sebastian might spend Christmas with – it didn't feel right that he might have a family of his own, that he might have priorities beyond football.

'Dad,' I called, knocking on my parents' bedroom door. 'I'm heading to the ground now. I hope you're feeling all right.'

'Good luck, son,' came back Mam's voice, replying on their collective behalf.

'Maybe see you at the ground, yeah?'

'Maybe, pet,' said my mother. 'We both love you, okay?'

Our Boxing Day fixture was against Watford, meaning that for my first league start of the season, I would be facing down Kyle in the opposition goal. I hadn't exchanged a word with Kyle since his departure. This choice to ghost him wasn't conscious – I simply had other priorities, and evidently so did he.

Owing to a muscular injury to Watford's first-choice keeper back in October, Kyle had cemented a place in their starting line-up. From what I'd gathered, his performances had been deemed competent, if unexceptional. He'd saved a penalty against Norwich but let in six goals against Liverpool.

It was a bright, midwinter morning. Weather my dad would have described as perfect for football. Through our warm-up, the pitch glimmered, manicured and evergreen, dusted by a film of sprinkler dew.

Stepping into the dressing room, I was surprised to see Samson, sat in his bay, dressed in dark jeans and a white shirt.

'Hi,' I said, approaching him, casually reaching into my cubbyhole for a towel.

'Hello,' Samson said, bestowing me a smile.

'I thought you were in Paris?' I said, towelling off my hair and neck.

'I come back,' Samson sighed.

'But, what about your mam?'

'Mama, she has another Christmas today. She visits others in Marseille. She is very loved, you know?'

'But, you wanted to be here? Instead of staying with her?'

'What I want – this does not matter. I need to work, to train.'

'Oh, right.'

'And I am back to support!' he said, standing and nudging me affectionately. 'A big day for you, no? I come here to support my friend.'

Friend, my brain registered. *You're his friend.*

'Here,' Samson said, pulling a compact black box from the pocket of his jeans and handing it to me. 'Merry Christmas.'

Inside the box was a necklace, adorned with a small platinum crucifix – more minimal than his own. Modest, but quite beautiful.

'Samson – thank you. It's great. I didn't—'

'You have given me enough,' Samson anticipated. 'Forgiven me enough. I am pleased you like. I chose this myself.'

He let me hug him, right there in the changing room, in front of everyone. Just for a moment, I could love him without fear.

'I decided that I'm going to sign with Sebastian,' I told him, letting him loose.

'Good,' Samson said, smoothing out his shirt, nodding his head slightly. 'This is a good choice for you. Congratulations.'

'You don't mind?'

'Why do I mind? This does not affect me. The choice is yours.'

'Thanks,' I said, stuffing the towel back into my space, placing my gift gently on top.

'Here, Samson,' Bert said, approaching us, topless, slinging an arm up and around Samson's shoulders, 'All them little kiddywinks at the hospital were asking about you.'

'I am sorry I miss this.'

'Ah, you're grand. We managed, didn't we?' Bert said, motioning to me.

'Yeah – it was good. I mean, good for the kids. It went okay.'

'So Samson,' Bert said, 'How do ye reckon our lad here's going do today?'

'*Magnifique,*' Samson said, bringing his fingers to his lips in a playful chef's kiss.

'Mag-nif-eek,' Bert attempted, punching me in the shoulder. 'You hear that? That's what I'm expecting from you now. Mag-ni-fuckin'-eek.'

After wishing luck to the rest of the squad, Samson

excused himself, heading up to the director's box, where he'd be watching the game alongside the owner.

With five minutes to kick-off, there was a knock on the dressing room door.

'Everyone decent?' Doctor Léonie said, popping her head around the frame.

'Please,' the manager said warmly, gesturing for her to enter the room.

'I'm just here to wish you all luck,' she announced, stepping inside. She was dressed in a dark blazer and pencil skirt, her hair tied back in a neat ponytail.

'Believe in luck, do you, Doc?' Bert quipped, adjusting his shin pad.

'Ah, good point!' Doctor Léonie said, 'Who needs luck when you can have the confidence of Bert Kendall!'

'That's what I'm all about,' Bert said, 'Confidence is king. Come on then boys, let's get out there.'

As the team filed out into the tunnel, Doctor Léonie stepped into my path, pulling me aside.

'So, you are starting.'

'Yup, I guess so.'

'And how do you feel about that?'

'Pretty good. Very good, actually.'

'And have you been visualising? As we discussed?'

'A bit,' I said, rubbing my arm.

'Just a bit?'

'Well,' I said, stupefied by her stare, 'not really, to be honest.'

'Okay – that's fine. Let's try it together now.'

'But,' I blustered, 'I've got to get to the tunnel. Everyone's out there.'

'Don't worry about that,' Doctor Léonie said breezily. 'We will have time.'

'But—'

'Take a seat and close your eyes for me,' she said firmly, guiding me back to my space, then hitching her skirt and squatting down in front of me, placing her hands on my knees.

'Now take a deep breath – in through your nose. And now out through your mouth.'

I closed my eyes and inhaled.

'One more time – in through your nose. And out through your mouth.'

The sensation of being watched was intense. I felt the warmth of her hands. The floral smell of her hair. Compliantly, I breathed.

'Good. Now: I want you to picture yourself in front of the goal. I want you to pay attention to the goalkeeper. Which way is he leaning?'

I hesitated, unsure of whether or not I was supposed to reply.

'Um, I'm not sure.'

'Look closer,' Doctor Léonie said.

I scrunched my eyes in mock focus. In my head, a dozen images flashed by like a flick book. I saw the children from the cancer ward, their yellow skin and sunken eyes. I saw Dad's face, contorted and red and crying. I saw Samson, kneeling and praying by his bed. I saw Samson, his necklace bouncing off his chest, in time with his thrusts. I saw Samson, bearing down on the goal, cutting inside, chipping the ball with effortless grace. I saw Samson, Samson, Samson.

'Focus. Breathe and focus.'

Somehow, through the haze and distortion, came a blurred picture of Kyle – his stance low, legs wide, arms splayed like Gormley's *Angel*.

'Left,' I told her, 'He's leaning left.'

'So what way will you shoot?' came Doctor Léonie's voice, her tone certain, expectant.

'Right,' I said.

'So shoot for me,' she said, squeezing gently on my right knee.

The image of Kyle had crystalised. As I pictured myself striking the ball, I felt the muscles in my leg tense up under Doctor Léonie's hand.

'Keep your eyes closed,' she commanded. 'Now watch the ball – see how the net bulges? See how the keeper reaches and fails? See yourself running off, running to celebrate? Tell me you see this.'

'I can see it,' I said, my heart pounding.

'You will make this possible,' Doctor Léonie said. 'Repeat for me.'

'I will make this possible.'

'I will score today.'

'*I will score today*,' I parroted, adopting her tone.

'Good,' she said, releasing my knees, then tapping on my thighs, as though to set me free. 'Go on then, it's time to get out there.'

Opening my eyes, the dressing room seemed luminescent, filled with a numinous, ethereal glow. I felt a little dizzy, as though my head were being gripped and twisted by a ghostly hand.

Doctor Léonie was stood by the door, straightening out her dress.

'Come on!' she said, her voice loaded with sudden urgency.

In the tunnel, I joined the back of the line, taking the hand of my mascot – a little blonde girl, who didn't seem to recognise me.

'This is my Christmas present,' the girl announced.

'Oh, cool.'

'But I wanted a dog. We were supposed to get a dog.'

Seconds later, with a single shout of '*LET'S GO BOYS*', Bert was leading us out of the tunnel, climbing the steps, onto the pitch. Above and beside me, fans threw out their arms from the stands, clawing at the air, calling our names, begging for our attention. An ersatz version of 'Right Here, Right Now' played through the speakers above us.

My heart had returned to its regular rhythm, but I could feel from the mascot's slipping grip that my palms were sweating. The girl had clearly been prepared for what to expect, and almost led me through the procedure, filing down the line, clapping hands with the referee, linesmen and each Watford player.

Meeting Kyle's gloved hand, I offered an amicable smile, but in return, he stared blankly ahead, professional, unmoved.

Our general plan for the match was to press with a high line. *L'oracolo* had identified that the majority of Watford's mistakes came from their indecisiveness – their players didn't trust each other, retaining the ball for far too long. By putting them under pressure, we could make interceptions and play on the front foot.

The referee blew his whistle and I kicked us off.

49

Football has always been a sanctuary for me. While I'm on the pitch, nothing matters but the game. I can zone out the crowd, the chants, the entire world. For ninety sacred minutes, I am reduced to a body – to the crude, physical contest of skill and strength.

Five minutes into the match, we won a corner. As we hoarded their box, Kyle bellowed instructions at his defenders, dictating their positions in the wall and on the line. He seemed louder than I remembered him, physically larger and more imposing. Clustered at the six-yard line, I found myself next to him.

'Fucking useless, you are,' Kyle hissed, shoving me, his gloved hands bunched into fists. 'You snidey little faggot. You've always been useless, you know that?'

Baba's corner swung wide, over our heads, out to the edge of the box. I stepped away from Kyle, back into space, but he kept my eye, a vicious smirk on his lips.

Throughout the half, Kyle attempted to draw my attention. Each time we were in proximity, he yelled at me.

'Fucking embarrassing,' he hollered as I pulled a shot wide. 'Where's that Samson when you need him?'

His tone had a desperate, jejune quality. These were the

insults of someone who had been humbled – who carried a burden of insecurity. I would not react to his words.

The game was playing out as *L'oracolo* predicted. Watford lingered on the ball, drifting out of position, leaving open space for us to exploit. As half-time approached, I spotted their number seven hesitating on a pass. I ran in from a tangent, throwing my shoulder into his side. He tripped forward, shifting his weight to shield the ball.

By instinct, I flicked out a foot, but caught the player high and late. I watched as he fell dramatically, his face drawn into a cartoonish, anguished gasp – pain that could never be commensurate with my challenge.

The referee blew his whistle – harsh and sharp, cutting through the roar of the crowd.

'You all right?' I said, bending over the number seven, offering him my hand.

The player disregarded me, choosing to continue his writhing and whimpering.

Our home fans screamed from the stands:

GET UP, YE FOOKIN' NANCY.
IT'S A MAN'S GAME, SON.
DIRTY DIVING BASTARD.

Turning, I saw that Kyle had rushed from his goal to join a pack of players surrounding the referee, both sides hounding him, lobbying for a favourable decision.

Off, off, off, chanted the away fans.

I stood with my hands on my hips, breathing heavily, fearing the worst. Nose to mouth, nose to mouth.

'Proper nasty one, ref,' Kyle squealed. 'That's an ankle-breaker, that is.'

Time felt swollen.

The air in my lungs was cloyed and thick.

I spat on the floor.

Nose to mouth, nose to mouth.

Somewhere above me, Samson would be watching. Judging. Knowing what he'd have done differently.

Nose to mouth, nose to mouth.

Eventually, the referee drew out a yellow card, brandishing it in my direction. Behind me, our fans jeered.

The Watford number seven rose to his feet, wincing through a hobble, before breaking into a light jog. As the gaggle of players dispersed, Kyle lingered, squaring up to me.

'Nowhere left to hide, mate,' he growled. 'I know what you are.'

At half-time, the score remained nil–nil. The manager said broad, reassuring things about how we were well on top, how we needed to be patient, to attack at the right times, to wear them down.

With the team listening in, *L'oracolo* honed in on me, warning me to be careful, to avoid any more silly tackles, to keep up the good movement, the smart runs. He spoke to me like a man – the equal of every other player. But between his words, I heard his true meaning: *don't make any more stupid decisions; don't make the staff regret playing you; don't let the world accuse us of relying solely on Samson.*

Don't let us down.

Finishing his team talk, the manager crouched in front of me, lowering his voice.

'Léo, she talks with you, yes? The doctor, she knows how to think – how you must use this brain.'

With a congenial smile, he rapped gently on my head with his knuckles, as though knocking for luck.

'It is a good head, no? You must use it for me.'

We started the second half more fluidly. Watford began resorting to scrappy, messy challenges. It was evident that they would be satisfied with a point away from home.

Kyle started to waste time, spending twenty, sometimes thirty seconds on each goal kick, launching the ball in long, hopeful arcs.

TRAITOR CUNT, yelled our fans. *FUCKING TRAITOR SCUM.*

Kyle responded by goading them, cupping a gloved hand to his ear. Eventually, the referee was pressured into showing him a yellow card for time wasting.

With less than ten minutes of ordinary time remaining, Dami picked the ball out of the air, controlling on the half volley and releasing me through the middle. Taking the pass in my stride, I ran with the ball, lifting my head, looking up at the keeper's position. I saw panic in Kyle's eyes.

Shifting the ball with my left foot, I lashed hard with my right, twisting through the shot, throwing my entire body off balance. As the ball crossed the line, beyond the reach of the diving Kyle, I stumbled forward heavily, just about maintaining my footing.

There were no thoughts in that moment. Only feeling: a raw adrenal rush. I opened my mouth and ran to the stands, bawling a guttural sound, lost to the din of the fans, bouncing off a wall of jubilant, virile noise.

With my throat burning and my body surrounded, grasped from all angles by the hands of my teammates, I recalled Doctor Léonie's advice – I tried to engage with my emotions, to anchor that feeling. This was why I played. This was why it mattered. This was what I desired.

Eventually, they released me. Running back to the centre circle, by instinct, I looked up to my father's usual spot. The seat was empty.

At the full-time whistle, the manager walked onto the field, beelining to me, drawing me into his arms for a zealous hug.

'Excellent,' he said, thumping my back. 'I am very proud.'

My goal had lifted us five points clear of the drop.

Kyle approached, offering out his glove. 'Nothing personal, yeah?' he said, winking.

'Nah, you're all right,' I said, ignoring his hand.

Kyle's mouth twitched. 'Good luck to you, mate. Love to your old man, yeah?'

Samson had made his way down from the director's box, stood at the top of the tunnel. As I moved to pass him, he stepped into my path, swinging an arm around my shoulders.

'What are you doing?' I asked, as he led me back onto the pitch, back towards our lingering, victorious fans.

'So defensive! A great performance deserves praise, no?'

I moved willingly, but Samson's arm remained, leading me in-step back onto the pitch, into the noise. With a slight tug on my shoulder, Samson inclined his head towards my ear, beckoning me with his mouth. The hairs on my neck bristled.

'You must enjoy this,' he said. 'You deserve it all.'

Releasing me with a little shove, I pulled away from him, feeling the electric trace of his touch fade from my shoulder. Stepping forward a reasonable distance, I raised my hands above my head and clapped to the crowd. They chanted my name.

SECOND HALF

50

I signed with Sebastian's agency in the New Year, meeting a woman called Claudia in one of the club's corporate lounges. She introduced herself as Sebastian's senior executive assistant. Claudia was tanned and conventionally attractive, but her business suit looked boxy, as though it might have been inherited.

'You are the first English,' Claudia told me, sliding over yet another page to sign. 'You know this? A big, big honour.'

'An honour for you?'

'No!' Claudia laughed, 'An honour for you! To sign with Mr Astor. He is very – how you say? – very particular about his players.'

'Oh, right.'

'Mr Astor, he prefers to do this himself. Everything himself, if he can. But he is so busy today! So much transfer business in January, you know?'

'Yeah, of course.'

'And your friend – this Samson – every day, the calls about Samson. Samson, Samson, Samson. It is all we hear for weeks.'

'What calls? Calls from who?'

'Oh, you know,' Claudia said, brushing a hair from her lips. 'Managers, owners, they are all asking to sign Samson – asking how long they must wait.'

'But he's here. He's with us.'

'For now, yes!' Claudia said, 'But every contract is just paper!'

She fluttered one of the freshly signed sheets from my contract, miming a rip down the centre, smiling jovially.

It struck me then – the inevitability of Samson's eventual departure. He would be removed from my life as swiftly as he had been gifted to me.

Since our Boxing Day win against Watford, we'd played another three games, drawing one and losing two. A general weariness was beginning set in. Not quite apathy, but a deep-set physical fatigue. Jean-Claude's remedy for this collective lethargy was to permit the squad to determine our own gym routines for the week – to exert some rare autonomy over our own bodies; to take heed from our muscle and marrow and work at a pace that felt germane.

Returning from the meeting, I walked back across the car park to the training complex. I passed Theo, unlocking his car.

'Hey, how was the gym session?'

'Yeah, mate. Decent one. I put on some absolute old school bangers. Chemical Brothers, Fatboy Slim, Basement Jaxx. The lads were loving it.'

'Nice,' I said, hesitant to mention Samson immediately. 'You the last out?'

'Nah, couple of stragglers,' Theo said, slinging his bag into the car boot. 'Milo's doing his hair. I think Bert's in a session with the shrink. And Samson's still in the gym, going at it.'

'Still? Weren't we supposed to finish at two?'

'Yeah. Crazy endurance, that boy. Works like a slave. Must be genetic.'

'Come on, mate,' I protested, 'Don't say things like that.'

'*Oooh*,' Theo said, fluttering his fingers camply. 'Okay, Mister Politically Correct.'

I moved to step past him, 'I've got to go grab my stuff and catch up with Samson quickly.'

'Woah, woah,' Theo said, his huge palms spread out, calming me like a bucking horse. 'Do you know something I don't?'

'It's nothing.'

'In a big rush for nothing, aren't you?'

'Look,' I said, dropping to a whisper. 'I think there's a chance Samson might leave. This transfer window.'

Theo's expression changed – shifting into a minor dread.

'And you're going to convince him to stay, yeah?'

'I dunno,' I said. 'I just – I've got to say something.'

'Too right you do,' Theo concurred, slamming his boot closed. 'I can't afford to get relegated. Not at this point in my career. No offence to you or nothing, but we're fucked without that boy. Like proper, proper fucked. Go see where his head's at. Say whatever you need to.'

'Right.'

'And make sure to mention that tidy little piece he's banging – that Holly bird, from off the telly.'

'Yeah, okay.'

'You wouldn't wanna let one like that go in a hurry, right?'

51

As Theo had said, Samson was still in the gym, pedalling unsupervised on an exercise bike. His face was drawn in a grimace that seemed to suggest tenacity, but might have been cramp.

'Found you,' I said.

'I do not hide,' Samson said, slowing his legs and sitting upright, arms crossed over his chest. 'You have now signed?'

'Yeah, all sorted.'

He took a long swig from his bottle, glugging the water around his mouth – his cheeks blown out, as though he was preparing to spit it over me.

'And how does this feel?' he said, swallowing.

'It feels good, I think. The woman, Claudia, she was nice.'

'*Clau-di-a*,' Samson posed, stretching out her name, seemingly trying to picture her.

'She's Sebastian's *executive assistant* or something.'

'I do not think I know this one.'

'Well, she definitely knows you. She mentioned that she's been handling a load of calls about you.'

Samson smirked, sipped again from his bottle, and recommenced cycling. 'January,' he said. 'This is normal, no?'

'Are you going to leave?' I asked, more panic in my voice than I'd hoped for.

'Who says I will leave?'

'No one. I mean, Claudia mentioned the calls. She implied there was a chance you could leave this window.'

'This is football,' Samson said, casually stretching out his neck, pedalling faster. 'There is always this chance. Remember what they always tell us, these old men: *your career is short, enjoy it while it lasts.*'

'Yeah, but you wouldn't actually do that to us. You wouldn't abandon us.'

I said it as a statement.

'For now I play here,' Samson said, now stood on the pedals, shoulders down, his bum elevated into the air, almost presenting.

'But it's your choice, right? Ultimately you get to decide. Staying with us – it's up to you.'

'*Oui.*'

I stood there dumbly. It felt as though I should have prepared something more. I should have been able to instantly present him a list of reasons for why he should stay, inserting myself somewhere towards the bottom, so as to remain modest.

'Well, for what it's worth, I want you to stay. I would miss you.' Looking over my shoulder, I surveyed the room, confirming we were alone. 'I'd miss us.'

Samson stared forwards, his legs pumping ferociously, as if he were trying to escape, to cycle away from my words. It was an unsustainable pace. His arse now swaying, Samson began intermittently releasing frustrated little grunts, breathing hard through his parted lips. If I could hold my nerve and remain steadfast on that spot, I knew that I could outlast his exertion.

I was close enough to feel the heat emanating from him. The familiar smell of his sweat; his slick, glistening skin. I felt my cock twitch.

With one final, mighty roar, Samson slumped forwards over his handlebars, grabbing for his gym towel and draping it over his head. Breathing in gasps, he rubbed down his neck and shoulders with dramatic vigour.

'You should want me to leave,' Samson said, emerging from his shroud, his eyes narrowed and severe, sweat beading down the bridge of his nose. 'This should be your mindset. Where is the man who once confronted me? That boy who treasured his *ten*. The precious position you fought for. Where is this fight today? Why must all these hopes depend on me? All this pressure, always for Samson. Where is your role in this?'

'We both know that I could never replace you. I can't *do* what you do. I can never be you.'

Samson exhaled, wiping the sweat from his hands.

'Then be yourself, eh?'

Whipping the towel back over his handlebars, Samson set about retightening the straps on his feet.

'I like yourself,' he said, tugging at a strap, speaking to the floor. 'I like—'

Shaking his head, as though to purge the thought, he sat up and faced me.

'Later, I will call Sebastian. I will let him know my preference.'

With that, he pressed down on one pedal.

'Please, go now. I must ride.'

I don't know how long he remained there after I left. Only Samson determined the kind of punishment his body deserved.

52

In the weeks since Christmas, I had been spending my Wednesdays alone. A whole day and night to fill.

Eating breakfast, I watched the latest transfer speculation on Sky Sports. Old white men in suits and ties, pointing to a ticker total, tracking upwards with unseemly numbers as deals were confirmed for seemingly everyone other than us. The presenters celebrated each transfer like personal triumphs, willing the tracker to rise higher and higher, to a daunting red line that indicated the previous season's spending record.

Earlier in the week, word had filtered through to the media that Samson was almost certain to remain with us for the rest of the season. Supposedly, Barcelona had already reached a provisional agreement with Monaco to sign Samson, with the understanding that the Spanish giants would need to wait until the summer to formally secure his services.

L'oracolo's only official comment on the matter was that Samson was enjoying his football and that he was prepared to fight for our survival.

Aside from some potential departures, we were unlikely to be involved in any business. The sale of the club seemed no closer than it had been back in August, and the owner was holding firm to his promise that there'd be no transfer budget made available prior to the club's sale being confirmed.

Mam called me just before ten. She had been checking in more frequently.

'Are you enjoying your day off?' she asked.

'I guess,' I said, pressing the phone to my ear with my shoulder, spooning up the last of my oatmeal. 'It's really odd. Without Dad, you know? I never know what I'm supposed to do with myself.'

'Just rest,' she said, her voice a balm, like permission. 'You've earned a good rest.'

'Yeah, but I can't be doing with just dossing about all day.'

'Well, have you thought about your summer yet? You could start planning for that. Is there anywhere you'd want to go for your holidays?'

'What, on my own?'

'That's up to you, pet,' Mam said. 'I'm sure your friends are off somewhere. Maybe you could join them?'

'There was some talk of a stag in Vegas for Milo, but nothing concrete yet.'

'Well, if not, I'll come with you somewhere!'

'You're all right, Mam,' I huffed, tugging a wilted leaf off my spider plant. 'Not sure how much Dad'd be liking that anyway.'

'You don't need to be concerned with him. He's a proud and silly man, but this drama between the two of you doesn't need to have me dragged into it. I won't be made to take sides in this.'

'I miss him, Mam,' I said.

'I know, love. He's still not ready just yet. Be patient with him. Remember what it was like when Grandad died? Your da must have been at the pub every night for a month, but eventually, he came round. Life goes on.'

'Is he drinking that much?'

'I didn't say if he was. And even if he did, that'd be his choice. You get to make your choices, and he gets to make his. Now listen, if you're really sick and tired of being inside, get out of the house for a bit while the sun's out.'

'Thanks, Mam, speak to you later.'

Before I dropped Dad as my agent, I'd never thought about money as a meaningful aspect to our relationship. At nineteen, the gulf of wealth between us was already so large that we had bypassed any potential awkwardness. I could comprehend that earning double, maybe triple Dad's income might have been emasculating for him. But five, ten, twenty times more? It was a comic book inequality – a disparity that he seemed to derive pride from. The money was a definitive, numerical measure of my success – something he could brag to his friends about.

The only time I really felt rich was stepping into my spare room. The notion that I could afford entire, unused rooms in my house felt like an absurd extravagance.

Growing up, we didn't have an inch to spare, let alone a whole room. All our expenses were measured in meals. A full tank of petrol cost us a week and a half of food. A new pair of football boots was around the same.

'I wish you didn't keep growing so bloody quickly,' Dad once told me, inspecting my shoes like there might be some way to extend them.

On Saturday afternoons, I used to accompany Dad to a pub around a quarter of a mile from the stadium, nursing a small lemonade for the duration of the match. On still summer days, we could reliably hear the roar of a goal a few seconds before it became manifest on the television broadcast.

From my mother, I learned to cherish the things I owned. I cleaned my boots with the reverence and affection that one might treat a piece of jewellery. I kicked at footballs until they were grey and flayed, suited only to be a dog's chew thing.

Over the school holidays, I spent all my time in the park, lingering by the football pitch until a game would form. I'd play with anyone who'd take me. Before too long, everyone at the park knew what I could do with a ball, and the balance of teams was calibrated around me.

Most years, our big summer trip would be a week in Scarborough or on the Isle of Wight. Some years, Aunt Grace would join us, making it known that the trip was her *little treat to us*.

Sometimes, Dad and I would escape my aunt's company to comb the beach for shells, building sandcastles and fishing in rock pools for tiny crabs, swishing through the water with a miniature net.

Come September, I'd have spent the entire summer outside. Returning to school, I lied to my classmates, boasting of the fashionable destinations I'd travelled to, presenting my tanned arms as though they were all the evidence I required.

Switching off the television, I opened my laptop and loaded an incognito tab. Through these long, lonely weekdays, porn had become an increasingly frequent means of distraction.

Somehow, the algorithm retained my preferences. I never paid for anything, never set up an account, relying solely on the seemingly infinite bank of young, beautiful boys from across the world who uploaded their pleasures every single day. I tended for videos reminiscent of my first encounter with Samson: solo, amateur footage of men masturbating. I sought out videos where I could see their faces – the glorious, almost painted contortions of their pleasure, their tongues wagging, stomachs clenching. I favoured vocal men – performers who embraced the exhibition, who thrust into their hands, rather than letting their forearms do all the work.

Switching from tab to tab, I searched for the perfect moment to finish to – slowing my stoke, restraining myself, alternating between an endless supply of bold, free men who refused to hide, who invited the world to watch. I wanted to match their pace. I wanted to share in their joy.

Moments after I came, my sense was restored. I purged my laptop of all evidence, deleting my history and clearing my cache.

Thoughts of my father crept back in.

I felt alone.

For my jogs, I tracked a five-mile route that lapped around, then through the fields where I used to play. It was still deep winter, and the turf was frozen over. With each step, the earth jarred back up through my legs, as though it had a point to prove, reminding me of the debt I owed to this ground.

My eyes streamed with the wind and cold. I ran in a tracksuit, with my hood up, suitably inconspicuous, my own incognito mode. There were no other runners in sight. The world was at work, hidden indoors, refreshing their phones – watching as the transfer ticker tracked ever upwards. My only company in the fields were a few dogs and their owners. The dogs bounded joyfully around the space, sniffing and digging for buried treasures – abandoned barbecues and lager cans from every summer since the dawn of time.

53

For our home game against Arsenal, Samson had flown his mother over to watch us play. Emmanuella would sit with Sebastian in the director's box, alongside the owner. Before the match, Samson escorted his mother into our home dressing room. She was dressed in an outfit tailored for a warmer climate. A white pantsuit with sharp black lapels and open-toe sandals, her hair in chunky braids, arranged in a high twisted bun that added a few inches to her diminutive stature.

Bert made a thoughtful fuss, complimenting Emmanuella's style, while the manager embraced her.

'Your Samson, he's a good boy, yes?' the manager said. 'Good values. Stays out of trouble.'

Samson stood there meekly, hands behind his back, head bowed, his mouth a thin, wrinkled stitch.

'He goes far, this one. You keep him on the ground for me, okay?'

Samson applied no special emphasis on my introduction. I shook hands with Emmanuella, smiling genially. I wondered what, if anything, she'd been told about me. I wondered what other sides of Samson his mother knew, sides of him that I would never see. I wondered whether through my intimate knowledge of his body, I might claim to know him more completely than her.

As we fed out into the tunnel, Sebastian pulled me aside.

'Why so serious, my friend?'

'It's nothing, don't worry. Just focused.'

'But I have news for you.'

'What news?' I said, my chest seizing.

'You start the next game,' Sebastian said, beaming, slapping my back. 'Against United.'

'What? Really?'

'Have I lied to you before? *L'oracolo* and I, we speak this morning about your chances, your work rate. He agrees that this is your time. You start alongside Samson. We will see how you combine.'

'Oh, great. Amazing! Thank you.'

'Tell no one though, okay? Keep this secret for now. After the game, I will come and find you. We speak more, my friend. Many things are planned. Many big things are on their way for you.'

With his mother watching on, Samson played with an unrelenting intensity. Each movement and action laden with purpose and pluck. He kept shape with the team, tracking back as required, even clearing a ball off the line from an Arsenal corner to prevent a certain goal.

He's here because of me, I told myself. *He's stayed for me.*

We were one–nil down with twenty minutes remaining. Picking up the ball just in front of our back line, Samson set off on a slaloming run, cutting inside and out at tapering tangents, veering forwards to the right flank. Finding himself surrounded by the Arsenal midfield, Samson spotted a stretch of vacant grass ahead of him: he kicked the ball long, as though passing to a future version of himself, then dipped his head and chased down the distance, arms pumping, setting his marker one metre, two metres behind.

Approaching the penalty area at pace, Samson shaped his body to shoot with his left, dummied back onto his right, leaving the Arsenal keeper toppling backwards. He stepped inside the area and casually flicked the ball into an open net.

Over the following weeks and months, that goal was replayed a million times. Though we went on to lose the match two–one, the game was destined to be remembered only for Samson's individual brilliance. It was the type of goal that invited comparisons between Samson and the greatest of all time.

'We can be positive, boys,' the manager said, addressing us after the match. 'For many, many reasons – this is one of our best games all season. Believe me, you must not dwell on this. On Monday, we will watch back together, and you will realise how close we were.'

With that goal, Samson had reached double digits in the league. He was the top-scoring player in the division outside of the big six clubs, and the first player from our club for twenty-nine years to find the net ten times before February.

Emerging from the shower, Samson left in a hurry to join his mother.

I lingered alone in the players' foyer for twenty minutes, waiting to meet with Sebastian, only to receive an apologetic text, explaining that he needed to accompany Samson and his mother to dinner, promising to call later that evening. If not, then potentially on Sunday.

Okay, I replied.

54

As the end of the transfer window approached, we were the only team in the league to have made no acquisitions. Despite Samson's individual heroics, it had been a fallow Christmas-period, and we'd slipped to eighteenth in the table. In the gym, the atmosphere was despondent.

'I told you,' Dami said, his voice jolting as he jogged on a treadmill. 'There was no chance. Swear down, that owner's a tight, stupid prick. He doesn't give a shit about us.'

'Two strikers,' Mario said, swishing a hand between me and Samson, 'A team with two strikers – two *kids* as our forwards. In the Premier League? The richest league in the world? You've never heard such stupidness.'

'It will be a miracle,' Dami said, 'if we stay up. A fucking miracle.'

'When we stay up,' Bert corrected, sitting up from the bench press. 'When we stay up, it'll be a miracle.'

In the papers, Samson had been pictured with Holly again. She'd forgiven him, apparently, though the article didn't specify what she'd forgiven him for. An 'exclusive' source claimed that Holly was a major factor in keeping Samson at our club through the window. They named prices for Samson ranging from a fifty to a hundred-million pounds, setting numbers on his head as though he were a bounty, coveted by all.

That afternoon, I was scheduled for another session with Doctor Léonie. Leaving the gym, I headed straight to her office, still in my shorts, warm and sticky with effort.

'Did Maud have a good Christmas?' I asked, taking a seat, motioning to her computer screen.

Doctor Léonie looked at me with a curious expression.

'Yes,' she said, removing her glasses. 'Yes – Christmas and her birthday are very close.'

'Two, right?'

'Yes,' she said, almost suspicious. 'She is two.'

The doctor paused, shuffled some papers unproductively.

'You are very sensitive to family, aren't you?'

'Maybe,' I said, 'Isn't that your job? To figure out my head?'

'Again, I remind you: I am not a psychiatrist. I am a sports psychologist. But I am sympathetic to the pressures that affect us beyond the game. Money, families, sex.'

She let the word hang there for a moment.

'We are complex creatures. What is true today may not be true tomorrow. A problem yesterday is forgotten today.'

Doctor Léonie spoke at a volume that invited me to lean in, as though we were speaking of the intimate – of dangerous, volatile things.

'If you wish,' she said, 'we can speak about your family. I understand that you have recently changed your representation.'

'Ah,' I said, sitting back again. 'They tell you everything, don't they?'

'Was this a secret?'

'I mean, no – but it's not like I'm out there bragging about it.'

'Is it something to brag about?'

'I know what you're doing,' I said, rolling back my shoulders. 'I can see where this is leading.'

Without comment, Doctor Léonie picked up a pitcher, poured two glasses of water and slid one across the table to me.

'Wouldn't it be better to speak about how pissed off everyone out there is? How hopeless it seems at the moment? How that cheap bastard is trying to sentence us to relegation?'

With the water in front of me, I found myself immediately thirsty. It felt like a trick – a power play. Indirectly, this was her way of communicating that I would need to speak first.

'Fine' I said, capitulating. 'He was my agent. My dad was my agent and now he's not. He's not even speaking to me.'

Doctor Léonie made no comment, sipping at her water as if the taste were worth savouring.

'And I haven't really tried to speak to him, but why should I? Why is it my responsibility to be sorry? I'm just trying to look after my own best interests. He thinks he knows best, but he doesn't really. He's never been part of this world. He doesn't know football. He's only ever seen one club. And he's only ever seen the good bits. He's completely blinded by his loyalty. And it's not like he knows business either. It would be different if he knew how to negotiate or something. If he had connections. But he doesn't! He doesn't know *anything*. He wouldn't know where to start with looking at contracts and image rights and all that stuff. And he kept telling people that we're the same. Me and him. That we're the same person. Like he wants to be me so badly. He thinks he can just say it and it becomes true. But there's no way he could understand. How could he understand all the sacrifices? He doesn't know what it means to say no to anything. He's got no idea. He doesn't know what it's like to work this hard every day. Every. Fucking. Day.'

Refilling my glass, I drank in one long, panting, messy slurp. When I eventually looked up, Doctor Léonie was holding a pen, straight and stiff, as though she were measuring perspective.

'Your new agent,' she said, flat and neutral. 'His background is football?'

'Yeah,' I said, sniffing. 'I mean, he knows football. He knows loads of people across the league, across Europe. He's really well connected.'

'And he played himself?'

'Oh – I don't think so. I'm not sure.'

'You hadn't heard of him as a player?'

'Um, no.'

'So his background may not be in football?'

'Does that matter?'

'You say it matters about your father.'

'That's different though.'

She nodded. Clicked her pen, punctuating the point.

'And how is your mother?' Doctor Léonie said, her eyes flashing to the computer screen.

'Mam's fine, yeah. She doesn't really get involved with football stuff.'

'But she is involved with your life?'

'Yeah.'

'And your life is football.'

'Yeah . . . '

With that, Doctor Léonie set down the pen.

'I admire the decisions you have made,' she said, in the tone of a conclusion. 'It is very brave to know what it right for you. To have identified what you want: what is best for your own happiness. Your own future.'

'Thanks,' I said, now holding the arms of the chair.

'Family is very important. Here, at the club, we are one type of family. But we are not a replacement. We cannot compete. Nothing can compete with blood.'

'But it will get better, right? Dad will get over it. He'll move on.'

Doctor Léonie smiled – a mother's smile – benevolent, but tinged with worry.

'I'm not sure,' she said. 'Perhaps we should address your previous concern. This imminent relegation. This is what you believe? That you are so doomed? Or this is the collective sentiment?'

'I think that—' I paused, unsure of what I'd say next. 'I think that we win together and we lose together, so it's the collective belief that matters most. Even if I think I'm good enough, everyone else has to believe in me. They need to trust me, to pass to me. The manager just needs to trust me enough to put me on the pitch.'

'In order for them to trust you, you must believe in yourself. Do you trust yourself?' Doctor Léonie asked.

'I do.'

'Do you believe in yourself?'

'I do.'

'They can rely on you?'

'They can rely on me.'

'You trust yourself. So, say this again.'

'I trust myself.'

55

It felt good to be starting games. Following a strong performance against Manchester United, I'd kept my spot alongside Samson. Perhaps in part due to Sebastian's interventions, but equally thanks to my own efforts. With nothing better to do, I had been staying for longer at the training ground, even visiting on days off. I felt strong – I could see and sense my muscles responding, developing, believing. Hours in the pool, on the squat rack, the bench press, they were manifest in my limbs, labour carried forwards in the flesh.

On the field, I had been playing effectively, linking well with Samson, scoring and making goals. Though we were still hovering around the foot of the table, we'd lifted ourselves out of the relegation zone. We were losing by tight margins, sometimes salvaging a draw. It was the start of February, and we had finally developed into the thing the manager valued most: we'd become a team who were hard to beat.

'The boys,' *L'oracolo* told the media, 'they make my job easy. All I ask is that they work hard, yes? That they listen and use their heads. It is a smart group here. Some very, very smart boys. They understand things very well, very quickly. Now, they must believe.'

The win against Burnley was hailed as our finest, most accomplished performance of the season. Samson scored first. From a free kick at the edge of the box, he struck the ball along the grass, hard and true, a textbook daisy-cutter, rifling under the thicket of leaping legs, straight into the bottom corner.

My own effort came ten minutes later. As Baba's cross flew in, time seemed to lag and the light flared – the optics of the stadium seemed to shift. Pushing off from the ground, I saw everything around me in a panoramic sweep: the ball's path like a dotted line on a plotted trajectory, destined for my head, my leap, my goal.

It was our first three-points since the Watford game. After that win, the owner felt empowered to speak out, arguing that our reasonable form was a vindication of his transfer embargo – as it turned out, the squad had been adequate already. Any additional signings might have potentially disturbed that latent harmony. Who knows how different things might have been?

Fans saw through his nonsense. Overnight, the protests returned. Banners were stitched. Signs were painted. More effigies were burned.

'Never mind all that,' Jean-Claude demanded, wafting away the figurative smoke, tooting his whistle, calling upon us to focus, to train.

I wondered whether Dad might get involved in the protests, whether I'd spot him among the crowds on television, steaming drunk and furious. Relegated back to being an ordinary fan, how might he make his feelings known? I couldn't quite picture Dad being destructive, but I could easily imagine him condoning violence, even enabling it. I could picture Dad stealing bricks from Uncle Nick's construction yard, ferrying them to the stadium in his hatchback, handing them out to the more thuggish protestors, the ones who were ready and willing to inflict damage on the thing they loved most.

I felt my father's absence like a cramp: a tender space in the pit of me. I'd made a conscious decision to follow Mam's advice. To be patient. To give Dad the space and time he needed to accept my decision. Before any progress could be made, Dad would need to accept that our relationship had been permanently altered.

On the night before our away game against Aston Villa, I sat on the edge of my hotel bed while Samson spoke over the phone to his mother. His voice was full of a warm, tittering affection. I could tell he was teasing her. It was tone that never carried over to his English – this easy, playful exuberance.

Later, after the video games, Samson prayed by his bed, fingering his crucifix.

When he stood, I cleared my throat, calling his attention.

'My dad's still not speaking with me,' I told him. 'Since I signed with Sebastian. I think he's really angry.'

'So what?' Samson said, softly enough to offset the cruelty of his indifference.

'So, what do you think? How can I fix it?'

'For this, I am not the person to ask. I have no father on this earth. Just one Father in heaven.'

Samson turned his eyes upwards, pressed his crucifix to his lips.

'My mama is all I need. She is smart. She is strong. And she knows who to trust. She learned this, you know? She has survived so much. You do not survive this much without knowing who to trust. She survives the camp, the journey to France. She comes to Paris, makes a home, secures a good job. All around her: racism, bullshit, very bad men. Everywhere you turn in this world, terrible men. Racist men. I have no father because my mama is very selective.'

'Right,' I said, wary of pressing further, of questioning the precarity of his logic.

'So if my mama trusts Sebastian, I trust Sebastian. And so should you.'

He turned away then, moving with a skip and a whistle to the bathroom, signalling the start of our ritual. I heard the toilet seat raised heavy-handedly, clinking violently against the porcelain.

'Your papa,' Samson called over the thunderous flow of his piss, 'he has raised a good man. That is all that matters.'

'Thanks,' I said redundantly, clicking off the light and removing my underwear, rolling onto my front.

56

My mother had begun spending more time at my house. She found wholesome excuses to visit, calling ahead to warn that she'd be popping over with some casserole. Dropping by to check whether the plant had been watered. She claimed that the light in my home was better for reading, that the reception was crisper on the radio. She suggested new possibilities for future projects – a conservatory, a water feature in place of the shed.

I didn't mind my mother's company, but I couldn't bear the implications. My mother, who venerated her own home, suddenly forced out by the stagnant, sulking, drunken presence of my unemployed father.

One afternoon, I returned from training to find Mam sat with Aunt Grace in my kitchen.

'I hope you don't mind love,' Mam said, taking my boot bag straight from my hand. 'Gracie's just here for a coffee and a natter. Better than paying those extortionate prices for a tea in town.'

'Yeah, no bother. Hi, Aunt Grace.'

'Hasn't your mam done a lovely job with the house?' Aunt Grace opined, drawing her arm across the room in the manner of an estate agent.

'Yeah, it's really nice.'

'You crack on with what you need to do, pet. I'll get your boots cleaned and we'll be out of your hair in ten minutes. Half an hour maximum, I promise. I've left you a nice chicken salad in the fridge for dinner.'

'Oh, great.'

'Won't you say thank you to your mam?' Aunt Grace prompted.

'Yeah, thanks, Mam.'

'Gracie's got to be off to church in a bit anyway,' Mam said.

'Church on a Tuesday?'

'I'll be going to confession,' Aunt Grace said.

'Oh, right' I said, opening the fridge to inspect the salad. 'I didn't know that happened on Tuesdays.'

Both women laughed. The syncopated laugh of sisters.

'Bless you,' Mam said, suddenly pious.

'Confession is one of the seven holy sacraments,' Aunt Grace said, using her most formal tone. 'None of them are tied to a specific day, love. They're all there as and when you need them most.'

'Oh. Okay.'

'As Catholics, we can be absolved of all our sins at any time, so long as we are truly contrite and pay penance.'

'Does it work?'

Aunt Grace guffawed. 'God always works.'

'So, no matter what you do, and how many times you do it, God will forgive you? You can just get away with anything?'

'Well,' Aunt Grace stumbled, 'I wouldn't put it quite like that. But God loves all his children and there is always forgiveness for those who truly seek it.'

'Right,' I said, closing the fridge.

Retreating upstairs, I listened for a while to my mother and aunt – the easy peal of their conversation: their long, concerned vowels and squalls of tight, measured mirth.

I had no one to speak with in that manner. Not really. That profound, familial connection was entirely off-limits to me. Instead, I had the club. I had Samson. I had the upcoming game against Crystal Palace.

I had everything I'd ever dreamed of and all of it hurt.

57

At home, I stood before my bathroom mirror, tensing and flexing, excited by the pronounced firmness, recognising in myself the features that my brain deemed worthy of desire: the attractive swell of my forearms, the sculpted slant of my abs, leading the eye down and down and down. I felt the strength in my thighs, the kinetic thrum of sinew and muscle, the power to sprint faster, push harder.

I contemplated purchasing new clothes that might flatter my developing muscles – tight-fitting shirts, tight-fitting everything. I tried to gauge what outfits might be worthy of Samson's approval. I fantasised about what he might like to rip off me.

Heading to our home fixture against Crystal Palace, I dressed in my club-issued suit and tie. With the protests ongoing, I wanted to abide by the public image that had been curated for me: the home-grown working-class lad, living the dream, doing his city proud.

Outside the stadium, clusters of men stood in the February rain with banners and megaphones, chanting for the owner to sell the club and never return. By contrast, the atmosphere inside the ground was buoyant. Samson's name rang round the stands throughout our warm-up.

We were expecting Palace to play a physical game. They typically fielded a compact back four, outmatching us in height and size. Lining out in the tunnel, all my newfound body confidence was dwarfed by the hulking presence of their central defenders.

'Come on then boys,' Bert yelled down the tunnel, slamming his left fist against the flimsy plastic wall, prompting his young mascot to pull free from his right hand and cower into Theo's trunk-like legs.

Around the quarter-hour mark, Samson put us ahead, poking home a rebound from my long-range effort. But within ten minutes, Palace had it all-square: an obvious shirt tug from Bert to concede a needless penalty.

At half-time, Dami pulled me aside while the manager laid into his captain.

'Watch your back,' he warned, 'Looks like their big ones fancy a piece of you.'

With the game still even after seventy minutes, Baba won a free kick around forty yards out, to the left of the area. Since the manager had anticipated a scrappy game with lots of fouls, we'd spent time in the week practising routines from this general distance.

When Milo gave the signal and took the free kick, I pulled off my marker to the left of the box, dashing up the touchline in anticipation of the cross. My role was to collect the ball and drag two men wide, before cutting back and releasing Samson in the centre. Sprinting, I watched the cross from over my shoulder, my eye on the ball.

The blow caught me from a blind spot to my right, hard and surprising and wild, twisting and lifting my body, my ankle still rooted behind. I heard the impact before I felt it. The crunch and then the scream: a raw, animal panic, erupting out of me, beyond my control. I rolled prone, my forehead pressed into the turf, my leg raised in the air like a white flag, a plea for help.

In replays, it's easy to project a determined malice into the tackle. I don't believe that the Palace player intended to cause any harm. He deserved the red card, but slow motion makes everything look premeditated.

As my teammates crowded the referee, grappling and screaming for justice, Samson kneeled by my side, desperately waving on the medical staff. Through the blurring, thumping pain, I felt his hand in my hair, a rushed whisper of assurances: 'It's okay – they're coming, they're coming'.

Somehow, through all the physical duress, my body registered his gentle, affectionate touch, and translated this into the stirrings of arousal.

Not now, I thought, siphoning air through my gritted teeth. *Please not now.*

Suddenly, my body was being handled from all directions. Turned and manoeuvred, eased upwards into a seated position. For what seemed like an eternity, they prodded and pressed, debating over me like a ticking bomb in desperate need of defusal. I felt nauseous and pulled my shirt over my head to avoid looking down at my ankle. I bit down on the shirt to help me bear the tide of pain, my teeth clamping down on the club badge, gifting the photographers their lead image for the back pages.

I barely registered the cheer of the home supporters as my assailant was issued his red card.

58

There is remarkably little sympathy for injured footballers. Injuries are perceived as a standard, unremarkable part of the job. Our damage is reported in precise, inhuman terms, framed primarily as an inconvenience, a problem for a manager and squad to navigate and overcome. The severity of an injury is determined entirely by its duration – how long the player will be out of the side.

As they carried me from the pitch, I lowered my shirt and covered my eyes with the inside of my arm. Peripherally aware of some benign applause, I raised my thumb in acknowledgement of the support.

I had little say in what came next. An oxygen mask. A shot of something in my arm. Sirens and an ambulance. Three X-rays and a private room. Mam by my bedside, Dad lingering in the hall. Low, hushed tones. I was drowsy with painkillers, catching only words and phrases.

Not as bad as we thought.

Around me, therapies were proposed and discussed. I was promised a world-leading expert – a woman who had spent her whole career profiting from the misfortune and pain of athletes.

In our sport, many stars are ridiculed for the failure of their bodies. Their proneness to injury. When time in the medical room outweighs time on the pitch, a player is labelled a drain on resources. Ex-professionals turned pundits harken to an age where they played through pain, both mental and physical. By comparison, my generation are accused of being soft things with unearned feelings.

This is what I know for certain: beyond a certain age, almost every player is pushing through some kind of pain. In this profession, no one is ever 'fully fit'. Injuries can cost us everything: our place in the squad, our value in the market, our entire legacy. Every footballer you can name wakes up stiff and goes to bed sore. One injury is destined to lead to another. You subconsciously favour one side, shifting weight, recalibrating instinct.

I know I'll live with the injury to my ankle for ever. In every step, I can feel the damage. It is a dull, grating click: bone on bone. In the years to come, once I am retired, surgeries are inevitable. Arthritis is inevitable. These are the risks we implicitly accept by setting foot on the pitch.

The game against Palace ended one–one. In his post-match interview, the manager dismissed the result from conversation, stressing it had been overshadowed by my injury. In my absence, the club had been reduced to a single out-and-out forward. Our hopes for survival would rest on Samson, and Samson alone.

59

That evening, my name was trending. The most popular tweet was a video of the tackle from a direct angle, played in slow motion. You could see my ankle buckle, my mouth split open in a wide, silent howl, anguished before I hit the ground.

From the hospital bed, I searched every variation on my name, all the misspellings, fan-created nicknames and abbreviations. I scrolled and scrolled, absorbing all of their comments and vitriol. I felt woozy from the drugs – the scrolling seemed like a comfort, a means to focus my attention, to distract from the throbbing.

On my bedside table, grapes, flowers and a card written in Mum's hand.

We love you – back stronger!

Dad had signed his own name.

They decided against surgery. By avoiding an invasive procedure, the doctors predicted I would only be out of the squad for between four to six weeks. I would need to wear an orthopaedic boot and report to the training ground for physiotherapy, hydrotherapy, cryotherapy – every type of therapy they could offer.

In the days following my discharge, I brooded on my couch,

punching pillows and snapping heartlessly at my doting mother as she brought me fruit and cups of tea. The fruit was from Sebastian – an overflowing basket and flowers, a card promising to check in more regularly.

After an initial flurry of commiserating texts and well-intentioned messages, I was left alone. The squad group chat maintained its banter. The media cycle changed to midweek press conferences and fourth-round FA Cup ties.

I lay there, staring down at my ankle like it was a foreign object, entombed in plastic and gauze. I felt let down by my body, betrayed by my precious, magnificent leg – my long-term ally – the origin and source of all my achievements.

I was angry because I was vulnerable. I was housebound, at the mercy of my mother's will and pity, with no way to burn off the energy, to vent the frustration. Worst of all, the injury had denied me time with Samson, cutting me out of the team for a significant portion of the season's remaining away games. A dwindling, precious commodity. I seethed, convinced that even after I'd recovered, there was no conceivable way of returning to bed with him. Our routine had been shattered and I'd been rendered utterly undesirable.

Mam enjoyed the excuse to fuss over me. Throughout my recovery, she slept in one of my upstairs bedrooms, busied herself with a seemingly endless stream of odd-jobs and housework. She was a self-appointed nurse, receptionist, chauffer and carer. She helped me into and out of the bath, unabashed in the face of my nakedness.

'Come on you wally, I've seen it all before.'

We scarcely spoke about Dad. On each occasion that Mam needed to make a trip home, she'd return in a solemn mood,

informing me that that Dad sent his love. She reminded me
that he was an adult man, and was perfectly capable of feeding and taking care of himself.

'One day, you'll have a nice girl to do all of this for you,'
Mam said, setting down a tray of scrambled eggs and grilled
vegetables for my lunch.

'Yeah, because that's definitely my priority right now,
isn't it?'

'Now listen here,' Mam said, squaring her shoulders and
raising a finger. 'Injured or not, I won't stand for that tone
young man. Now sit up and eat your tea.'

'Whatever,' I mumbled, submissively moving my leg off the
sofa with a stiff, shuffled drag.

'And you'll say "thank you" when I take the effort to make
you food.'

'Thank you, Mam.'

'You're very welcome. Come on now, eggs'll go cold.'

60

It was Thursday and Mam was driving me to the club's training ground for another round of therapies.

'I'll miss this, you know,' she said, eyes on the road.

'Miss what?'

'This! You, ye silly git! I'll miss having an excuse to be
around you. I'll miss you when you get poached away by
Real-bloody-Madrid or some other bastard club halfway
across the world.'

'I'm not going anywhere, Mam.'

'Don't be daft. Of course you will.'

She spoke with a certainty that I wasn't sure how to process: smiling, quite content, tapping the steering wheel on
beat to the radio's music.

'No one would want me like this.'

'Not with that bloody attitude. Don't pretend like a little
knock on your ankle's going to stop you. You'll have forgotten
all about this by the end of the month. Come the summer,
there'll be nothing in your way.'

'Well, you could always come with me. Not that I'm planning on leaving. But if I did – you could come too.'

'You say that now, but you don't mean it. Once you've got

settled with some pretty young thing, you'll want nothing to do with me or your da. I know how the world works.'

'I'm just saying—'

'Well you can forget saying it. You just get your head right and focus on getting better, okay?'

Hydrotherapy pools are most commonly used for post-game recovery. The medical and technical teams can vary the depth and temperature of the water to curate the intended effect. To maintain my cardiovascular fitness, I was required to spend at least an hour in the pool most days, transitioning from lane swimming to deep-water running, which would habituate me to putting weight back onto my ankle.

Wading up and down the centre of the pool, I moved with minimal floor contact, hopping and bobbing, relying on my arms to propel me forwards – wide, cresting breaststrokes, purposefully parting the underlit water. With every length, I focused on my breathing – willing myself to heal and purge, channelling every breath down and through me, straight into my stupid, swollen ankle.

It was just past midday. I knew the squad would be winding down their training session, ready to head inside for an early lunch. Dipping my head below the water, into the hollow silence, I could picture it all so clearly: the tussling debates over who got the last touch on a winning goal; the academy scholars lingering behind, gathering cones and wayward balls in their frostbitten hands; the tart chemical smell of Deep Heat in the changing rooms; Samson removing his kit – always his shirt before boots.

Since the draw with Palace, we'd been roundly beaten by Tottenham in London. A four–nil loss, with very little by the way of consolation. It was a game we were expected to lose, but the manager never spoke in those terms. I knew the team would be hurting.

The new social media manager that Sebastian had appointed for me put out a tweet from my verified account after the match – some vague platitude about 'going again next week', accompanied by a professional photo of the North Stand. It had garnered a few thousand likes.

'How's it been?' I asked the pool guard while treading water. 'You know, since the weekend.'

'Ah, no surprises really, son. No one likes getting battered. Especially when you know it's coming and there's nowt any of you can do to stop it.'

'Right,' I said, reaching into my swimming trunks to adjust myself.

'They're missing you out there.'

'Did someone say that?'

'I'm saying it,' the guard said, smiling broadly and unlocking his phone, as though to end the matter.

'Thanks, mate.'

Heading out to the car park, I spotted Samson and Baba, deep in conversation, exchanging agitated French.

'Hey, hey, wait up,' Baba called to me, eyeing my crutches. 'How you feeling, bro?'

'Yeah, a little better thanks,' I said, swinging myself towards them.

'You look shit,' Samson said, his tone piqued, arms crossed.

'Be nice, eh?' Baba said, slapping Samson in the chest. 'He is in one of his bad moods, you know? All training, cussing us out, calling us this and that. He hates to lose, this one.'

'Oh, right.'

'All the team, we tease, we say it is because he misses you.'

'Fuck you, eh?' Samson barked, stomping off to his car.

I leaned back on my crutches as Baba rolled his eyes and turned away.

61

I learned a new shape to sleep in. My leg raised, slightly beyond comfort, swaddled in pillows. Just as I had settled into a comfortable position, my phone rang. It was Sebastian.

'How did you like the fruit basket, my friend?'

'Yeah, it's good. Thanks Sebastian.'

'Did you try those blueberries yet? Straight from Poland to your mouth. So good, believe me – very in season, excellent anti-inflammatory. Antioxidants, you know? Excellent for recovery.'

'I'll try some in a bit.'

'You are in training tomorrow, no?'

'Yeah. Well, not full training. Still just the gym and the pool, I think. The gaffer prefers to keep the squad separate from us lot – the injured players.'

'And your head? What do you feel?'

It sounded like Sebastian was driving. This welfare check had been slotted in between his other, more important meetings.

'My head's okay, I guess. It's all pretty boring. I'm ready to get back. The ankle's getting better. A little pain, but nothing I can't handle.'

'I know your type, my friend. Always rush, rush, rush. Throw me back in. I am ready, I am ready. Please, for me, listen to your body. Do not feel the pressure of the club. Your career is long – you must be so sensible with these things. If you change your mind about my private physiotherapist, you must tell me. Maria is the best in Europe. I promise that no one will be better.'

'I think I'll be okay. The club are doing a good job. I'm feeling good – I promise.'

'Okay,' Sebastian said, indifferent. 'That is excellent. I will let you rest. I am here when you need me. Samson is there too. You must use him. He loves to help you, okay?'

'Sure,' I said, smoothing my hand over the duvet.

'Sleep well. *Bon nuit.*'

The co-codamol tablets had left me constipated and bloated. My core felt dense. All mass and heft and tenderness. As a result, my appetite had changed. I ate my mother's soups with dutiful politeness, forcing myself to spoon and swallow, spoon and swallow. I chewed on the wholewheat bread she procured fresh each morning until it was reduced to a stodgy, nutty paste that my throat could reluctantly accept.

Each day, following my rehab exercises, I lay on the sofa and passed the time in an infinite scroll, alternating between apps and porn. Reading the group chats, I mentally willed someone, anyone, to message me personally. I dared myself to reach out to Samson.

I miss us, I drafted, then deleted. I turned off the Wi-Fi and buried my phone between the sofa cushions. A performance of restraint.

At night, I thumbed the *Get Well Soon* card from hospital,

running my finger over Dad's signature, feeling out the texture of my loss.

On Valentine's Day, at the nadir of my isolation, Doctor Léonie came to my home. Mam had abandoned me to spend the day with Dad, so I had the space to myself.

For the past week, the team WhatsApp group had been in a battle of romantic one-upmanship, duelling with flowers and jewellery and private concerts. The bar had been set by Milo, who had bought his fiancée an Audi convertible.

From the chat, I knew that Samson had a date scheduled with Holly that evening – dinner reservations at one of the city's most exclusive restaurants. Bert had helped him to secure a table.

Doctor Léonie sat on my sofa, watching me like a house cat. Inward and suspicious, silent and fixed. I was dressed in a tracksuit, ungroomed and slouched – all petulance.

'Healing is difficult,' Doctor Léonie said, steepling her fingers and leaning forwards. 'I understand that it is hard for you right now, but believe me, things will become easier.'

I scoffed. 'What do you mean you understand? What is it you think you understand? What is there to understand about this situation? It's not exactly a mystery. It doesn't take your brilliant brain to tap into how I'm feeling.'

'Well,' she said, 'why don't you assist me by telling me how you're feeling?'

'I feel like shit. Obviously. Just useless and shit.'

'What would you prefer to be doing?'

'I want to be playing. I want to help the team.'

'So you are guilty?'

'Guilty? I guess – I don't know. Maybe. I'm just bored

of *this.*' I gestured down at my leg. 'I hate the boot and the crutches and I hate people feeling sorry for me. I'm bored and tired and lonely.'

'Lonely?' she said, latching onto the tail of my sentiment. 'You still miss your father?'

'Sure,' I said. 'Yeah, I miss him.'

'And you have attempted to speak with him?'

'Not exactly.'

'What is it you think your father is feeling? Might he also be feeling bored and useless?'

I stuffed my hands into the pockets of my tracksuit.

'I guess.'

'And is there a way you could use your influence to address his feelings? To find some means of resolution? Could there be an opportunity at the club for your father? Some use for his skills?'

'Okay, you've made your point.'

'The world is made small by injury,' Doctor Léonie said. 'In suffering, we are forced to live inside ourselves. One of the best means to escape this is to think beyond our own anguish. To regard the pain of others – to bear witness and gain perspective. You are a remarkable young man. You have a great capacity for empathy – you care and feel deeply. These are strengths that not all your teammates possess. I hope you will use your influence for good.'

The following morning, the newspapers published pictures of Samson and Holly dining together. Clean, stage-managed angles. His smile from three different vantage points. Holly's nails painted in the blue, red and white of the French flag. Samson's hair etched with a love heart.

Fuck empathy, I thought. Only my pain mattered.

62

In my absence, we had gone four games without a win, including a defeat to Aston Villa that saw us eliminated from the FA Cup. With the score tied after extra time, the match had gone to penalties. Stepping up for the deciding shot, Samson had his spot kick saved and we were denied a place in the fifth round.

Samson was disconsolate, sobbing on the pitch. The photographers captured him in tears, Bert's arm around his waist – a Baroque portrait of suffering. The slumped anguish of his naked shoulders, our club shirt bunched in his fist. The embossed love heart still in his hair, faded and broken.

Though the squad and our fans promptly forgave him, Samson remained in a terrible strop, stomping around the training ground, dropping weights and eating alone. Things only became worse the following week, when he was overlooked once more for France's national squad.

'I wouldn't even try yet,' Bert warned me, as we rested between laps of the pool. 'He's not in the mood to be consoled.'

Thinking of you, I texted Samson, ignoring Bert's advice. *I'm still here if you need me. I miss us.*

I received no reply.

63

The physiotherapists were pleased with my recovery. I had regained near full mobility in my ankle and was deemed ready to return to light, contact-free training.

It was March and spring was budding. At the training ground, the air was crisp – sweet crocus and primrose, alive with the tremulous chirps of blackcaps and peppy chaffinch tweeps. Banks of daffodils lined the pitches, blooming like a warm welcome.

As I jogged onto the field, Samson was stood on his own, at a distance from the squad, grinding his toe into the grass like a punished child.

'Here's our man,' Bert said, pulling me into a headlock. 'Took your fucking time, eh?'

'I'm still meant to be careful,' I said, shoving him off.

'All right then precious. I'll play nice.'

For the entire training session, Samson avoided my eye. He played with a selfish determination – refusing to pass but rebuking others when they failed to pass to him.

'*Putain!*' he spat. '*Brûle en l'enfer!*'

Hours later, when Jean-Claude finally excused us, Samson hurried straight inside, stripping and heading to the steam room.

'Go and try to have a word, would ye, lad?' Bert said. 'Typical Frenchie – loves being a little madam. Striking and making a fuss, you know?'

'What do you think I should say?'

'You're mates, ain't you? You know how to call your mates out when they're being daft.'

'All right, fine.'

'Good lad,' Bert said, punching me in the arm, 'Proper glad to have you back in action, son.'

Stripping off, I prepared an excuse about the heat being therapeutic for my ankle. It had been over a month since I'd been alone with Samson.

'Hello?' I said, opening the door, stepping tentatively forward into the mist, both hands extended, blindly reaching for a surface. 'It's just me.'

'Close the door, eh?' said Samson, somewhere to the right of me. 'Hurry and sit.'

'Would you prefer me to go?'

'You can do as you please.'

Through the steam, I could just about make out the hazy outline of his body. He was leaning back, one knee bent, like an emperor in recline, awaiting grapes and sweetmeats. I positioned myself on the opposite side of the room. The steam settled and he disappeared entirely from my sight.

'Don't expect me to talk,' Samson spoke into the mist.

'I don't expect anything from you.'

He snorted at me, harsh and brutish. 'Sure you don't.'

'I mean, I don't expect that—'

'I am not interested,' he spat, 'in anything you have to

say. About what you expect or don't expect. Just keep your mouth shut and leave me be.'

I sat back against the baking wooden wall and stretched out my legs, my heart and lungs adjusting to the enveloping warmth. With my eyes closed, I began my yoga breathing exercises. In through the nose, hold for ten, slow release through the mouth. In through the nose, hold for twenty, slow release through the mouth.

'They overlook me became I am in this team,' Samson said, unprovoked, interrupting my count. 'You understand? This shit, useless team that I must be the one to save. Because I am stuck here in this stupid country. I am stuck for another three months and then never again. I will never play in England again.'

I wiped my hands along my thighs and weighed up an appropriate response. I knew he was trying to provoke me. My immediate instinct was to be logical – to name the numerous players in France's national team who hailed from English clubs.

'You may be right,' I said.

'Of course I am right. Every day, the Rwandans, they call me. *Every. Day.* They have my number. My email. They call and they beg: come to us, Samson, play for us, save us, please. Everyone needs for Samson to save them. They promise me everything. This country I have never known, never visited. Leave France and we will fix everything for you, make your dreams come true. We will take such good care of you. Such good care of your mama.'

'You could just listen to them?' I said, attempting to shape the suggestion into a question. 'Or speak to them and tell them no.'

Samson huffed. 'It is not so easy, eh? Once I decide, I

am a traitor. I am so greedy, they will say. I forget myself, betray them for the enemy. The colonial bastards who steal everything. Who turn away and let us suffer. Who cause so much of the hurt. They will turn Rwanda against me. And my mama, they will turn on her too.'

'Does your mam know that they're hounding you?'

'Mama, she knows what matters. She knows how to survive. Mama, she always tells me to smile. *Always be smiling, Samson.* When the Black man smiles, he is not a threat. He is friendly. And so always you see Samson smile. I make myself smile, no matter what I feel.'

'I'm sorry,' I said. 'I didn't realise.'

Samson kissed his teeth. '*Sorry,*' he repeated back. 'It is so easy for you to be sorry, eh?'

'I'm sorry you feel you're stuck here,' I said into the steam, as calmly as I could manage, 'But you can't blame me for any of this. I can't help the way you feel. Or the way I feel about you. And I'm not the one who signed you. I didn't force you to stay in January.'

'Ah,' Samson chuckled, 'But of course you did.'

My heart lurched.

'What do you mean?'

'You beg me to stay, so I choose to stay. Then you never wear the necklace I gift you. And then you get injured? You abandon me?'

'I didn't realise that you wanted me to wear it. I wouldn't do anything to hurt you.'

'And now you and Sebastian, eh? He loves his pretty little white boys. So well behaved. So easy to control. He has you watching over me, eh?'

'Samson,' I said, my tongue cloying, 'You know it's not like that. I would never—'

'*I would never, I would never* – this, I believe this, you know? Your whole life is a never. You would never dare to do anything. Nothing that matters. Safe here in your precious club where it is all so easy for you. Where you can hide your secrets. Where there are no expectations. You get injured, so what? The team goes down, so what? The team stays up, so what? Look at yourself! Look at this life!'

He spoke without pause. I listened, awaiting the chance to interject. To defend.

'Samson, I know you—'

'Listen here, eh? You don't know me. You know nothing, you hear? Believe me, you could not last a day where I am from. *Not one day.* Mister *I Would Never.* Big man at your little club, thinking you're the king. You are the king of *merde.* This is all you will ever see. This ugly little town. The racist fans and foolish owner. This is your kingdom? This is all you are worth? You can keep it.'

With this, he stormed out of the room, the steam swirling behind him like a grand finale, the flourish to his theatrics.

I stayed put until the heat began to wane and the mist parted, a path forwards now clear.

He stayed for me, I thought, holding on to that fact.

I was Samson's confessional. I was the safe place where his insecurities and fury and sins could be laid bare. I could be his constant – show him the love and forgiveness and acceptance that he so clearly craved. I may be the king of shit, but he was here because of me.

64

My name was trending again. According to a number of newspapers, I was growing increasingly frustrated with the uncertain future of the club. Both Arsenal and Tottenham were lining up summer moves to sign me, contingent on how I performed post-recovery. Barcelona were also now allegedly 'seriously considering' a double deal, pouncing for both me and Samson.

One piece contained a quote, apparently from the office of my agent:

> In football, nothing is impossible. Big teams need big players, and I believe my clients to be big players. And for the young ones, they are big players who dream the biggest. Who am I to stop their dreams? For young ones like him, everything can be possible.

I called Sebastian.

'My friend, so good to hear from you. How is the ankle?'

'Yeah, doing better thanks. Listen: did you speak with any journalists about me?'

'Why? What do they say this time?' Sebastian chuckled.

'They've got a quote from you here, saying that I'm dreaming of a move away from the club.'

'Is that right?' he said demurely.

'Yeah, it says "everything is possible" for me.'

'And how do you feel about these words?'

'Confused, frankly.'

'My friend,' Sebastian said, 'You must trust me. I know how this game works. They take my quotes about one thing and twist for all the juice. I have been playing at this game for a long time – many, many years. In time, you learn to let them play with their own words.'

'But did you say that? Did you tell them I'm dreaming of moving?'

'We say just enough to create an appetite, you see? The interest of big, big clubs – it is very good for your sponsorships. Very good for everything. When the time comes to negotiate, all these things? They are our weapons. We need many weapons to fight. As I say, my friend, you must trust me on this.'

'Right,' I said, still unsure whether my question had been addressed.

'I will make sure there is more fruit for you soon, okay? I have to go now. Business never stops!'

65

Upon my return to full-contact training, the medical staff seemed to linger in my periphery. They guarded the touchline with an air of inevitability. For those first few days back on the pitch, I felt acutely attuned to the pains and strains of my team-mates, the injuries they were pushing through in our fight for survival, the damage their bodies had weathered and gleaned.

Samson continued training with menace, demanding more from everyone. He chided every wayward pass, rebuked our muddled runs. Not even I was immune from his beratement. I was off the pace and it was evident – my close control was more clumsy than usual. As I shanked a shot wide, Samson laughed at me.

'Why don't you lay off,' I flared at him, punting a water bottle in his direction and watching as it flashed by the right of his face.

I sensed the team tense up. The air sucked from their lungs: a vacuum of hostility.

Samson kissed his teeth. 'Grow up, eh?'

'Hey!' Jean-Claude yelled at Samson. 'Stop this! You are not so perfect, you know this? You aren't so smart, believe me. I have coached men who would eat you for breakfast.'

'And now?' Samson retorted, 'Now you are here, coaching these lazy fools?'

Sizing up to each other, they switched to French, parrying each other's insults, calming only once Bert stepped forward to separate them.

'Easy now,' Bert warned, shoving Samson in the chest, creating some distance between the men. 'Come on, lads. Let's all calm down for a second.'

'I am calm,' Samson sniffed, his jaw tense. 'But I ask you this, Captain Kendall – why does everyone yell only at me?'

Raising his hand, Samson pointed to me.

'Why is the teacher's pet free from blame? So nice to be everyone's favourite, eh? Nice to be treated so softly.'

'All right, listen up,' Bert announced to the group, his beefy arm now locked around Samson's shoulders. 'It's good to care. It's good to demand these standards. To push each other. But we won't be getting anywhere by being a bunch of poncey little faggots.'

Directing his attention to me, Bert beckoned me forwards, restraining me with his other arm. 'First week back and you're already causing me grief?'

'Just a bit rusty,' I said, wary of conceding too much, of accepting fault.

Bringing his arms together like a chest fly press, Bert drew me face-to-face with Samson.

Meeting his eyes, I could sense no real anger. I reassured myself that it wasn't me that Samson was frustrated with; I was merely a safe conduit for his discontent. I was the embodiment of this club, this town, this country. I was the reason he stayed. I was proof that he still cared.

Samson dropped his eyes to the floor, jerking his shoulder, clearly desperate to be relinquished from Bert's grip. Somehow I had forgotten how young Samson was, how much he simply loved to play.

'Now shake,' Bert demanded.

'I'm sorry,' I said. 'I'll try harder.'

66

Our first game after the international break was an away trip to Wolves. Following our final training session of the week, the manager invited me to his office, letting me know that I was back in the match-day squad, and would be returning straight into the starting eleven.

'You are ready,' *L'oracolo* told me. 'I know this. I see in your eyes. Jean-Claude is pleased with your progress, the effort you apply. So you come along, share again with Samson, it will all be well.'

Upon leaving the manager's office, I called home immediately.

'Oh, that's great news, pet,' Mam said. 'You've worked so hard on your rehab. I know you'll do great.'

'You could come, if you like. To the game. Both of you. The tickets aren't a problem. It'd be good to see Dad.'

'I'll have a word,' Mam said, then lowering her voice. 'But I can't promise anything. It's still hard for him, you know?'

'I know,' I said. 'Just let him know I offered.'

'Okay, pet. I'll go and tell him now. Well done again. We both love you very much.'

Still eighteenth in the table and two points from safety, we had eleven games left to secure our survival. Six away fixtures remaining to room with Samson; to preserve our ritual, to offer him everything I could, to show him I was prepared to try harder, to fight.

In my absence, Samson had been sharing a room with Dami. Leaving *L'oracolo*'s office, I headed to the weights room to update them both on the room arrangements.

Through the heavy gym doors, the deep bass thrum of European techno, punctuated by the clank of iron being heaved and racked. From the hallway where I stood, hesitating, rehearsing what to say, I could already smell the acrid, chemical sting of rubber and disinfectant. Above this, heady top notes of body spray and deodorant – floral and citric perfumes, masking the musk of effort.

As I lingered, Dami shoved his way through the doors.

'You're welcome to him, bruv,' Dami responded to my rushed explanation. He laughed with a force that seemed excessive. 'That boy – the chaos! Clothes everywhere! I literally can't. It's not right, bruv. I can't be living like that.'

'Yeah,' I said, 'He's definitely messy . . .'

'Messi, messy,' Dami pondered. 'Maybe your boy takes his inspiration a bit too literally, you know?'

'Maybe,' I said. 'Hey Dami, he didn't mention me, did he? Samson didn't say anything about sharing with me?'

'Nah,' Dami said, beginning to walk away, 'But you're a proper saint, my brother, tolerating his nonsense all season. That boy blows so hot and cold, you know? Someday, you'll look back and you'll ask yourself: why did I put up with that shit?'

Inside the weight room, I found Samson with his

headphones in, performing weighted squats in front of the mirrored wall. Making eye contact through the mirror, Samson dipped his head to acknowledge my presence, his lips pursed with exertion. I stood by, waiting for him to finish his set, respectfully admiring the heft of his thighs, the pertness of his arse.

'Counting,' Samson said, breathlessly, removing one headphone. 'I was counting.'

'Don't worry. I know. I just came to let you know that we're sharing again. I'm back in the side.'

'Oh,' Samson said, scratching at his crotch, turning back to the mirror. 'Good. That is good news.'

'It can be just like before,' I told him, holding his gaze through the reflection. 'Back in flow. Back to normal.'

'I'll be ready,' Samson said, reinserting his headphone and flexing his knees, beginning another set.

67

On the coach to Wolverhampton, I received a phone call from an unknown number.

'Hello?'

'Aha, it is good to hear your voice.'

'Oh – hi Doctor Léonie.'

'I apologise that we didn't get to speak before you travelled. Back in the squad – this is such great news! Some recognition for all your courage. I had been meaning to check in – to see how you're feeling.'

'I'm okay,' I said, squeezing past the slumbering mass in the seat beside me, moving quietly to an emptier section at the front of the coach. 'I think I'm all right.'

'You think you are?'

'I know I'm all right,' I said, understanding her prompt.

'You must trust your body,' Doctor Léonie instructed. 'You are the one in control. Without this faith, you cannot perform. You decide how ready you are.'

'I'm ready,' I told her.

'What are you ready for?'

'I'm ready to score. I'm ready to win.'

'Say it again for me.'

'*I'm ready.*'

68

Our room was on the top floor of a chain hotel. Even lower budget than our usual fare. The windows were tall – they filled the room with an unsentimental spring light, every speck of dust set dancing.

Samson emptied his suitcase onto the floor by his bed, rummaging through the wreckage for a phone charger.

'*Merde*,' he spat, 'Can I borrow yours again?'

'Just like usual?' I joked, trialling the possibility of a reconciliation.

'Yes, like usual,' Samson smiled, taking the charger from my hand.

Standing, Samson drew a deep, deep breath – enough air to lift his whole body. His shoulders raised high, eyes closed.

'I want to say,' he said, 'that I am sorry to you.'

'Oh,' I said. It came out quickly, like a cough.

'You know – for saying – these things. In the steam. I do not mean these things. It is not fair to say these things to you – I think you are good, you know? A good person, good player.'

'Right,' I said, sat on my hands. 'Thanks.'

For a while, he just stood there, swinging his arms to and fro, like a child waiting to be excused.

'Look,' I said, pulling down my collar to expose the necklace he'd bought me. 'I really do love it.'

Samson nodded his approval.

'I will wash now,' he eventually said, hurrying to the bathroom, shutting the door heavily behind him.

Sitting on the side of the bed, my mind swam. He'd apologised. Not the forced concessions and mannered clarifications that I'd heard from him in training, but a real apology. A genuine acknowledgement of fault. I was still sat there in a stupor when he re-emerged.

'Right,' he said, clapping his hands loud enough to startle me.

Dropping to his knees, Samson began to pray, his lips moving in silent communion. With his eyes scrunched in absolute focus, he held his own crucifix, rubbing it between his thumb and forefinger like a wish. There was something voyeuristic about watching him in prayer. It felt like a violation of something impossibly intimate. He finished by opening his eyes, dotting his head, chest, shoulders and lips with his thumb – the sign of the cross, sealed with a kiss.

'What do you think about?' I asked. 'When you pray – what do you think about? How does it work?'

Samson stretched, rose to his feet. 'Many things. I think about my blessings. All the thanks I owe. I think about my mama. I ask God for her safety. I ask God that I have the strength to play well, to honour the gifts he has given me.'

'But, like – does he – does God answer? Do you hear him?'

'I do not need answers,' Samson said. 'It does not matter to hear answers. Blessed are they that have not seen, and yet believe.' He crossed himself reverently.

'Right,' I said, touching my crucifix to suggest that I understood.

Samson walked around the side of the bed and sat, facing me.

'How is it?' he said, gesturing to my ankle.

'Yeah, all right. Pretty much there.'

'Good to play?'

'Yeah, I reckon so.'

'So,' he said, as nervous as I'd ever seen him, 'for later – for after the lights, you know – do I need to be – to be careful?'

My heart leapt. A surge so sudden and full that it must have looked like panic.

'So, you still want—'

'If you think that it is okay . . .'

'I mean, yeah,' I said, suddenly bashful. 'Yeah, it'll be fine. Maybe a be little careful, just to be safe.'

'I am glad you are better,' he said. 'Without you, it was different. Everything was harder.'

'But I'm back now,'

'Yes,' Samson said, holding my gaze, 'You are.'

My face felt very hot. I was newly aware of the space between us – the coiled charge of the air. I felt as though my desire had its own gravity.

'Can I kiss you?' I asked.

He paused, but then bowed forwards – his eyes shut, consenting.

Samson's lips were soft. All that imagining and yet he could still surprise me. I kept my eyes closed – enjoying the moment for all it was, for all it meant. Then it was over and he leaned back. Samson looked to the window, as if to double check the curtains were closed – as though the kiss carried greater risk than anything else.

'Thanks,' I said.

'It's okay. You have kissed before?'

'Was I bad?'

'No,' Samson said, scratching at his shoulder, 'I just wonder – if there were others. Like us.'

'No,' I lied, shocked that he even deemed it possible. 'It's only you. It's only ever been you.'

Samson stood. He cleared his throat, shook out his hands like shock.

'The doctor,' he said, his back to me. 'Léonie, she wants me to have a celebration.'

'Oh yeah?' I said – looking down, conscious of his tonal shift. 'She told me the same thing.'

'Will you help me? Help me decide this?'

'I mean, yeah – why not? I can try.'

'I will not copy anyone,' Samson said, swaying on the spot, side to side. 'Nothing that has been done.'

'That's going to eliminate a lot of options.'

'Yes,' he smiled. 'This is why I need your help. You are good at this – you think well.'

I felt myself blush.

'I guess we could create a dance? You love to dance.'

'Any dance with no music is stupid.'

'Well,' I considered, 'how about one of your nicknames?'

'I told you, in Paris, they call me *Megs*.'

'I'm not sure about that one,' I said. 'A little too feminine. I don't think it lends itself well to a trademark celebration. I was actually thinking about how Sebastian calls you his *goat* – the greatest of all time.'

'Goat?' Samson gagged. 'In Paris, the *chèvre* is an insult. This means a terrible player.'

'Yeah, well – maybe you can reclaim it. You can change the meaning. What do you think of when you picture a goat?'

Samson paused. 'In my mama's country – in Rwanda – the goat is very important. The goat, it can be raised anywhere. Even on poor land, dry land. The goat does not care where it is. It fertilises the ground – brings life back from the soil. And from the goat, there is enough milk for all the family – enough to sell the spare, to make the cheese, the yoghurt. To make money to provide.'

'That sounds perfect to me,' I said, jumping up, off the bed. 'How about something like this?'

I stood with my index fingers pointed backwards, behind my ears.

'It is so simple,' Samson said, looking at me sceptically.

'Yeah, but maybe that's a good thing. The simple celebrations are better – more iconic. They're good because people will imitate you.'

'And the people, they will know this is a goat?'

'I guess they'll know if you tell them.'

'Okay – when I score and do this, I will think of you.'

That night, we used his bed. At first, he restrained himself, easing into me, controlling his body to a gentle, measured pace, overly careful to avoid my ankle. Things stayed that way until I brought myself to whisper a single word.

'*Harder*,' I said.

Harder, he complied.

After I'd cleaned, he motioned for me to join him, to come back under the covers. After some shifting and shuffling, we found a position that worked, settling into each other: flesh on flesh, man on man.

He fell asleep long before I did, one arm slung possessively over my chest. For some time, I lay awake, listening to the rhythm of his breath, the regular percussion of his heart.

At some point in the night, Samson's phone buzzed above us – electric and jarring. Samson stirred, but did not reach to check, pulling me closer, snuggling further under the covers.

Between us, something had deepened. A peace had been reached.

69

We both scored against Wolves. Then again the following weekend, at home against Brighton. The pundits claimed that Samson was back to his best – noted that our partnership was instrumental to his revival. One commentator described us in musical terms: the harmony of our movement, the contrapuntal nature of runs. Major and minor. Tenor and bass. Scale and score.

After each goal, Samson used his new celebration. The media embraced the narrative, beginning to associate him with other goat-like qualities: stubbornness, adaptability, agility, balance.

With nine games remaining, we were out of the relegation zone for the first time since the turn of the year. Among the squad, spirits had turned.

'It's alreet for you young 'uns,' Bert reminded me, 'But for us war-torn bastards, having a relegation against your name is a fucking anchor. You'll only ever get dragged further and further down. Keep up your scoring, and you'll make a lot of old cunts extremely happy.'

Following the Brighton match, our fans developed a chant:

His name is fuckin' Samson
And he's the fuckin' GOAT
And if you try to mark him
He'll stick it down your throat.

He passes with his left foot
He passes with his right
And when he rams another in
We'll sing this song all night.

70

After that night in Wolverhampton, there was a new sensitivity to Samson. A willingness to engage, to acknowledge my presence, my body.

Our sex improved. Though I still faced away, and though the lights were always off, he'd become attuned to my rhythms. That music from the pitch had extended to our bed. We performed as a duet. We were beat and pulse, sharp and flat, then catching breath – a lull in the middle of the movement, leading into a surging, swelling crescendo. I became confident enough to use my voice, to tilt back my hips, to reach under myself, to hold and tug without fear.

After, we'd rest, my head on his chest, his crucifix swung to the side. There, in the dark, I'd tell him stories about the club, the long history of our rivalries, the lost glories of days past. I spoke low, barely whispering, speaking to the pace of the rise and fall, rise and fall, his breath growing shallow, then imperceptible. Time would drift, the present and the past, all sounds and thoughts converging into an abyss of deep, peaceful sleep.

In April, the club cut ties with Patrick O'Shea. He'd been filmed in the pub, drunkenly spouting inexcusable, racist sentiments. He'd complained about how the 'darkies' were ruining football, how they should fuck off back to where they came from.

The club's actions were swift and their language was condemning. The press release suggested that Patrick's opinions were a shock revelation, as opposed to long-held, ingrained sentiments that our toxic leadership was all too aware of.

In the dressing room, Bert shot down the suggestion of a whip-round for Patrick. He could go without a leaving gift.

In a statement to the players and coaching staff, the club committed to reviewing their process around hiring representatives. Patrick's departure had created a vacancy at the club for an ambassador and a player liaison coordinator.

I decided to use my influence.

71

In late April, Samson's hotel room was broken into. Initially, Samson was reluctant to report the invasion – to involve the police at all. But upon Sebastian's insistence, he acquiesced.

The police determined that the raid had been conducted by fans. They left the room's safe untouched, stealing only shirts, underwear and boots. The hotel launched an investigation and promptly fired two members of staff, thought to be involved with helping the group gain access to the room. Somehow, the newspapers acquired the police's report. They led with headlines about the suite's exorbitant cost per night and the various amenities available to Samson, publishing stock photos from the hotel website.

Samson was forced to issue a statement, posted to Instagram, using Sebastian's words, assuring the world he was okay. That he was focused. That we'd keep pushing on, fighting to the end of the season.

Privately, the violation of his space had shaken Samson. At Sebastian's suggestion and with minimal resistance, Samson moved into my house for the remainder of the season. All parties concurred that it was a practical and sensible short-term solution.

I felt very grateful to those thieves. There he was, under my roof, under my sheets, complete with the blessing of our manager, Samson's mother and Doctor Léonie. Suddenly, Wednesdays were a blessing. From daybreak to dusk, we shared each other's company. There he was, at the mercy of my questions, an increasingly willing subject. In my home, Samson seemed more relaxed, more human. I found myself chastising him for his messiness, for his disregard of order. Scolding him, I heard my mother in my voice.

I observed novel quirks in him that delighted me: the way he shimmied eagerly in place while waiting for the microwave to ping; the sounds he made while shaving, sucking air through his teeth as the razor pared over his perfect face; the way he bounded up the stairs to retrieve his ringing phone from the bedroom, inclined fully forwards, his hands padding the steps.

Summer had arrived and the days felt long and glorious. As it became warmer, Samson would happily walk naked around my home, strutting as he spoke on the phone, unbothered by my adoring gaze. Despite this intimacy, he remained resistant to kissing. All contact between us was made on his terms.

As we lay on the sofa one evening, my head in his lap, I felt woozy with happiness. I breathed in the intoxicating smell of his body, suspecting that the universe had conspired to grant me all my wishes at once – that from henceforth, my life would never reach this peak again.

And yet, still I longed for what could have been. Nearly a whole season of wasted time – both of us treading around our feelings, resisting a connection that had been present from the off.

I had claimed him for my own, and I wasn't ready to let him go.

72

Two weeks into his stay in my home, Samson was nominated for the league's Young Player of the Year award.

'How should we celebrate?' I asked.

'What is there to celebrate? I have won nothing.'

'It's hardly nothing. You're the second youngest on the shortlist! It's a recognition of your work.'

'For now, it is nothing. Your country, they make these awards for the English. For you pretty white boys.'

'You're being stupid,' I said, nudging his arm, then gauging his reaction. 'Listen, I insist that we celebrate.'

'*Noooo*,' Samson said, leaning away, employing the tight, tender voice of an unconvincing protest.

'Let's go out somewhere. Let's go for a dance or something. You love to dance.'

'Together?' Samson kissed his teeth. 'You know this is not an option for us. Don't be so mad, eh? And I am warm. It is nice here. I do not want to get dressed.'

'Fine then, I'm going to order us a massive pizza.'

'Pizza is not the fuel for award winners,' Samson said, joshing.

'I don't care,' I said, pulling out my phone to open a delivery app. 'Call it a cheat day or something.'

'Cheat day?'

'Cheat – as in break the rules.'

'So now you love to break rules?' Samson teased.

An hour later, we were sat on the floor, eating pizza. It felt indulgent and earned. It was first junk food I'd consumed since Christmas. For those first few bites, I found myself salivating at the pulpy smell of the cardboard. I luxuriated in the gooey, greasy cheese, the synthetic, pliant give of the rugged crusts. But after just three slices, I was bloated – my mouth felt tacky and dry. Gargled, groaning sounds came from my stomach.

'I think I'm done,' I said, pushing back my box. 'It was probably a mistake to order the large.'

'Yes,' Samson said, dropping a half-eaten slice, as though my concession had granted him permission to stop. 'I will get us some water.'

As he walked to the kitchen, Samson's phone began to vibrate beside me. *Mama*, read the screen. For a moment, I considered answering on Samson's behalf, taking the opportunity to properly introduce myself. But as usual, I'd thought too long, and the moment passed.

'It's your mam,' I called towards the kitchen. 'She's ringing you.'

With a clattering of glassware, Samson dashed back into the room, snatching the phone from my hand.

'Mama!' he said with a smile, immediately retreating upstairs, the phone pressed to his ear.

From where I sat, I listened to the distant sound of Samson's voice. It was heavy with a joyful patois that I'd never really managed to elicit from him. Somehow, his French laughter felt fuller, more genuine.

For ten, maybe fifteen minutes, I eavesdropped, stealing words here and there, typing them into Google Translate. I gleaned *Dieu* for 'God', *avion* for 'aeroplane', *coûteuse* for 'expensive'.

Eventually, he returned. I'd moved myself to the sofa, setting up the TV for another night of *FIFA*.

'Everything okay?' I said, handing him a controller.

'Yes,' he said, pouring the remainder of his water into our spider plant. 'All is good.'

'Is she happy for you?'

'Yes, very happy. She was annoyed that I did not tell her – how you say? Immediately. About the award, you know? She says she finds out through her cousin. Very embarrassing.'

'So is she going to come over? For the ceremony?'

'Maybe. Maybe not. We will see.'

'You miss her a lot, don't you?'

'Of course. Every day. But that is the price of this life. As Sebastian says – for the football, this is the choice we make.'

Plugging his phone back in to charge, Samson lay on his back and hung his legs over the side of the couch, flicking them girlishly.

'Are you glad you came here now?' I asked, selecting our club.

'Anywhere I choose, anywhere I go, there is good and there is bad. Monaco, Barcelona, London – wherever I go, my mama, she supports me.'

'But why not bring her with you?'

'My mama.' He laughed. 'She sees too much. I cannot lie as well as you. I cannot hide this from her.'

Samson motioned to me, an invisible cord tethered between us.

Us, I thought.

'When you leave here,' I said, my hands tightly gripped around the controller, 'do you think there's anything you'll miss?'

I turned from the screen to look at him, willing him to consider me.

'Maybe,' Samson said, staring forward, unmoved. 'Come on, let's play.'

For the rest of the evening, sat beside him, I let numbness overtake me, safe in the knowledge that eventually, grief would come. It would arrive later, detached from this quiet moment, and when it came, it would be solitary and dense and complete.

73

On my twentieth birthday, we secured survival. A one–nil home win against Sheffield United. Following my return to the squad, we'd secured four straight victories, pushing us past the magical forty-point mark: mathematically safe for another year.

That night, we celebrated. A double party, Bert assured me. At the Roxy, I was to be the guest of honour. I could have whatever girls I liked, as much drink as I desired. The city, the world – they were ours for the taking.

Twenty – the true death of childhood. An age not worth lying about. Nineteen had felt like such a reassuringly liminal state – a cusp, a horizon view of all life had to offer, still loaded with teenage possibility. But twenty felt unseemly.

Mam had visited in the morning, bringing a cake and another card, signed by both her and Dad. She wouldn't leave until I agreed to eat a slice. The cake was delicious, moist and light, filled with coconut and raisins. I thanked her, wrapping the cake in cling film and placing it in a Tupperware.

By the time I rediscovered that cake, it was weeks later. It was dry and stale and Samson was gone.

Returning to the nightclub, we were led to the same booth

from Christmas. The experience felt identical. It seemed to me that the girls were duplicates, the music unchanged from five months prior.

I drank slowly, nursing a single bottle, sat on the leather while others roamed the dance floor – bodies among bodies, bobbing heads under pulsing lights, inchoate and wild.

Except that night, Samson chose to remain by my side, equally sober. I hadn't requested this from him, but there he was. It was the finest birthday gift I could possibly hope for. Chatting, he leaned into my ear, cupping his voice over the music. There, in the booth, his touch was a warm, glowing sedative – an assurance that for now, I was his and he was mine.

At 1 a.m., with the night still just beginning, we excused ourselves, five minutes apart, returning in separate Ubers to my home, to the dawn of the third decade of my life.

74

With three games left to play, we had little left to compete for. On a warm and languid Tuesday afternoon, Doctor Léonie brought the squad indoors to deliver a talk about retaining focus.

'It is not me who motivates you,' she said, clicking through a PowerPoint. 'You must motivate yourselves. This motivation, it comes from inside of you. You must ask yourselves, what is my goal? How can I be the best version of myself? What do I expect from my body?'

Later, coming out of the showers, Theo imitated Doctor Léonie's voice, asking Samson what he expected from his body while whipping at him with a wet towel. Samson squealed playfully, running away, nude and unashamed.

'Ahh, I'll proper miss you, lad,' Bert said, catching him and putting him in a headlock. 'Don't forget about us, will you?'

'Never.' Samson choked.

At training, Jean-Claude iterated the same arguments as Doctor Léonie, speaking about the importance of a strong finish – of setting a points target to beat for the following season, of rewarding our fans for their support through a difficult period.

For many in the squad, their words meant nothing. The fans meant little. The season was effectively over. It was time to relax, to eat well, and enjoy the perks of a Premier League lifestyle.

In the gym, Mario lectured me: 'Thing is, if I do apply myself – if I really push on and keep trying, then I'll be a sore thumb in this side, and the fans will claim I'm playing for a move come summer. You're damned if you do, and fucked if you don't. So if they think I'm going to deny myself a barbecue and a few pints, they're having a fucking laugh.'

75

As promised, Sebastian secured me a litany of endorsements and sponsors. There were separate contracts for my boots, my shirts, my suits, even sunglasses and watches. I had been committed to these brands on four and five-year deals, taking me into my mid-twenties, to the peak of my abilities.

Before our away fixture against Fulham, I sat with Sebastian in the lobby of a fancy west London hotel, a stack of papers between us.

'It is important to sign these deals on a high, you see,' Sebastian explained. 'We negotiate while Samson is here, while *L'oracolo* is here. We make the most of these blessings.'

'So, do I need to like, read everything?'

'This is your choice, my friend,' Sebastian said, casually sipping from a steaming cup of coffee. 'But I have read all these a hundred times. This is what you pay me for – to read for you. I promise you, I have a very good eye. These are very safe hands.'

Contract by contract, I scrawled my name on dotted lines, inside enclosed boxes. That same signature I'd practised inside the backs of schoolbooks, staring out of the window, imagining the future I'd now secured. When all was done, my annual income had tripled.

'This is just the start,' Sebastian said, gripping my shoulder. 'Another goat on the farm.'

76

In early May, Samson travelled to London with our owner for the Player of the Year ceremony. I watched on TV as he walked the red carpet, dressed in a black tuxedo and a flamboyant pink bow-tie that I'd persuaded him to wear.

No one on Twitter cared about his outfit. They focused on his hair – on the neon green goat he'd had shaved above his right ear.

Before he went inside, an interviewer caught him.

'Samson, you're nominated tonight for the Young Player of the Year Award, what does that mean to you?'

'I'm very happy to be here. It is nice to be recognised. I just thank my teammates and my manager, and we will see what happens.'

'And we love your hair – can you tell us a little about this?'

'My boy Remy, it is his design. It is a goat – *greatest of all time*, you know?'

'And can we expect to see you back here again next season?'

Samson laughed. 'Only God knows this.'

Despite being the bookies' favourite, Samson missed out on the award. Instead, it went to a talented English forward from Manchester United.

I watched as the camera panned to Samson's face, applauding impassively as the rival player made his way to the stage. Samson's goat appeared to rear in disgust.

Many called it an outrage, pointing out that the Manchester United player had two fewer goals and three fewer assists. But almost immediately, everyone forgot. Everyone moved on.

In the papers the following day, Holly was pictured leaving a London nightclub holding hands with a player from Leicester City.

MORE HEARTBREAK FOR SAMSON AS BUSTY EX WOOS NEW BEAU, read the headline.

'Heartbreak,' I said, turning my phone to show him over breakfast.

'It hurts so much,' he teased, a hand to his forehead.

That Sunday, I taxied Samson to St Mark's for their midday service. Heading towards the city, I drove with the windows down, opting for a scenic route. We twisted past freshly ploughed fields, fragrant with sod, budding wildflowers, life in bloom.

I recognised that my perspective had shifted. Previously, Samson had awoken me to the provincial banality of my existence, my narrow fidelity to the only place I'd ever known. But that day, cresting one final hill, spires and cooling towers punctuating the horizon, I felt full of warmth and affection for this land, my city, my supremely blessed life.

On the radio, pundits caterwauled about Saturday's results – the perceived injustices, the dramatic consequences of refereeing decisions, the grand, potential financial implications of a single penalty kick.

'Turn that off please,' Samson requested, 'I am done with these men.'

Throughout his time in England, Samson had attended mass whenever it was viable. He had spoken fondly of the Ghanian parish priest, his soft cadence and generous spirit.

'You should come inside,' Samson said, as we pulled up to the church grounds. 'Come join me.'

'Are you sure? Would that be okay?'

'All are welcome,' Samson told me.

Stepping inside just before the hour, we sat towards the back of the church, a discreet pew in a transept, angled towards the altar. Above us, an oil painting of the Virgin Mary, her face stoic, lips plump. At the centre of her chest, an exposed heart, pierced with a sword and coronated with fire. She cupped this heart with both hands, her fingers troubling its surface like a ripe fruit.

Throughout the service, I remained seated while Samson moved through the motions of prayer and contrition, variously standing, kneeling, singing and bowing.

'Praise to you Lord, Jesus Christ,' he said, echoed by the congregation. For a moment, I registered my own accent in his voice. A subtle inflection. A marker of me, of this city, transposed into him.

As he returned from Communion up the nave of the church, a handful of people reached out to Samson, keen to shake his hand, to bump his fist. Before reaching our seat, Samson gestured for me to stand and follow him outside.

'But mass isn't over?' I said, stepping through the grand, oak doors.

'Near enough,' Samson told me. 'I don't like to be a distraction from God.'

Buckling back into the car, I asked Samson if he was desperate to get home.

'I'm easy,' he said. 'I have served my duty for today.'

'I've got an idea,' I told him. 'Indulge me. I think you'll like it.'

'Okay,' Samson said, rolling down his window. 'I trust you.'

It didn't take long for Samson to deduce my plan. On the motorway, driving south from Gateshead, Gormley's *Angel* dominates the horizon.

Walking up the slope from the parking lot, Samson paced ahead, leading the way, occasionally turning back to me with an expression of gleeful delight, beckoning me to hurry up.

Reaching the base of the sculpture, it seemed we had the space almost entirely to ourselves. Looking straight up, I felt a mild head rush, almost woozy, overcome by the scale.

'I can touch?' Samson said, his hand already reaching.

'Go for it,' I told him. 'I won't stop you.'

Laying his palm flat against the steel, Samson shut his eyes, his lips moving in a silent prayer.

'I haven't been here since I was a boy,' I said, mostly to myself. 'I must have driven past thousands of times. All the way through school, through the academy, on the team coach. It's always been here. For my whole life.'

'This is now a pilgrimage,' Samson told me, removing his hand. 'Now you will see this, and you will remember me.'

'I don't think there's any risk of me forgetting you.'

'Okay,' Samson said, rolling his eyes. 'Perhaps I wish to make sure.'

With this, I reached for Samson's hand, but he pulled away.

'*Excusez-moi, monsieur,*' Samson called, waving one arm, drawing the attention of an anoraked man further down the slope. Jogging towards him, out of earshot, I saw Samson present the man his phone, clearly requesting a photograph.

Sprinting back up to the base of the *Angel*, Samson put his arm around my waist, pulling me tight to his side.

'Smile,' he instructed. 'This will be your remembrance.'

The photo came out beautifully. The angle low and sky clear. The *Angel* filling the frame, the sun just cresting over one wing. And us at its base, joined at the hip, wide smiles and matching heights.

'Could you send me that, please?' I requested. 'My mam and dad will love this. I bet they get it printed out. Another treasure to put on the mantlepiece.'

'*Bien sûr,*' Samson said, tapping at his phone while wandering, walking around the back of the sculpture.

'Aha,' he announced, pointing down the embankment. 'Come look. This is where they have been hidden.'

Behind the *Angel*, at the bottom of the mining hill, were two full-sized football pitches, games underway on each.

'Oh!' I said. 'It's Sunday league!'

For a while, we stood there, watching the amateurs play, side by side in that gentle summer breeze. Balls lofted high and hopefully into the air. Panicked clearances, booted long to no one, chased down breathlessly. Roughshod tackles and foul throws. Among them, men and women wearing our kit, our numbers, even our names. This was real sport, played only for the joy of the game.

I felt happy. No matter what came next, I imagined this moment could sustain me.

77

Returning home from our final Friday training session, we heard a clattering. A physical, blustering sound – movement and tumult and muddling. The noises came from the kitchen.

My heart hammered, from my chest to my throat.

At the door, Samson raised one finger to his lips – a call for silence. A vow between us, that we would deal with this ourselves. That together, we would confront the danger.

My mind conjured up some deranged intruder, violating our space, here on a tip, staking out possible malicious rumours about us. About the things we did with each other in the holy privacy of that house.

Scanning the hallway, there were no obvious weapons. Desperate, fizzing with adrenaline, I grabbed my old crutches, still balanced idly by the door. Handing one of them to Samson, we inched up the hall, towards the kitchen door.

With a nod, I flung it open.

It took me a second to spot the bird, long enough for Samson to yelp, to flatten himself back against the wall.

The creature was a tiny brown blur, spilling about the room

in a state of rash panic, swerving on hidden vectors, flapping and crashing from counter to window to wall – the desperate fanned snap of its tiny wings.

'Fuck,' I said, relief flooding through me, loosening my grip on the crutch.

'Fix this,' Samson said, now cowering, his elbows shielding his face, as though braced for impact.

'It's just a bird, Samson.'

Without thinking, I found myself taking out my phone and calling my father. He would know what to do.

'Son?' Dad answered, near enough immediately, intuiting my panic. 'What's wrong?'

'Hey – Dad – there's a bird. In the kitchen. We just got here. I don't know how – I don't—'

'I'm on my way,' he said, cutting the line.

By the time Dad arrived some fifteen minutes later, Samson had retreated to the bedroom and the bird had settled, perching on a lamp by the window, admiring its own reflection.

'It's there,' I told my father, pointing from the doorframe.

Dad had come equipped with a net. I recognised it as one I'd used as a boy, for crabbing and fishing in the rock pools on Scarborough beach.

'Open the patio door then,' Dad said, unruffled, practical.

Casually, he walked over and swung the net, catching the bird first time, then ferrying it swiftly out of the room, back into the air.

Side by side, we watched it take flight, steady, then riding high on a bow-bend of wind, gliding westwards, towards the setting sun.

'The small ones,' Dad said, 'they're always the most

anxious. The angriest. They have to fight so hard to stay alive, to find enough energy to stay up there.'

'Right,' I said, shifting my weight from heel to toe.

'Remember this old thing?' he said, extending the net.

'Yeah,' I beamed. 'I loved those summers. Really good memories.'

'The best,' Dad said, still looking to the sky.

'How have you been?'

'All right,' he said, pulling up his trousers. 'Keeping busy. Staying out the way of your mam, you know.'

'Right,' I said. 'Good.'

'Big game on Saturday then,' Dad said after a pause. 'Nice one to end on.'

'Yeah, I'm starting again. Should be a good one.'

'And so you should. Glad they saw sense. Well deserved, son.'

'You could come, if you like?'

'Ah, I might be busy. I'll have to check.'

'All right. Just let me know. If you can make it, it might be worth having a chat with some of the staff. There's a job at the club, I think – because of Paddy's video, you know? They're looking for a player liaison person. Mostly supporting the kids out on loan and the ones coming through. They want someone who knows the club. I've already had a word to recommend you.'

'Well, if you think I'd be any good,' Dad said, measuring his words, clearly not wanting to betray his enthusiasm. 'Then yeah, thanks, son.'

'No problem,' I said, pulling him in for a hug.

78

Samson finished the campaign with sixteen goals and six assists across all competitions. I had scored eight and set up four, for exactly half of his combined return.

After our final home game, the squad brought their wives and kids out onto the pitch, taking selfies, enjoying the mid-summer heat. The crowd lingered behind, their shirts off, tattoos bared, applauding wildly as Baba's four-year-old girl dribbled the ball over the goal line.

GET HER SIGNED
GET HER SIGNED
GET HER SIGNED

Despite our objective mid-table mediocrity, there was a party atmosphere. A collective feeling of hope for a bright, uncharted future where everything was beautiful and nothing hurt.

I waved to my father in the crowd, back in his seat, his spiritual home. Hands in the air, he led a chant for Samson.

His name is fuckin' Samson
And he's the fuckin' GOAT

And if you try to mark him
He'll stick it down your throat.

He passes with his left foot
He passes with his right
And when he signs for Barca
We'll sing this song all night.

That evening, Samson let me take him in my mouth.

Kneeling in the dark, it felt like my own form of prayer, of worship. Altar and sacrifice. While other players danced and made merry into the wee hours, we chose each other.

I laid him back and kissed him tenderly, from the jutting contours of his hip bones to the sculpted cut of his obliques, the sheer, taut muscle of his thighs, the coarse, adolescent curls of his pubes. Taking silence as blessing, I ran my tongue up his dick, hard and prone, flexing expectantly against his abs.

I'd prepared for that moment. I'd researched how to please him – the theory and the technique. It was yet another skill where the physical met the mental, demanding that you push past your limits, discovering yourself to be deeper, more limitless and more capable than you'd ever believe.

Tasting him, steering him, I'd never felt closer to his body. That level of control, that complete and total intimacy. His body was my body – I knew when he was close, then closer: sensed the sounds, the tensing, shuddering reward.

And afterwards, his body at peace. The tamed bulk of him, his elbow cocked, rested across his face, shielding his eyes, as though to preserve whatever fantasy he'd conjured, whatever lie he required. It would only have to sustain him for a few more days.

I took responsibility for packing his bags. For his final hours in England, Samson sunbathed on my lawn while I scampered about the house, gathering up his possessions: socks thoughtlessly flung into corners, Man of the Match awards strewn across surfaces, underwear stripped at the foot of our bed.

Sebastian had arranged for a driver to collect Samson, to take him to the airport and out of my life. Initially, Samson would be returning to Paris to spend a week with his mother. From there, his destiny was unmapped.

With the task complete, suitcases ready by the door, I stepped out into the garden. As I approached the patio bed, Samson did not register my presence. He lay there dozing, unperturbed by the future, headphones in; a fine gloss of perspiration shimmered on his perfect chest, his abs.

Feeling bold, I took a photo of him. The athlete in repose. One final artefact, just for me.

Crouching by his side, I kissed Samson's shoulder, rousing him.

'It's done,' I said. 'All packed. The driver will be here in an hour.'

'*Merci, mon ami,*' Samson said, rubbing his eyes and slouching up onto his elbow.

'You might want to do a quick double-check. There's a chance that I'll have missed something.'

Samson batted his hand indifferently.

'I trust you with this. You are very thorough. If anything important remains, you will send it to me.'

'To Paris?'

'To wherever I may be,' he said, lying back down. 'You will find me.'

'Don't you want to have a shower? Get ready for the driver?'

'The driver will wait,' Samson said. 'Let me enjoy this. I want to enjoy what remains of this time.'

79

Soon enough, my mother came to clean, to strip the sheets, to wash away the smell of him. I watched her do it – desecrate that holy ground, cleanse my life of the vestigial traces of him; standing there, I could think of no grounds to protest.

L'oracolo left shortly after, with the club still under the owner's control, no further towards securing a suitable buyer. Before his departure, the manager claimed in an interview that the club didn't need to worry too much about replacing Samson, because they still had me. He stressed that I could go on to be just as good, if not better.

In the wake of the news of *L'oracolo*'s departure, one betting site offered comically enhanced odds on our club being relegated the following season, going viral in the process. The world laughed at our misfortune.

On the day Samson signed for Barcelona, I spoke to him over the phone. He couldn't say what part of the city he was in – not because he was being coy, but because he genuinely didn't know. It had been a covert operation, smuggling him into Spain via private jet in the middle of the night, whisking him off to some remote, anonymous hotel, all corridors and conference rooms; private security men stationed by every door.

Barcelona were worried that another club might poach him, Samson explained. Steal him from under their noses at the last second. It had happened before.

'They say it should be done by the morning. Then I have to do the photos, the media. They present me at Camp Nou. Twenty-thousand fans they expect.'

'Woah.'

'My mama, she is so bored here. She just wants this to be over so we can visit the beach. I promised her that when we come to Barcelona we will visit the beach. We will swim in the sea. I buy her ice cream.'

I laughed.

'Why do you laugh? You laugh at my mama?'

'It's just good to hear your voice,' I said.

Samson grunted dismissively. 'Sebastian, he says the negotiations are very long. Very precise. The Catalan, they are tough at the business. Much tougher than you English.'

'Is he trying to negotiate your shirt number again?' I asked. 'Will you be trying to steal someone's pride like you stole mine?'

He laughed – a full genuine cackle. It felt like an indulgence. 'No,' he said, 'At Barcelona, it is different. Everything is earned.'

'Well, either way, you'll need a new celebration, I suppose. You can't be the GOAT in that squad.'

'We'll see,' Samson said.

'I miss you.'

'Not now,' Samson said. 'They're coming. I have to go.'

80

After that, we spoke less frequently, with longer intervals between each occasion. It was always me who initiated contact. Soon enough, I ran out of excuses to bother him. Ran out of compliments and reassuring words, the small kindnesses that sustain a friendship across borders. From this distance, I was just another fan.

In July, Dad started his new job at the club. At the end of his first week, I visited my parents' home for a family dinner.

'They're a good bunch of lads,' Dad told us, carving into his chicken. 'A proper laugh. And the atmosphere's much better than I'd reckoned, given the circumstances. Everyone's saying that with the right manager, we'll have a good chance.'

'Uh huh,' I said, spearing a carrot.

'Because there's a spine there still. That's what really matters. The gaffer, he's left something behind that can be built on.'

'Enough football now, Adrian,' Mam said, 'Honestly, he's been at it all week. Like a kid in a sweetshop.'

'Sorry, pet,' Dad said, chuckling, pecking her swiftly on the lips.

'Ew.' I cringed. 'Gross.'

'Don't be daft, love. Now, tell us about your summer! What do you have planned?'

While Mam disappeared to clean the plates, I sat with Dad, keeping him company while he finished the last of the wine.

'Bordeaux,' he read, showing me the label. 'That anywhere near Paris?'

'I'm not sure, to be honest.'

'Have you heard from your Frenchie mate? From our Samson?'

'A bit,' I coughed. 'He's pretty busy, you know. Media, training, another new language to learn. I don't want to bother him too much.'

Dad nodded ponderously and set down his glass, as though he were readying himself.

'Smart lad. All those languages.'

'Yeah. Pretty clever.'

'It's okay to miss him, you know?'

I paused, disarmed.

'I'll cope,' I said, as though that were sufficient.

'It's hard to lose a mate,' Dad began, leaning forward, almost whispering. 'There was an understanding between you two – anyone could see it. The way you played together, the way you complemented each other's game, that's a rare thing. He brought out the best in you. People wait their whole careers for a partnership like that. Most of 'em will never come close to what you had.'

His tone was uncomfortable, but sincere. From across the table, I explored his face for possibilities: for the possibility that somehow, he might know.

'So yeah,' Dad said, taking a breath, picking his wine glass back up, 'it's okay to miss him.'

Processing those words, I stared at him, suddenly recognising what others saw. I saw myself: there, in his jaw, in the curl of his lips, in the emerald and hazel of his eyes.

'Listen, I know I'm just a fat old sod, and I know you're your own man, but I'll always be here. I won't disappear again. If you need me, for anything, I'll always be here.'

'Thanks, Dad,' I whispered. 'I love you.'

81

Without comment, Samson removed himself from our team WhatsApp group. Soon after that, his number went dead – I figured he must have switched to a Spanish phone. After a few days of hesitation, I mustered the nerve to call Sebastian and request Samson's new number.

'My friend,' Sebastian said distractedly, 'it is not my place to give out this number.'

'What do you mean? I'm his friend – what's the problem?'

'Right now, Samson is making new friends. He is very focused on his transfer and his play. This is an important time, you understand?'

'Yeah, I get that, but I'm not going to hassle him. I just want to say hello, check in, you know?'

Sebastian sighed – a piquant, composed frustration.

'In time, you can say hello, but for now, you are not his priority.'

'He lived with me, remember? He chose to move into my house. We're good mates.'

Sebastian laughed.

'My friend, there are many things in life that we choose, but this move, it was not Samson's choice. This is one thing that I demanded. After the robbery, I insist that it is you he lives with. For this deal with Barcelona, they look at more than the player. They are a special club – when they do business, they care about certain qualities. Personal discipline, good behaviour. Samson – you will agree – he does not always have these qualities. But I knew that with you, under your roof, he would be free from trouble. Out of the papers, no?'

I remained silent, processing his words.

'I will be very honest, my friend. You are a good boy – very safe. Very grounded. I am very pleased to have you, to work with you and represent you. But for now, Samson comes first. There can only be one true GOAT, okay?'

Sebastian took a breath.

'I have to go now. But do not linger on this, okay? In this life, there are different paths. Eventually, some paths may cross again. For Samson, he knows who you are, he knows where you are. When he is ready, he will find you again.'

82

That summer, the owner cut the academy's funding, pointing to the poor return on investment delivered by the sale
of recent academy graduates, and the paucity of players who
had gone on to play for the first team. I was the outlier. The
survivor of a weak yield. The product of barren land and
sterile soil.

Not the greatest of all time, but the best we had to offer.

INJURY TIME

83

Towards the end of July, Milo got married in Las Vegas, Nevada. He invited the whole squad.

It was my first time in America. I flew from Heathrow with Mario, Dami and Theo. First class seats, a private attendant, all the food and champagne we could wish for.

'I know you're not a drinker,' Mario encouraged me, 'but make the most of it. These seats ain't cheap. Gotta get value somehow.'

It was night when we arrived. Waiting to land, the plane circled over the desert: a vast expanse, studded with halogen twinkles.

'Here we go, boys,' Mario said, pinging his sleeping mask across the aisle at Theo's face. 'The fun starts here.'

Free from the club's dominion, our group had elected not to share rooms.

'Fucking stupid system anyway,' Theo argued. 'Treating us like we're babies.'

'I personally enjoyed it,' I said.

'Ah, yeah,' Theo sniffed, 'proper pity Samson ain't coming. When he wasn't being a stroppy French cunt, he could be a good laugh. Remember his song in Doha? That was wicked.'

We'd chosen not to stay in the same resort as Milo, his bride and their extended families, instead opting for suites in the MGM Grand, where there were daily pool parties.

Within ten minutes of claiming a room, there was a knock at my door.

'Allow me some deodorant,' Dami said, barging past me into my room, topless and dripping, a towel round his waist.

'Oi, what's the point in paying for separate rooms then?'

'To shag, you prick,' Dami scoffed, spraying what seemed to be half the can under each arm. 'Don't worry, I promise not to be too loud.'

'Whatever,' I said.

'Why the mood? You jet-lagged or something? Couple of drinks and you'll sleep better anyway. You brought plenty of jonnies, yeah?'

'What? Oh – no, actually.'

'Hold on then,' Dami said, jogging out of the room, his towel now hanging open, arse bared.

'Here,' he said, returning with a fistful of condoms. 'They'll rip you off in the toilets in this place. Learned that the hard way last time.'

'Thanks,' I said, spilling the foil squares onto a dresser.

Though it was already gone eleven, the squad had decided to head out, to push through the time difference. We were headed for the Wynn, a monolithic structure at the north end of the strip. Our plan for the evening was to meet up with Bert, Baba and the others, working our way down the strip, stopping for drinks at each casino. Both Bert and Baba had brought along their families.

'The missus insists on it these days,' Bert told me in the Wynn lobby. 'She's seen too much.'

As we stepped onto the casino floor, a stout woman pushed her arm into my chest.

'Imma need to see some ID there, sir,' she drawled, chewing on something.

'I'm twenty,' I said, producing my passport.

'Casino floor's for twenty-one and over, sir. Imma have to ask you to leave.'

'What?'

'Imma have to ask you to leave, sir,' she repeated. 'In the state of Nevada, all alcohol and gambling is illegal for minors.'

'He's bloody twenty,' Bert said, stepping between us. 'How's that a fucking minor?'

'Sir, please do not use that language towards me.'

The woman spoke with a weariness that seemed hard won – the fatigue of years on the front line of hindrance.

'It's fine, guys,' I said. 'I'll just go home. I'm pretty tired anyway.'

'Like fuck will ye,' Bert said, yanking me towards him, an arm around my waist. 'This is a lads' trip, and we'll fucking well stick together.'

'Hey,' Dami said, a smirk on his face, 'I know where we could go.'

84

The firing range was a fifteen-minute taxi journey from the strip. After some light persuasion from Dami, the rest of the group agreed to his suggestion, childishly excited by the prospect of weapons, willing to forgo alcohol until the pool party the following afternoon.

'This is the ready area,' our instructor stated, hands on her hips, a baseball cap containing her braids. She looked even younger than me – a foot shorter than anyone in our group, but she spoke with military sternness.

'Only one person in the ready area at any time – got that? When you've entered the ready area, I'll step forward with you to the firing point and hand you your weapon. You're gonna point your gun straight down the range, towards your backstop. You do *not* move your gun away from the backstop at any time, okay? You do *not* remove your eye and ear protection at any time, okay?

'Now the gun you're going to be firing is a standard-load Glock 19. This gun has an effective fire rate of eleven hundred rounds per minute and a range of fifty metres. You're gonna put the gun in your dominant hand, and step forward with your dominant foot, okay? You keep your finger off the trigger until I give the all-clear to fire.'

'Jesus,' Theo whispered to me. 'Lot of rules, eh?'

'Well, it is a gun range, Theo.'

'I can't believe they didn't do a breathalyser or something,' Mario whispered, craning his neck for a better angle of the range.

'Hey, Mario,' Bert said, nudging him in the side, nodding towards our instructor, 'How much for ye to pinch her arse?'

'You're mental.' Mario laughed. 'She's got a fucking gun, Bert.'

'Ten grand?'

'Get fucked.'

'All right, how about twenty?'

'Seriously? You'd actually pay?'

Bert shrugged. 'Fuck it, yeah, why not.'

Mario scratched under his safety goggles, pursing his lips as though he were seriously considering the offer.

'Nah, mate,' he eventually said. 'I fancy a go on the gun anyway. Don't want to spoil it for everyone else, do I?'

'What about our little minor?' Bert said to me. 'Twenty grand enough to tempt ye?'

'Nah,' I said. 'You're all right, mate.'

'Yous lot are boring,' Bert sniffed. 'S'pose it's a shit arse anyway.'

In turn, the lads stepped forward and unloaded a magazine of fifteen rounds into a hanging target – the plain outline of a person – a canvas to channel hate straight into.

Contained within that concrete room, the sound of the gun was louder than any of us anticipated – a shock of noise, booming and patently deadly.

I was the last to step up to the range. Around me, the squad were high on sleepless adrenaline, still abuzz with the power they'd just wielded. On my go, they cheered my name, braying and thumping my back, as though I were stepping up to take a penalty kick.

'Ready?' said the instructor, handing me the gun before I could reply. It was heavier than I expected – a weight that required conscious lifting. Raising the gun, I found myself winking to establish a line of sight.

I don't know why I pictured him. I don't know why it was Samson who appeared in that outline, manifest from some hidden part of me. But there he was – barefaced, his palms open like acceptance, like contrition.

The instructor pressed her hand on my shoulder, bracing me, anticipating the kickback, the confusion, the guilt.

'Okay,' she said. 'Fire!'

85

I was too over-stimulated to sleep. Through the wall, I could hear Dami snoring – terrible fits and chokes of nasal sound, uncontained to any rhythm.

Lying there, the gunshots still ringing in my ears, I willed myself not to think any more about Samson. Instead, I spread out my legs like roots, and found myself thinking fondly of home.

I thought of my parents' house: the clutter of stuffed toys and gifted affections. My childhood bed, almost certainly made – ready and waiting, whenever it might be needed. I thought of rolling green horizons and sod-pocked fields, of battering rain, sweeping across the stadium's North Stand. I could picture it all so clearly, and yet home seemed impossibly far away – at a complete disconnect from this manicured simulacrum. Were these the stirrings of homesickness? Was it plausible that I might pine after less than a day? Was this what Samson had suffered all season long? This scrambling, bracing ache of a feeling? A feeling that begs to be filled, that demands to be drowned out by any means possible? Was my body just his means of escape?

86

I awoke around midday, disorientated, my mouth dry from the air conditioning. The pool party was due to start at two. Milo had planned for the party to function as his stag – a chance for the squad to meet up with his other friends and relatives.

I brushed my teeth and sat on the toilet for a long time, scrolling through my phone. I'd developed a bad habit of reading an article, then circling back to one of Samson's social media accounts. It was a lazy, compulsive form of stalking.

When I eventually stood, my legs had gone dead, buzzing with pins and needles. It felt like my body's way of chastising me.

There was a knock on my door – a manic energy that could only be Dami.

'Here,' he said, handing me a sandwich. 'You've missed breakfast.'

'Oh, thanks, mate.'

'All right if I use the deodorant again, yeah?'

'Yeah, I guess.'

'Get that down you quick. Gotta line your stomach, innit. There's a long day of boozing ahead.'

'Yeah, should be good.'

'Actually,' he said, pulling off his shirt to spray the deodorant, 'could you do my back while we're here?'

'What?'

'Slap some cream on there, would you? I'll do you after.'

'Oh – yeah, all right then.'

'Don't worry,' Dami said, noting my expression, 'nothing gay, like. Just don't fancy looking like a burned prick come dinnertime. Not the best look, you know?'

'I get it, it's all good, mate.'

'Tell you what,' he said, motioning for me to remove my T-shirt. 'I'll show you how it's done.'

Lying on the bed, Dami stood over me, moving his hand in small, looping circles, gliding back and forth over the slim peak of my spine. It was not an unpleasant feeling. With my eyes closed, I could imagine his hand was Samson's – that same rough, gym-calloused surface.

'You still miss Samson, innit?' Dami said, as though he could read my thoughts through my skin.

'Um,' I mumbled in shock. 'A bit, I guess.'

'Yeah, we can all tell. It's nothing to be ashamed of, you know? It's hard at first, when your mates leave. Especially when you're young, and when they're leaving for something bigger and better. But it'll be all right. It's not like he's dead or nothing. You'll forget about him come next season. It's basically always all right in the end.'

'Thanks, mate.'

'All right,' he said, slapping me wetly. 'That's all done I reckon. You do me, then let's get down to the water.'

87

The pools at the MGM Grand were one-and-a-half times the size of a football pitch, Milo boasted to us. The water was not intended for swimming, but more for a human-version of grazing, accommodating up to sixteen hundred people. The water was one level, waist-high throughout, surrounded by bungalows, hammocks and cabanas, three different bars and an elevated DJ booth.

The party operated a token system, seemingly designed to moderate the pace of our drinking. With prepaid tickets and drinks tokens, I wouldn't have to worry about being checked for ID.

On entry, each of us was handed three paper tokens without question, but with no bag or pockets to secure them, I decided to cash in all three immediately, before the queue grew too large.

Alone in line, I looked out across the pools from behind my sunglasses. The American men seemed to favour smaller swimsuits – our group mockingly referred to them as 'budgie smugglers'. I looked out at that throng of men, with their tight buttocks and their packed bulges, feeling nothing other than a quiet resentment. I was weary of it all, bored by the burden of want. I just wanted to drink and forget. Forget about him.

After five minutes in the queue, I received three colourful cocktails, served with decorative umbrellas and useless sprigs of plastic.

'You're starting fast,' said the woman behind me in the queue. She was an exclamation mark of a person – a tall, brilliant blonde, the light gilding her hair. She stood confidently in her orange bikini, as though she'd spent the year conditioning her body for this exact occasion. Her accent was perilously unplaceable – perhaps Canadian.

'Here,' I said, handing her one of the cocktails. 'You can have one. On me.'

'Don't mind if I do,' she said playfully. 'I'm Noelle.'

'Enjoy, Noelle,' I said, registering the shock on her face as I walked away, a drink in each hand.

With everyone shirtless, it was surprisingly difficult to relocate my teammates. After a few minutes of wandering, I eventually spotted the group in a private cabana area by the DJ booth.

The sky was a sheer blue, with both the sun and moon somehow visible, as though rules did not apply to this strange desert land. Vegas, where the horizon is a panorama of all things, all the world's disparate treasures, pale imitations of their real forms. Where beauty is a bare-faced trick; where even the presence of water is a terrible, impossible deception.

While the group accelerated their drinking, I excused myself, easing my body into the water, I rested there, my elbows spread back on the pool's edge, bobbing gently, my back flush with the wall – the cool of the tile against my skin. I breathed slowly – my chest open and eyes softly closed under the sunglasses, enjoying the hypnotic lap of the water, the way it gurgled through the drains with a hollow grumble, as though it were complaining – *I do not belong in this place.* The air was perfumed – sun cream and hard spirits and the distant waft of barbecue.

If this was a life without him, I might just survive it. I might yet learn to live beyond his influence. Samson was right all along: *no pleasure is simple.* There is sadness and terror in all things, in all the world's bounty. But for those who dare to seek it, who venture to act, beauty waits, impatient and fading. I stood there, buoyed by the water, consumed by the same old fears, yet happy all the same.

Then a voice, cold fingers on my shoulder. I started and turned, recognising the girl from the bar. Noelle was lowering herself beside me, into the pool, offering to buy the next round: presenting her emptied glass like a contract that had been forged between us – a promise of things to come.

'My friends think you're cute,' she told me.

'I'm twenty,' I said like an excuse.

'That's okay,' Noelle said. 'That can work.'

Behind us, I saw Theo and Dami in the cabana, looking straight at me. Catching my attention, they put their thumbs up, great gurning smiles spread across their faces. Placing his hands on his lower back, Theo broke into a thrusting motion of encouragement.

I was trapped.

'So what do you?' I asked Noelle, conceding defeat.

She spoke quickly, as though to expedite the process, hurrying through the requisite platitudes and civilities before we could begin kissing. Listening to her, I felt thankful for the sunglasses, their partial masking effect. Though I could form a smile with my mouth, my eyes could remain appropriately disengaged.

Returning from the bar with fresh drinks in hand, we slipped back into the water, wading to the centre of the pool. The DJ was playing thumping techno. Around us, people raised their drinks aloft and swayed to the music. Floating there, Noelle pressed herself against me, using me as ballast against the human tide, her fingers roaming round my sides, squeezing my bum. Her hands were smooth and her nails were long.

'You're so adorable,' Noelle told me. 'Where are you staying?'

'Here, actually.'

'Let's go upstairs,' she said, biting her lip.

'Now?'

'Yeah, why not?'

Leading me by the hand through the water, Noelle dragged me back through the bodies, out of the pool, and past my whooping teammates.

'Go on, son!' Bert yelled.

88

In the privacy of my suite, Noelle removed my sunglasses and kissed me, peppering my lips and neck and chest with small, eager kisses.

'You like that?' she said.

'Yeah.'

'Tell me you like it.'

'It's nice. I like it.'

Backing me towards the bed, Noelle untied her bikini top, sticking out her chest expectantly.

'You're really tall,' she said. 'Like, the perfect height.'

'Thanks,' I said.

Laying me down on the bed, she pulled off my swimming shorts with a short, sharp tug – like a magician's big reveal.

'Look at these thighs,' she said, running her nails up my legs. 'You're like an actual proper athlete, aren't you?'

'Yeah,' I said, my voice stalling.

Releasing my legs, she grabbed my dick firmly, as though she were trying to tame it. I remained still as she ran her tongue from my balls to the tip of my cock, lapping eagerly, then licking her lips, as if she wanted to savour the chlorinated taste of me. I felt myself respond to the grip, growing hard in her hand.

'I'm ready,' she said.

'Right. Me too. Obviously.'

'Do you have condoms?'

'Actually, yeah,' I said, walking over to the dresser, presenting a condom like a drink token – a passage for entry.

'How do you want me?' Noelle asked, removing her bikini bottoms, shuffling back up the bed.

'Face down,' I said. The words fell out of me like instinct.

And as she rolled over, there he was, back in my thoughts, shocking through me like trauma. It was our old routine – our roles suddenly and terribly inverted. For the first time, I would be the one doing the fucking. I would have to become him. Another pale imitation on the Las Vegas strip.

Somehow, the situation felt like a test. Like something I'd been building towards. This was something that Samson had been unintentionally training me for.

'Is it okay if we close the curtains?'

'Whatever you want, baby.'

All those hours on the pitch, following his lead, learning his tricks and flairs, borrowing the nuance of his movement, his style. I'd learned to become his body. Thanks to Samson, I intuitively knew how to fuck: how to position her hips, how to angle myself, how to buck back and find purchase.

'So strong,' Noelle cooed, guiding me.

Moving inside her, I felt the fear recede. I could do this. My body could do this. My hands were his hands, my cock was his cock – channelling Samson, I could do no wrong.

'Fuck me, Daddy,' Noelle said, performative and forced, as

though she were quoting someone else – referencing something that should have been instantly recognisable to me.

Even from behind, the smell of her was potent – a floral sweetness; quite chemically different from all that I favoured.

I exerted myself silently and soberly, pushing through the motions. There was no emotion to the act, only two hard bodies, fulfilling a biological imperative.

When it was over, Noelle dressed quickly, suggesting that we should return to the party. But as we stepped out to the corridor, there was a huge roar, my teammates springing from either side of the door, bundling into me, shoving me to the floor.

From my pinned position, I watched as Noelle screamed and ran away, back down the corridor, towards the lifts.

'Fucking legend,' Mario yelled into my ear.

'You filthy bugger,' Theo said, groping between my legs. 'Cost me a grand, you have.'

'What?' I said, struggling upright, shoving Mario off.

'Bet with Bert, didn't I? He laid me a grand at evens that you'd get laid in Vegas.'

'Oh,' I said, standing up, rearranging my hair. 'Sorry, I guess.'

'No bother,' Theo said. 'I'm happy for you, lad.'

'Aren't you gonna chase off after that little sort then?' Mario asked.

'Nah,' I shrugged. 'She knows where I am.'

With that, another roar, Mario knocking me back to the ground.

89

The next day, Milo married Tijana in an Elvis-themed chapel in downtown Las Vegas. There were sixty of us, crammed into a tiny air-conditioned room. Almost all the squad were hungover and suffering, me included. Thankfully, the ceremony lasted a mere ten minutes.

'Uh huh huh, thank you very much, ladies and gentlemen. A round of applause for the happy couple.'

Once the papers had been signed, we travelled as a group by limousine to a banquet room at the Luxor resort – an Egyptian-style casino at the foot of the strip, adorned with a huge black glass pyramid.

There, in front of his friends and family, Milo led Tijana in a slow waltz to the same Nat King Cole song he'd rehearsed with me months prior.

Unforgettable, that's what you are
Unforgettable, though near or far.

After the dance, Milo broke away and approached me.

'How I do? How was posture?'

'Perfect, mate,' I told him. 'You were perfect. Congratulations.'

90

Come winter, Samson's goat celebration had been pro-
grammed into *FIFA*. I felt sure this would be the legacy of
my influence. Intangible but undeniable evidence of our
time together. A period when he was mine and I was his.
Thanks to that silly celebration, I'd forever have a place in
Samson's story. I'd remain part of him, somewhere buried
and repressed.

Eventually, we did speak again. On the week of his long-
overdue international debut, Samson texted me from a new,
Spanish number. He would be playing for France against
England and wished for me to join him at Wembley as his
guest.

He offered no apology. No acknowledgement of fault, of
neglect. Just an invitation to bear witness.

I didn't reply straight away, nursing my feelings for a full
day. What power would I allow him? Would our future
always remain on his terms?

Once I'd prepared myself, I rang the number, fingering the
platinum crucifix around my neck.

'Who's this?' Samson joked.

'A friend,' I told him. 'A very proud friend.'

Acknowledgements

I am indebted to the early readers of this novel, who proffered the advice, encouragement and friendship that was required for me to persist with what often felt like a ridiculous project. My deepest gratitude to Dr. Sam Oyesiku-Blakemore, Niven Govinden, Naomi Ishiguro and Niamh Mulvey.

Overwhelming gratitude goes to my agent, Max Edwards, who understood and championed both this story and me. I am eternally thankful for your kindness, your vision and your presence in my life.

My love goes to the entire Dialogue team for helping refine my craft and bring this novel into the world. Thanks to Hannah Chukwu for the deep care she has shown to my characters in her deft and considerate editing. To Sharmaine Lovegrove, for her advocacy and enduring belief in my art. To Adrian Noble, David Bamford and the editorial team for their attention, energy and patience. To Ned Green, Annabel Robinson and Emily Moran for helping GOAT find its readers.

Thanks to my pub friends who still maintain that the novel should be called *Man On*.

This novel is dedicated to all queer sportspeople, both closeted and out. We'll be ready if and when you are. You will remain loved.

Bringing a book from manuscript to what you are reading is a team effort.

Dialogue Books would like to thank everyone who helped to publish *Greatest of All Time* in the UK.

Editorial
Hannah Chukwu
Adriano Noble

Contracts
Anniina Vuori
Imogen Plouviez
Amy Patrick
Jemima Coley

Sales
Caitriona Row
Dominic Smith
Frances Doyle
Ginny Mašinović
Rachael Jones
Georgina Cutler
Toluwalope Ayo-Ajala

Publicity
Annabel Robinson
Ned Green

Design
Nico Taylor

Production
Narges Nojoumi

Marketing
Emily Moran

Operations
Kellie Barnfield
Millie Gibson
Sameera Patel
Sanjeev Braich

Finance
Andrew Smith
Ellie Barry

Audio
Dominic Gribben

Copy-Editor
David Bamford

Proofreader
Saxon Bullock